MW01595865

FAMILY DRAMA AND A SEXY NEIGHBOR CREATE DIVINE TURMOIL.

A family illness draws Serena home to face issues she's avoided for years: an absent father, an ornery sister, and steamy neighbor Brian Allen.

With one broken marriage behind him, Brian can't believe he's falling for Serena. She's a risk on heels -- spirited but vulnerable, and utterly irresistible. He'd be crazy to give her a second glance. She'll break his heart. Or his bed. Probably both...

DIVINE TURMOIL

By

Rebecca Rose

Lyrical Press, Inc.
New York

LYRICAL PRESS, INCORPORATED

Divine Turmoil
13 Digit ISBN: 978-1-61650-186-0

Edited by Camila Londono
Book design by Renee Rocco
Cover Art by Renee Rocco

Lyrical Press, Incorporated
337 Katan Avenue
Staten Island, New York 10308
http://www.lyricalpress.com

PUBLISHER'S NOTE:

This book is a work of fiction. The names, characters, places, and incidents are products of the writer's imagination or have been used fictitiously and are not to be construed as real. Any resemblance to persons, living or dead, actual events, locale or organizations is entirely coincidental.

The publisher does not have any control over and does not assume any responsibility for author or third-party Web sites or their content.

Published in the United States of America by Lyrical Press, Incorporated

First Lyrical Press, Inc electronic publication: November 2009
First Lyrical Press, Inc print publication: August 2010

Dedication

For Mark, Isaac, Leah, Jack, and Claire: without your love, support, and sacrifice, I would not have been able to make my dream a reality. You mean the world to me.

Oh, and thanks for the name, Doris!

Acknowledgements

I would like to thank my aunt Diane Crevier who at the beginning of this adventure was gracious enough to provide me with medical books/pamphlets to help me research crucial information. I love you.

I also need to thank my beloved friend Lorettajo. You gave me the confidence to put all my fears aside and go for it.

Author's Note

This novel was written with love for my Grandmother Bolduc who lost her battle with cancer. She showed only strength and grace during her illness and will always be my inspiration for all things possible.

CHAPTER 1

The blacktop stretched before her, dismal and unyielding. White dotted lines blinked by as she sped along with the windows wide open to force thick, heavy air through the car's interior. Serena clenched the steering wheel.

"Well doesn't life suck?" She turned on her blinker and switched lanes. "I could have sworn I left this place with no intention of coming back. What the hell am I doing? I'm talking to myself again, that's what I'm doing. This is too long of a friggin' ride."

She leaned over and turned up the volume on the old cassette player radio. "I need to stop talking to myself, even if they do say it's a sign of intelligence." She briefly wondered if it was true. "You're rambling again, Serena. Everyone says you tend to ramble."

The ride home was lengthy and exhausting. Most of the scenery had been long stretches of monotonous trees. Trees didn't spark an interesting view around New England except for their rebirth in early spring or the carnival of colors in the fall. But it was June, and in June there was either the chill of a winter that refused to pass, or the stifling heat of a drought-induced summer. Serena decided, as yet another mile passed, that getting her AC fixed would be an excellent idea.

She took the next exit to a rest stop a little too fast; Serena tended to take all corners that way. She slammed on her brakes and screeched the car to a stop, barely missing the minivan parked next to her.

"Three hours into this lousy trip and one to go. I need some sanity and food." She extended her arms and face to the sky and rolled up onto her toes to ease away the stiffness in her muscles.

"Mmm." Serena felt her stomach rumble. In her mind, there was nothing like a big burger made of God knows what, radiated to all hell, with some extra greasy fries, and a very big carbonated drink.

She could hear her mother now. "Don't eat that stuff, it'll kill you. Do you know what parts of the cow they put in there?" Serena always shrugged it off. "If it's good, who cares where it comes from?"

Scenes from long ago flooded into her mind's eye as the people around her became shadows to her vivid memories. Their voices faded to mumbles in the background and everything moved with a soulless animation. As Serena waited, her sister's irritated voice echoed from some hidden archive in her memory. "Are you serious? Serena, how could you move away with this guy? You just met him. He could be..."

"Ma'am. Ma'am! Your food is ready." Serena shook herself back to reality, and reached for her tray. What did it matter now what everyone thought then? I did what I had to do. I got out. I saw something different. I did something new.

Sighing, Serena sat down to eat. "Even if it was for only a little while," she said to her burger before taking a large bite.

Trapped. It was all she could think of as she got back on the highway to finish the last stretch of her journey. The four doors of the sedan might as well have been steel bars. The interior was packed full and made the tiny vehicle feel more claustrophobic than it actually was. She'd expected the trailer she rented to hold more and was immensely disappointed when she had to leave some things behind.

When the speedometer hit eighty, the wind whipped at her hair, giving her some sense of the freedom she craved and desperately pursued. Somehow though, even with her independence, happiness always seemed to elude her.

It was a few hours later when Serena's car came to a halt in her mother's dirt driveway. She could imagine the smells that should be inside her childhood home: fresh baked coffeecakes, meat pies, and homemade sauce, combined with lemon dusting polish. Her mom should be in the kitchen, the very heart of their home, busying herself with something. The kitchen was where board games were played when she was young, then card games once she was old enough to gamble her pennies, and later, drinking games. It was where important discussions were held and reprimands given and love shared.

Serena O'Neal climbed out of her weary car while it sputtered and complained about the long journey and the trailer it hauled. She thought about how someone once said leaving home is the hardest thing to do. Apparently, they'd never found themselves forced to go back.

"I promise I'll have you taken care of." Patting the hood, Serena shifted the duffel bag on her shoulder. Glancing at the home before her, she realized it still looked the same. Somehow, she had thought it would be different. It felt different. The atmosphere around it was overshadowed by the undeniable darkness of her mother's absence.

I should knock, Serena thought, as she approached the wide screen door. No, I should knock as I'm going in. No, I should just go in and announce that I've arrived.

"Only you can make yourself feel uncomfortable," she told herself aloud. So why was she doing this, standing there waiting for someone to make the decision for her?

Serena was so engrossed in fighting with herself she didn't notice the tiny face staring through the screen door. She'd forgotten that her sister and niece would be there waiting.

"Why you talkeen to you-self?" Serena glanced down and saw a beautiful, tiny, angelic face. Lizzy had the same reddish-brown curly hair as her grandmother Katherine and Aunt Serena. She also had the big round eyes that were a family trait, except hers were dark chocolate without the amber flecks that made the O'Neals easily identifiable. A button nose tied Lizzy's features together, making her appear innocent and harmless to unsuspecting victims.

"I always talk to myself. Don't you?"

"Yeah! Mama say I like my auntieee." Then with her eyes darting back and forth she cupped her mouth and whispered, "I guess she a little..." She rotated her finger by her ear.

"Crazy?"

"Yeah!"

"Wonderful." Serena threw her hands up in the air showing defeat. Her niece thought she was crazy, and Serena still didn't know if she should simply walk into the house. Deciding to go in, she reached for the doorknob. What's the worst that can happen? she wondered, silently this time. The little angel instantly started screaming, and then ran full force at Serena with fists swinging and teeth showing. Serena stumbled back against the rail, catching herself before falling down the stairs. She held on with one hand while trying to ward off her assailant with the other. The girl was quick and agile. She slithered around Serena, then sank her teeth into the flesh of her left leg.

Serena let out a holler. The little girl was tough and not letting up. Her tiny body seemed to predict every one of Serena's deflective moves. This being so, Serena decided to do the only thing that seemed smart: yell for help.

"Elizabeth! Stop that this minute!" Hope appeared in the doorway, hands on her hips.

"Damn, Hope!" Serena exclaimed while rubbing at her sore thigh. "You don't need an attack dog, do ya?"

"You could have knocked, Serena." The screen door creaked as Hope opened it for her. "This isn't your house, you know."

Sarcastically Serena said, "Welcome home, sis. I'm so happy you had a safe trip. I know it was very long. You must be tired. Come in.

Sit down." She spread her arms and puckered her lips for a kiss she knew she would never receive under the circumstances.

"Cut the bullcrap." Hope turned on her heel to head back into the house.

"Do you think I could get something for the bleeding?" Serena yelled, still eyeballing the little beast that bit her.

Hope glanced over her shoulder at Serena's leg. "Sorry about that. Lizzy has a hard time with people coming into the house, even if she knows them." She tried to suppress a chuckle and failed miserably.

"I would hate to see what would happen if she didn't know them." The mood lightened when Lizzy's grin spread from ear to ear.

"It's not pretty. Tell Auntie Rena you're sorry and we'll talk about this later."

"Sorry." Lizzy clasped her hands in front of herself and stared down at her toes.

Serena squatted down to the little girl's height. "It's okay, but don't do it again," she said ruffling her hair. "Now, go play."

Elizabeth did as she was told, leaving the two women wondering how to deal with what was next.

Reluctantly, Hope waved her sister into the house. "Come on, Serena. Let's fix you up."

The sun had dipped low into the horizon. It sent flashes of color out to streak the darkening sky. Lizzy was playing with her doll on the floor when Hope and Serena sat to talk, with hopes of actually communicating. It wasn't easy, considering they never agreed on anything and never could bend on their own opinions.

"Right now Mom's at Baystate Medical Center. If she hadn't hid the fact she was sick for so long, the doctors could have done more for her. She keeps saying she didn't want to worry us. She didn't even want me to call and have you come back." Hope threw her hands in the air and rose to pace the room as a caged animal would. "Like I can take care of her myself! She says she's not going to need help, but come on! She should have both her daughters here to help her. It's only fair." The patronizing tone in Hope's voice had Serena's blood boiling.

"Of course I would want to help. Jeez, Hope! She's my mom, too." Serena glared at her sister suspiciously. "I hope you never questioned that I would come back here and help out. You make it sound like you thought I wouldn't, and that I would leave it all up to you!" She pushed herself out of the chair.

Hope stepped toe to toe and eye to eye with her sister. "Serena, calm down," she seethed.

"Jesus, Hope, what kind of person do you think I am?" She was shouting now, and she knew it. What the hell was wrong with her sister? Is Hope that self-absorbed?

"Will you please keep your voice down? And I'm not the one who left in the first place. That was you." Hope demonstrated by jabbing her finger at Serena. "I stayed to take care of things around here, while you took off with some guy."

"First of all, when I left, Mom was fine. She's a grown woman who doesn't need a babysitter. You dote on her like she's a child. And I was twenty years old. If I felt the need to leave, it was my business. I didn't need to ask your permission."

"Like you would have anyway!" A vein in Hope's neck pulsated.

"Now who's yelling?"

"You know, Rena, you only think of yourself. It's all about you. Who cares about anyone else?"

"You're absolutely right. I quit my job, packed up most of my stuff, and I got here in two days. Two days! I'm sooo sorry, Hope, that I was living my life the way I chose to." It was becoming the same old argument, the one neither of them could win.

"So what do you want? A friggin' medal?" Hope took a step back and crossed her arms.

"No! How about, 'I'm so glad you could get here so fast, Rena. I know this is hard. It is for the both of us. Tomorrow when we go see Mom, she's going to be so happy the whole family's here.'" A small lump in her throat threatened to choke off her voice.

"Give me a break." Hope rolled her eyes. "You think now that you're here it's going to make things wonderful all of a sudden?"

"No. I think me being here and the two of us finding a common ground will make things easier on everyone. I'm not the bad guy here, Hope. Her cancer is!"

They both fell silent. It wasn't fair for either of them. They each had what the other wanted: one, a beautiful loving family to go home to; the other, the freedom to chase her dreams. Not that either of them regretted the choices they had made, but neither knew if they could stop looking at what they'd always wanted, and simply enjoy what they already had.

"Hope, we have to stop this." Serena fell back on the couch and took an exhausted breath. "Let's just agree to disagree and try to get along. We need to find some form of peace for everyone's sake."

"Agreed." Hope picked up her daughter who, with big watery eyes and a trembling lower lip, needed her attention. Hope made soothing noises and talked softly in her daughter's ear. "I might need your help with her, time to time," she told Serena without turning to look at her.

"As long as she doesn't try to chew on me again." Serena gave her niece a soft pinch on the arm. Lizzy was a fireball and she was going to give her mother a run for her money.

"She's so much like you," Hope affirmed softly.

"I haven't spent nearly enough time with her. I can't believe she's already three. My God, she looks like Mom." Her sister took the sigh Serena let out with a silent understanding.

"Scary, isn't it? She even has her smart mouth. Of course, that could be from her Auntie, too. Go get your pajamas, sweetie."

Serena watched Lizzy with a small smile as she ran to the next room. "She does have my hair."

"If she's lucky, she'll get your breasts." Hope forced a laugh.

"I'm telling you, they're not what they're cracked up to be. Most of the time that's what men are talking to, and you can't sleep on your stomach," she said pointedly.

"Yeah, yeah. Give me a real reason not to want something that bounces, besides my leftover baby fat." The conversation was a standard in the O'Neal home. Even though Hope was born first, she felt she was cheated in the breast and leg category. While Serena was hourglass-shaped with long thin legs for her height, Hope was flat-chested with a long torso, and short but very shapely legs. Serena never understood her sister's problem. As a teenager, Serena's arms were too long, so every shirt sleeve was too short. Her legs felt stretched too thin, so everything was short and baggy. And the curly mass on her head refused to be tamed into submission. Eventually though, she had come to a point of acceptance in her own skin, especially after the very awkward teenage years were finally over.

"Okay Lizzy, it's time for bed." Hope attempted to snatch the girl, who was out of reach. She let out a series of giggles and ran.

"Gotcha!" Serena scooped her up into the air and held the little girl upside down. "There's no escaping!" she announced while tickling the little beast.

"No bed! No bed!"

"Do you mind?" Hope placed one hand on her waist and cocked a hip. "You're getting her wound up before bed. Now she's never going to sleep."

Serena frowned down at Lizzy. "Sorry." She placed Lizzy back on her feet. "I was only trying to help."

"Well, don't. I don't need any help." Hope scooped up her little girl and headed to the bedroom.

Serena watched her sister stomp down the hallway, all the while making faces at her back. She wondered how two people could be so different despite being raised in the same household.

CHAPTER 2

Serena sat up most of the early night trying to sort through the chaos in her head. She still had a bunch of stuff to unpack from the trailer she'd towed. And even though Hope might complain a bit, it'd be nice having her help before she returned to her own place and husband. Rolling over in her bed for the hundredth time, Serena searched out the clock, then sighed at the late hour.

"Guess I'm not sleeping tonight. Maybe I should go for a walk." Pulling on some clothes and being careful not to wake anyone, Serena slipped out the front door into the warm night air. She could hear the crickets playing their tune, and the frogs filling in background vocals. The air smelled sweet from the flowers her mother used to tend to daily. She couldn't help but note that, these days, they were overgrown with weeds. The full moon, high above her, cast long shadows with silver linings on everything it touched.

Memories flowed back, like the tender breeze teasing her face, soft, warm and refreshing. There were nights, just like this one, when she'd tiptoe out and take long walks or drives with friends. She remembered, one time, sneaking out her window and being pulled over with a bunch of friends. The cop had said she was too young to be out that late. Serena smiled sheepishly and told him she was older than she appeared to be. With a mischievous grin, Serena remembered how she'd dated that officer's son. Oh, he had been a wild one. They soon discovered, though, they were better at being friends than they were at being boyfriend-girlfriend. So much so, they'd emailed each other regularly during the seven years she'd been gone. Now he had a wife, one child, another one on the way, and Serena didn't know what to think. Did settling down really make him happy? Can one person really have everything they want? "You ask too many questions, Rena," she reminded herself.

Coming upon the entrance to the neighborhood park, Serena realized she'd walked farther than she expected. It was a good mile from home, and she was surprised she still had energy to spare. "Oh, what the hell," she said while shrugging her shoulders and letting her feet lead the way. It was a beautiful night.

She strolled past the tree-lined dirt drive to the clearing and realized not much had changed. Some of the trees had been taken down in different areas for more sun, but it still felt the same. She could smell the water that no one could swim in, a fishy, musty smell that would get stronger at night and on humid days. Her thoughts wandered with the easy current. The crickets and frogs sang to the night breeze, and the water bugs skated on the pond like graceful ice dancers. "It's so peaceful," she said with a sigh, and turned her face up to bathe in the moonlight; then she heard something.

Serena's eyes grew huge when she turned to the commotion heading toward her. She let out a quick unconscious scream before beating back the urge to run. Fear became a twisted knot in her stomach as the dog came to a sliding halt, tackling her.

"Oh, shit!" The next thing Serena knew she was butt first in the mud, with a very big dopey dog staring down at her. And as ridiculous as it seemed, Serena could have sworn the dog was smiling. It was then she took noticed of his master. Now this is a man! Tall, broad shoulders, narrow waist, and a great face with its sharp chin and crooked nose. His hair was in disarray as if he'd been running his hands through the thick mass of it. Serena tried not to lick her lips. The man looked delicious. She dropped a protective veil over her eyes. He probably has a harem that follows him around.

"Bart!" The dog's owner was panting with his hands on his knees. "I'm sorry. I don't know what got into him. He never does that. Bad boy!" He scolded the dog and extended a hand to Serena. She placed her hand in his and felt a strong sexual current run from his fingertips to hers.

"Oh, he's pathetic!" she crooned, taking the man's hand to hoist herself up. Bart put his head down as far as he could and peeked up at Serena, his eyes pleading for forgiveness. "He couldn't hurt a fly, could he?" She turned to the stranger grinning.

* * * *

Brian's first thought had been one of annoyance. He came here late at night to be alone. But now, with this stranger, he didn't know what to say. He was too busy being enchanted by her face and smelling her wild yet subtle scent. He still couldn't make out the color of her eyes and hair, but her face was all soft curves like her body. She was short, when he'd been certain she'd be taller when he'd seen her from across the field. It was all that leg, all that long lovely leg, tiny waist and… I don't care one way or the other, but nice full breasts. Jesus, what am I, a teenager goggling at some lady? Brian pulled a hand through his hair. "Are you okay?"

"Yes, thank you." She swiped at the dirt on her butt.

"Sorry about Bart." It had to be a trick of the moonlight's reflection on the billowing water that did those wonderful things to her skin. She glowed silver, and tiny sparkling lights floated around her. The moonbeams reflected off her hair, creating a halo around her head. She didn't seem real, yet there she was.

The woman before Brian looked at his dog, who still had his head down. When Bart let out a moan, Brian knew it was his way of apologizing. Laughing, the mystery woman put her hand out to the furry beast. Taking this as complete forgiveness, Bart licked up her arm. "Yuck!" she exclaimed, wiping it on her jeans.

Brian's body hardened as a surge of lustful energy brought it to attention. "Sorry. I'm not kidding. He never does this. You must be sweet."

Serena snickered. "I guess it depends on who you're talking to."

"What are you doing walking here by yourself? What if Bart was some crazed animal with rabies and attacked you? Or I was?" Brian asked with an accusing tone.

"Are you?" she asked with a small challenge.

"What?" Annoyed with himself and with his reaction toward her, Brian planted his hands on his hips and furrowed his eyebrows.

"Some crazed animal with rabies?"

"No, not the last time I checked," he replied, dryly.

"Well then, I think the verdict is in on the dog not having rabies. And, as for you, I would have dropkicked your ass into the lake. Then left you to the fish and whatever else lives in there." She thumbed to the water. "That would have served you right."

"Good answer. I'm Brian," he said putting out a hand.

"Serena," she replied while taking his hand. Then she rolled her eyes. "Oh, crap." They both watched out over the field as a police car came into sight with its lights rotating red and blue. "What is it with this town? I swear the cops sniff me out."

"They here for you?" Brian asked with humor.

"Who knows? With the way word spreads around here, they probably knew I was coming home before I did."

"Serena O'Neal! I'd know that ass anywhere," the officer yelled while getting out of his squad car.

"Darren!" Serena launched herself at the newcomer and, wrapping her legs around his waist, hugged him tight.

Watching, Brian knew this little scene would be in his fantasies later that evening, but he would be on the receiving end of it.

"I'm glad you at least walked here with someone. He's a good neighbor." Darren put Serena down and turned to Brian. "She's always going places by herself. Used to drive me up the wall."

"Well, I'm glad I could be of service." Turning, Brian winked at Serena. "We were about to head back. Weren't we, Serena?"

Giving Brian a suspicious stare, she turned to Darren. "So, you two know each other?"

"Hell, Bri and I have been friends for what? Four years now? Had to put him in a holding cell for a night. He was drunk and disorderly," Darren explained.

"I was not disorderly," Brian said matter-of-factly.

"Right." Darren gave Bart a friendly pat. The dog grunted in what seemed like a hello. "And the bar bathroom floor was a great place to spend the night."

"I was out of the way and in the corner," he clarified for Serena. "You know, Darren, you're going to give this girl a bad impression of me."

Darren laughed as Serena gave him a joking shot in the ribs. "I think you've told me about him." Serena nodded toward Brian. "Is he the one who's always trying to pick up your wife?"

"That's him," Darren stated with pride.

"It's only a matter of time till she leaves you for me." Brian rocked back on his heels. "It's a known fact, I've got better legs," he told Serena.

"So I've noticed," she replied slyly. "Darren, why is it all your friends, including your wife, were arrested by you?"

"Hey! He did not arrest me." Brian was sticking to his story no matter what everyone said.

"I need to keep an eye on everyone." He turned to Brian. "Certain people I have to stay closer to than others."

"Like your father did for us? Don't let him fool you for a minute, Brian. I have sooo much on this man that I could..."

"You know I need to be going, Serena." Darren took a deep breath and released it slowly, with a sigh. "I'm sorry about your mother. If there's anything we can do, let me know."

"Thanks." Serena thought for a minute and then added, "If you're not doing anything tomorrow, I could use some help unpacking the trailer."

"I'll call you in the morning." He gave Serena a peck on the cheek and Brian a nod. After saying goodbye to Bart, Darren got into his car and drove off.

Together, Serena and Brian walked back to the park entrance in a cloak of silence. Their thoughts were with a sick woman who meant a great deal to both of them. Thoughts that had them seeking a place of solitude and darkness that night; what they'd found instead was the comfort and understanding of a stranger.

"I like your mom." Brian put an arm around Serena's shoulder and squeezed her to him. He couldn't say why he did it, but it felt good and it felt right. "She would always bring me cake or cookies."

"Best way to get to a man is through his stomach."

"Isn't that the truth?" Brian joked. "Funny you and me always missed each other."

Serena let out a long wistful sigh. "I didn't visit nearly enough."

"Come on! We all have to go our own way sometime." Brian pulled her close again. "You know living here isn't that bad. So what if everyone knows everything about you? So what if the roads never get plowed in the winter? Things could be worse. Bart here could have tried to hump you." The off-handed comment had Serena smiling up at him. "Thatta girl," he said while pinching her chin. "So, what is it you do for a living?"

"I'm a hairdresser. I gotta find a job now that I'm back."

"Oooh, I wouldn't mind you putting your hands on my head sometime." He wiggled his eyebrows at her and grinned.

"We'll have to see about that. And what is it you do, Mr. Smooth?" Bart bumped his large head against Serena's hip and sent her into Brian. "Sorry."

"Not a problem, any time." He laughed when Serena rolled her eyes. "I'm a mechanic," he told her.

"Really? Do anything under the table?"

"That's a loaded question, babe."

"With cars, Brian. I—" Serena was cut off by Bart's whole body hitting hers. It sent her barreling into Brian, who caught her in his arms. Their bodies pressed intimately together, their breaths mingling as their eyes stayed steady on one another's.

"You've spoiled him," she whispered.

"Nah," Brian's eyes went from her eyes to her full lips and back again. "He simply likes you." So do I. Damn, I'm falling for the girl next door. But, boy she doesn't look the part. Brian put himself in check. He'd already been down this road once before and that was enough. However, laughing with her like old friends, having her body so close to his, it all made not trying to get to know her that much harder.

Serena took a step back, and then started walking again in silence. "What?" she asked at Brian's concerned stare.

"Where did you go?"

"Sorry, I do that a lot. My brain likes to wander off. I know it's the rudest thing, but there's nothing I can do about it. You should have seen me in school. I think my best subject was mythology." Nervousness caused Serena's voice to move too fast along with her hand gestures. "Everything was a great big story of passion and greed. Of course, sometimes the passion consisted of father-daughter relationships, or son-mother, sister-brother. But, hey! It was exciting. All those make-believe characters! Some were so neat to imagine, walking around the Earth or in the sky, flying horses, and..." She stopped talking for a moment. "And I'm starting to ramble. I'm sorry. I tend to do that, too."

"I have a habit of doing it myself sometimes. Here's your house." He nestled a hand in the small of her back and led her toward the door.

"I guess you're right. Thanks for the company home." At the door light, Serena turned, then stumbled into Brian. Her hands went up to his chest, their bodies brushed and their eyes locked. The spring air warmed around them from the mixture of humidity and lust.

"You're welcome, Serena." Brian brought his hands up to the ones resting on his chest. They were smooth and small boned. He brought one to his lips and kissed the palm. "Let me know if there is anything else I can do." Like taste your lips, strip off your clothes, and make mad passionate... Really Brian, get a handle on your imagination.

"You'll be the first to know. Thanks again," Serena said and dashed into the house.

Mmm... This is going to be an interesting summer, Brian thought while rocking back on his heels. Serena O'Neal was going to be fun to figure out. He wondered what the rise of color in her cheeks was. The smile that stretched across his face was devious. I'm just going to have to find out. Brian glanced again at the door and wondered if he made her nervous. Yeah, he decided happily and whistled the rest of the way home.

CHAPTER 3

Serena slowly woke to the sounds of a child's laughter. Sleep hung over her the way thick fog would hang over a grassy field on a hazy night. Her eyes refused to open, even as her brain began the slow process of recognition. Not enough sleep, was her first thought. How can I function when I can't smell the coffee machine doing its job? Did I forget to set it for seven? she asked herself through the haze. Without coffee, morning cannot and will not be possible.

Serena moaned and blindly got out of bed. She then proceeded to walk smartly into the dresser where the door was supposed to be. "Crap!" Her senses cleared quickly as pain seared through her knee. "Crap," she announced again while falling back onto the bed.

Rubbing her knee hard and fast, Serena surveyed her childhood room and then sighed. "So you're home, Rena. Now what?"

The shadows of the impending day crossed her face. It felt as if doom would prevail in this fight. Yet she couldn't think about 'worst case' when it came to her mother. She could only think about what to do now. She hung her head in her hands, with a feeling of defeat. None of us have a lot of money. Now I don't even have a job. She thought about how the walk the night before had energized her. But as she stared out the window at the early morning light, Serena felt her precious energy slipping away.

"I need to get myself out of bed," she murmured, "and face the day."

Hearing the laughter down the hall Serena rubbed her knee, got her robe, and limped out of her room. She found the source for all the commotion behind the bathroom door. It was early morning bath time and Hope was trying to rinse Elizabeth's hair, while Elizabeth was trying to rinse her mother.

"Stop that! You're going to get the floor all wet. Now stay still." Serena could hear Hope's patience start to wane.

"No!" Lizzy screamed.

"Yes!" her mother argued.

"Boy, am I glad it's you and not me." Serena rested her body against the door jamb.

Hope scowled and the angel in the tub dumped a cup full of water out of it.

"Lizzy! That's it! When bath time is over you're going for a time out."

Lizzy began to wail as Serena took out some towels to help mop up the mess.

"Why don't you let me finish up, this way you can make some coffee?" Serena had seen the strain on Hope's face when she walked into the bathroom. She knew it was going to be a long day for the both of them.

"Good luck." Hope stomped out of the water-soaked bathroom.

"Why you giving your mom a hard time this morning?" Serena asked her niece. "She only wants to make sure you don't smell."

Lizzy sat quietly with a trembling lower lip as Serena slowly and carefully rinsed her hair and body. "You know, your mom didn't like to take baths either when she was younger. Of course, that's what Grandma always told me."

"Grandma's sick." The girl seemed so sad when she said it that tears welled up in Serena's eyes.

"Yes honey, she is sick. I hope she can come home soon."

"Me too! We were suppoz to go to the air together."

"You mean the fair?"

"Yeah!" Lizzy hopped out of the tub.

"Charter Day." Hope came back in carrying two large mugs of steaming coffee. "Mom takes us every year. It's next weekend."

"Well now," Serena said to her niece, "we can't miss an important day like that! There are rides to be ridden, prizes to be won, and food to be eaten. What do you say, Lizzy? Will you show me around the fair next week?"

"Sure! Can Briam come too? Grandma always has Briam come. He wins me big prizes. Last year he brought this girl too." At that, Lizzy screwed up her face. "I didn't like her much."

"I'll ask him not to bring her." Fully clothed, Lizzy was off and running as Serena's body warmed with the memory from the night before of a handsome man with strong muscles. He's not bringing some girl if I have anything to say about it.

"I can't remember if you've met Brian," Hope commented while handing Serena her mug of coffee. "He's like our adopted brother."

Serena downed half the mug after deciding coffee couldn't be held off any longer. "Yeah, I met him," she stated with a wiggling of her brows.

Hope laughed. "He has great legs... and a couple of other nice attributes." She gave Serena a wicked smile over her own coffee.

"Hope! You're a happily married woman. You're not supposed to notice things like that." Serena considered for a second or two. "Is he single? You know, just in case I happen to wander into a friendship with him. I wouldn't want to step on any toes." She playfully batted her lashes at her sister.

"Oh, I bet you wouldn't. Divorced, about three years ago. What a mess. That girl took him to the cleaners and didn't even bother to wring him out. Since then he's dated around, nothing serious. Bagel or muffin?"

"Bagel, thanks." Bad divorce. Serena, this is not a man you want to hook up with. He's got high maintenance written all over him.

The dry tone in Serena's voice had Hope turning to get a glimpse at her sister. "What are you thinking about?"

"Men, and how much I like his dog." She took another swig of coffee then rested her chin in her hand. "And how last night he was, oh I don't know, I guess comforting would be the right word."

"Wait a minute, Serena, what do you mean last night?"

Serena grinned up from her coffee deviously. "I snuck out last night. Escaped!" she said with her eyes growing big. "I walked down to the park and met the most beautiful creature on earth. He was big, dark, and handsome." She let out a sigh of appreciation. "Oh, Hope, he even kissed me."

"No way!"

"Yeah, I hope I see him today." Serena sighed dreamily. "It's so nice, he doesn't even drool."

"Rena, what do you mean he doesn't drool? Are you talking about the dog?" She gave her sister a look of disgust. "You had me going there for a minute. I thought maybe you and Brian had something going on."

"Sorry. No smut was going on last night. Although... when he walked me to the door I thought about what it would be like having him rip my clothes off."

"Mmm. Having your clothes ripped off by a very attractive stranger. That would be one of a woman's most seductive fantasies come true."

"Isn't that the truth?" Serena's smile was wicked and her eyes were dancing. "Maybe he'll take pity on us while we're unpacking the trailer and grace us with his hard, muscular, sultry body. I'm getting excited thinking about it!" Serena gave a not so subtle tremble and giggled.

Watching, Hope joined in the laugh. "You know Rena, the imagination you have is unbelievable."

"Actually, I just have a very corrupt mind." They were actually getting along, Serena noted with amazement.

Hope turned to the dishes in the sink. "I'm really glad you're back. This place has been way too quiet without you."

Serena knew it cost her to say that. She knew there was still a deep chasm between her and her sister. Therefore, she got up from the table where she'd been eating her bagel, and went to her. "I've missed you too, sis. And I'm not going anywhere." Serena wrapped her arms around Hope, and they both held on tight. This, Serena thought, is how we should have greeted each other yesterday. With support and understanding, not harsh words and angry stares.

"Stop." Hope pulled herself away from Serena. "You're going to make me cry." There were already tears there, teetering on the edge of escape, but pride would not let them fall.

Watching her sister at the sink, Serena couldn't help but wonder what happened to those two little girls who used to go on adventures together, who used to share secret spy information. Some of the time, they'd play dolls and house, or dress each other up and pretend they were going out. But that was when life was simple. Then their parents' divorce came and lives were changed. Nothing hurt as much as the feeling of being torn apart. If there was a single moment in their lives that defined who they would become and how they would handle the world, that was it. Hope took to being a second mother around the house. She took responsibility for things no ten-year-old should. She cooked and cleaned. Tried to comfort their mother in times of great stress. Then, eventually, Hope became somewhat of a boss. To this, Serena rebelled. She couldn't understand her sister's need to ride her back about everything. Slowly, Serena became increasingly independent and defiant. And though things did settle into a routine, a rift was formed with resentment in its crack. Later, when jobs and stability made things easier, their relationship began to build again. Nevertheless, there was always an air of distrust. Until finally one day, Serena gave up. She felt she couldn't please Hope, no matter what, and she was sick of trying. Therefore, Serena left, and Hope felt abandoned. And when all of Serena's visits ended in emotional blowouts, Serena stayed away for longer stretches of time, something that their mother didn't take too well. But when it came to discussing Hope and Serena's relationship, their mother learned fast it was better not to get involved.

The sound of the phone ringing brought both of the women back from their thoughts. "I bet that's Darren. He said he'd call in the morning to help with the unpacking."

Hope laughed. "Let me guess, you ran into the police last night on your walk."

"I swear they follow me! Hello," she said picking up the phone.

"Hey, sweetie!" Serena could hear Darren's smile in his voice. "I didn't want to call too early and wake you up."

"Don't worry, everyone gets up early in this house. We're going to see Mom around…" She pulled the phone away from her ear and looked at Hope, who signaled with three fingers. "Three o'clock."

"Then Meg and I will be over at eleven. She'll be expecting food."

"Yeah, I'm sure you are." Serena knew he was grinning on the other end. "Darren, you were always such a leech."

"Hey, the woman's expecting, you can't let her starve!"

"Yes we can, right Hope? We don't feed the help."

Hope yelled back to Darren, "Absolutely, bring your own food. We don't take in strays!"

"Then you get no help!" he replied.

Darren always knew what to say to make Serena feel better. When things were at their worst, Darren was at his best. That, Serena was convinced, was the reason he made such a good cop.

CHAPTER 4

It was eleven on the dot when Darren and crew came into the drive. He was long and lanky, with dark chestnut hair that was always in perfect order. Serena liked to mess it up whenever she could. The tall blonde that got out of the passenger side was a very soft-featured woman with the biggest blue eyes Serena had ever seen. With the exception, of course, of the little ball of blonde fire that was trying to get out of the back seat.

"Wanta see Lizzy! Wanta see Lizzy!"

"You will simply have to be patient." Meg glanced over at Serena with what could be described as a 'kill me now' expression on her face. She was getting so big with this child and looked as if she didn't have the energy to go on.

Meg let Emily go free, and then leaned heavily against the side of the car. "I don't want to do this anymore. I can't do this anymore. And you!" She jabbed at Darren's chest with a finger. "Can't make me have any more!"

"Of course you don't have to have any more, honey." His smile was wide as he led her to where Serena was getting the outside toys for the girls. "And it will all be over real soon."

"Yeah, right! The hard part hasn't even come yet!" Meg yelled at him. "Get your hands off me before I tear them off. You will never touch me again. You will sleep on the couch, and like it!"

Serena happily watched them. "Awww. Married bliss. It makes me so sentimental."

"Doesn't it? She loves me, you know." It was so sweet watching Darren wrap his arms around Meg who, to Serena's amusement, made half-hearted protests as he kissed her. "We're going through the 'men are good for nothing' stage."

"Don't you patronize me, Darren. I can make your life a living hell," Meg told him.

"Honey, it already is."

"Good! And don't forget who made it that way."

He kissed her one last time on the nose and headed next door.

"You guys are too much." Serena laughed. "I only hope my future husband and I can abuse each other so well." Both women attempted an embrace, but Meg's belly wouldn't get out of the way.

"There's way too much of me for physical contact." Meg put her hands on her enormous belly. "Two weeks, three days. I'm not counting down or anything."

"Oh, no. Why would you do a thing like that?"

"Because being pregnant sucks," Hope announced while coming out of the house.

"Hope! God, I've missed you." Meg tried the hug thing again and didn't do much better.

"Meg, you look great! Right?" Hope elbowed Serena, who was distracted by the tall dark blond walking with Darren. She had hoped Brian would come over to help, and was secretly glad she'd taken the extra time with herself that morning.

"Glad you have dark sunglasses on, Rena. He might think you're staring at him."

"Yeah, well he's staring right back," Serena said and started walking toward them. What a sight these two make. One tall, dark, muscular and yet lanky. And the other… God, I hope I'm not drooling.

Tall, broad, powerful and… calm down girl!

* * * *

The men were walking across the lawn when Serena headed their way with tiny jean shorts on, a deep blue tank top, and bare feet.

Darren told Brian, "You never get used to it. You just learn to appreciate it."

Brian looked over to see Darren grinning at him. "She's dangerous. And man," Brian said after taking a sharp spontaneous breath, "it's been a long time since I've wanted to do something dangerous."

"Down boy. She doesn't date much. Serena's always been more one of the guys."

"That is no guy. This is the girl Mom warns you about," Brian said firmly. "Shit, Darren. I have all sorts of impure thoughts going through my head." To this, Darren laughed.

"Hey guys! I could surely use some strong capable men to help me unpack. Do you think you're up for the job? I've got something in mind for payment." Face to face, Serena batted her eyelashes behind her sunglasses. "If you're interested," she added with a sultry tone. "I'm afraid that some of the stuff is a bit too heavy."

After batting her lashes again, Serena thought about what a wonderful thing it would be if Brian tossed her to the ground and had his way with her. It'd been too long since she'd felt a man's hands and mouth on her body. And now seeing him in the late morning light she realized they weren't going to make it with just being neighbors. Not if this pulling attraction continued.

"You really are too much, Rena. I'll go open the hatchway," Darren told them as he walked away.

"So what kind of payment did you have in mind?" Brian stepped close and into her space. He took off his sunglasses and, to Serena's surprise, revealed his eyes were a mesmerizing steel gray. They entranced her almost speechless and let her know, at that very moment, that anything Brian wanted he could have.

"Lunch," was all she managed in a strangled voice. Her brain had gone completely blank as she watched his hands sweep up to take her sunglasses off.

"I wondered all night what color those eyes are." His voice was smooth as silk wrapping around her thoughts.

"Brown."

"Oh, no. Brown, my dear, is much too plain to describe those. There's red fire in there."

Through the trance that had fallen over them, Serena and Brian could faintly hear a voice. "Hey! Get your butts over here and start helping, 'cause the pregnant one is not lifting a finger!" At the sound of Meg's voice they shot back from one another as if jolted from a dream.

Serena blinked twice at Brian as reality crashed around her. She felt something change inside of her. Her chest hurt and her brain couldn't quite register what Brian was shouting.

"Wow, she's bossy, Darren," Brian yelled at Darren as he came from around the house. "How can you put up with someone like that?"

"Love and absolute pure affection." He smiled at his wife, who flipped him off in return. "Come on, Bri, this stuff isn't going to move itself. And she promised us lunch."

After a quick and hard shake of his head, Brian grabbed the first big box with ease. "What do you have in here, plastic ware?"

"Don't you worry, honey," Serena purred. "I'll make you work for what you want."

He stopped as he passed by her and whispered in her ear, "God I hope so, because nothing is done right without a lot of sweat and hard, hard work."

Serena felt her knees go weak as Brian trotted off, leaving her with that thought. I really need to get a hold of myself, but jeez! Look at that butt!

* * * *

With Darren busy burning the burgers and dogs on the grill, Serena steamed corn on the cob inside with the girls. It hadn't taken very long to unpack and everyone was happily chatting and catching up.

"You know you shouldn't let Darren near the grill," Meg was saying. "I don't know why everyone always lets him, it's like eating leather."

"It's better than letting Rena cook." Hope laughed. "Remember the meatloaf we had to spoon out?"

"Hope's got a point, Meg." Serena waved the tongs at Meg. "You know I can make some very dangerous concoctions." She turned back to the corn in the pot and missed the look exchanged between Meg and Hope.

"God, I think the best thing I've ever eaten was the roast Bri made for us on Thanksgiving. Remember that, Hope?"

Hope made a sound of admiration. "Serena, you couldn't make it home that year. Boy, did you miss out!"

"Well, maybe I'll have to show off my cooking skills again real soon." Brian was leaning against the door jamb grinning like a Cheshire cat. "You know Meg, you're the only one he'll listen to—" He thumbed toward outside and Darren. "—and unless you want black burgers that are raw in the middle, which he has a knack for, you really need to get out there."

"I'll help you," Hope said as they both rushed out of the kitchen.

"You know I'm going to have to hurt him if he burns those burgers." Serena gestured with the tongs at Brian in a threatening manner.

"We wouldn't want that, now would we?" In a blink Brian had the tongs out of her hands, and her body trapped between the sink and him.

"You could hurt somebody with those. I might have to teach you a lesson."

"Oh really?" Serena tossed back her hair and threw up her chin. "And what would make you the one to teach it?"

He grabbed her chin in his hand and looked deep into her eyes. "Let's just say I like a challenge." Slowly he lowered his face close to hers. The defiance he saw in her eyes filled his body with need. "You've never met anyone like me. I won't treat you like a trophy."

"I have no need, or want, to be treated like a trophy." Serena had fire in her eyes and ire in her voice.

Brian wouldn't kiss her now, but man, he wanted to. "No, but everyone always has, haven't they?" He liked seeing that spark of anger. It excited him and made him want to see more, so he brought his face a little closer to hers.

"You really are an arrogant man, Brian." Serena narrowed her eyes and stood her ground. "I'm not sure I want to even be around you."

Their lips were a breath apart; their breathing deep and ragged. "I don't know what it is that we do to each other, but sooner or later we're going to find out." He wanted a taste of her, one small taste, but he knew one taste would never be enough.

"I take things very slow, Brian. I don't like to jump into anything." Serena gave him a lopsided smile. "And my life is completely out of order right now."

"I don't want to complicate your life." What Brian saw in her eyes made him take a step back. "I'm sorry, Serena." He cupped her face in his hands and kissed her forehead. "If ever you need anything, you simply have to ask."

"I know." Serena wiggled her eyebrows at him and they both laughed. "If you've ruined my corn, Brian," she said pushing him away, "I swear I'm going to have to hurt you."

"I get the feeling you have a lot of pent-up aggression in that little body of yours."

She snatched the tongs from him and went back to the corn. "You keep getting in my way and you're going to find out."

That's the plan, he thought.

CHAPTER 5

Brian had watched Serena all through lunch. It was easy to see the strain on her and Hope's faces and the black circles under their eyes. Silently, they had all agreed not to discuss why Serena had come home. The caring sentiment made the late morning more enjoyable for everyone.

After lunch, Darren and his crew said their goodbyes. When Brian went to leave, he had to fight back the urge to take Serena in his arms and protect her from the sadness, confusion, and need for answers where there were none. The grief in her eyes told him a story he was all too familiar with. And to Brian's surprise he decided, when the time was right, he would share his own loss and heartbreak with Serena. He only hoped it would help ease some of her pain and not add to it.

It was a while later when, looking up from under his car's hood, Brian saw Willie's car pull into the drive. He could tell Hope's husband had just gotten out of work. His clothes were filthy with a day's work, and he still had on his uniform cap. Ten minutes later, Brian saw two cars leave in opposite directions. Silently, he said a little prayer for all of them and went back to working on his car.

* * * *

Hope drove into the hospital parking lot with the ease and precision only a cautious driver has. Serena felt a tug of guilt as the car slid effortlessly into a parking spot. "I should have come yesterday."

"You talked to her on the phone and she was barely coherent." Hope put a reassuring hand on Serena's, and got out of the car. "The surgery took a lot out of her. It's okay."

They both fell silently in step, pursuing their own thoughts. When the automatic doors slid open with a swish, hospital smells—cleaners and antiseptics—immediately overcame them.

In Serena's mind, she heard the lingering silence of anticipated doom. As she and Hope passed people, she took in the different faces and expressions, each telling its own tale. Stories of great joy—a woman in a wheelchair, holding her new baby while being pushed by her husband. Or stories of great sorrow—the elevator doors slid open revealing a teary-eyed family with lost expressions on their faces. It's bad news. I can see it in their faces. Will people be able to see it in ours? Will that be us, leaning on each other, crying? Serena and Hope entered the elevator, the heavy silence between the sisters lingering on.

Hope took a quick glance at her sister. Without saying a word, she grabbed Serena's hand, gave it a squeeze, but continued staring straight ahead as the doors slid open to their floor.

Stepping out, Serena saw the signs for the cancer unit. Reality struck her rigid and she found herself unable to continue down the path. "This isn't happening," she whispered. "It can't be."

Serena looked at Hope and noticed, for the first time, there were tears in her sister's eyes. Hope tried to be smooth about wiping them away, but then the sniffles started.

"Now, how am I supposed to keep up a front of taking this well when I have you falling apart next to me?" Serena put an arm around her sister's shoulders so they could lean on each other.

"You know, Rena." Hope took a deep breath and wiped at the tears one more time. "You really are a jerk."

"I know. It's in the blood." Serena gave her sister a reassuring hug before they continued to search for the doctor's office.

The cold, uninviting corridors of the hospital caused Serena to shiver as they walked. Even though the place had plenty of positive colors and paintings, nothing could overcome the building's gloomy institutional atmosphere.

When they entered the reception room, Serena saw it was filled with the same bright cheerful pinks, yellows, and blues, as well as chairs that appeared to be soft and comfortable.

"At least no one's butt is going to fall asleep," Serena tried to joke. Her attempt was met with a bland stare.

They found the receptionist to be friendly enough. At least it seemed like a genuine smile, Serena thought to herself while sitting. She took a shot at reading a magazine to pass the time but soon spotted a fish tank. The fish inside swam without a care to what was going on outside of their world. One darted from the top of the tank down and back up again. Serena couldn't help but chuckle.

"Remember when I tried to keep fish?" She leaned over close to Hope and spoke softly, so as not to disturb the others waiting.

"Yeah," Hope said with little to no interest. "You killed them with the glass cleaner you used to clean the outside of the tank."

"How was I supposed to know you couldn't do that? Besides, your fish used to try to jump out of the tank." Serena felt the satisfaction of it being something they both failed at. "Fish, no matter what anyone says, are not easy to take care of."

"Yeah well, it doesn't really matter now, does it? It's not why we're here."

"I was just trying to lighten things up a little." Serena turned away and rolled her eyes as Hope began to rant.

"Don't. You never take anything seriously enough. Then it's left for me to figure it all out." She gave Serena a stern eagle eye. "So I hope you can pay attention in there to what the doctor's saying and not crack a bunch of jokes."

"Excuse me, but humor is how I handle things." Serena glared at her sister with contempt. "Oh, and I don't need to be told when I need to pay attention. I'm quite capable of being serious when the situation calls for it."

"Well, obviously not!" Hope's voice was starting to rise. "Otherwise you wouldn't be cracking jokes and talking about fish right now."

"I don't think this is the time or place for one of your parental lectures." Serena could feel her body getting hot from her temper rising. "Nor do I think you have a right to give me one, considering I am an adult."

Hope crossed her arms. "Then start acting like one."

"I don't know why I even bother." Serena waved her sister off.

"I wonder that myself som—" The receptionist interrupted, telling them quietly and efficiently they would be seen now. She showed the sisters into the doctor's office and then closed the door gently.

"Good afternoon, ladies. I'm Dr. Kinney." He shook their hands then gestured toward some more soft chairs, this time in seafoam green. "Please have a seat. Now, as your mother has requested this information be provided to both of you, we will start with her diagnosis. I realize some of this may be a repeat of information for you, Ms. Burk, so please bear with me while I bring Ms. O'Neal up to speed." His soft and soothing voice had Serena and Hope slowly beginning to relax as he told them about their mother's condition. "Your mother had what we would call a grade two tumor. It's an intermediate grade, between grade one, which is low, and grade three, which is a high appearance of unhealthy looking cells. Your mother's stage of cancer and how far it has advanced is what determined the treatment she chose to undergo. As you know, cancer of the uterus has a very good survival rate when detected early enough. The type your mother is battling is uterine carcinosarcoma, as evidenced by the tumor we removed."

"And do you feel this was detected at an early stage?" Serena was now sitting forward in her seat. She wanted to simply leap out of it and demand to know if her mother would live or die.

"Everyone reacts to the treatments differently. We'll know more once she starts the radiation. She's healthy. That fact gives her an advantage."

Dr. Kinney's hands were folded on the desk and he was looking directly at them. How many times, Serena wondered, how many times had he been that confident, said those words, and still been wrong?

"Your mother will be able to go home in a week. She will be restricted on her activities and will have to come back for follow-ups. These will include blood work to keep a watch on her white blood cells and platelets. I also want to see how the radiation is affecting her physically as well as emotionally."

"How often will she have to have the radiation?" Hope asked as Serena felt her stomach start to reject her lunch.

"Radiation is usually given five days a week for six to seven weeks. It will depend on how her body is responding to the treatment and how she is doing with its side effects. Each external radiation therapy session lasts about fifteen to twenty minutes. She will be getting the radiation for only a few minutes of that time. She will feel no pain during treatment. It's like having an x-ray done. You can't see, hear, or smell the radiation. She will be comfortable." He took his time, spacing his words evenly. "There aren't many side effects to the radiation, though some people tend to have more than others. We'll have to wait and see."

Serena took a large gulp of air. "How will we know? Is it days? Weeks?"

"Some people have side effects right away." Dr. Kinney made a steeple with his hands. "And others take months or even years to develop them. She'll most likely find she has some fatigue. Some low stress exercise will help with this, and of course proper rest and diet. Her skin will most likely change. I have discussed this with her already. I also told her it would be helpful to have someone drive her back and forth to her appointments. She's going to need to conserve her energy."

"Do you hear that, Rena? That's going to be your job, to make sure she doesn't overdo it. And—"

"I know why I moved back home, Hope. I think we should finish listening to what the doctor has to say before we battle out round two." Serena gave her sister a cocky grin, and Hope gave Rena a look of death.

"You each must remember that you both have your mother's best interests at heart. Fighting with one another will not only cause unneeded tension in the family, but could hamper your mother's recovery." He leaned forward to emphasize his next set of words. "Your mother needs to worry about getting herself better right now, not whether her daughters aren't getting along and she's the cause of it."

"Mom knows she isn't the reason we don't get along, and I highly doubt it'd be something we'd have to explain to her."

Dr. Kinney turned to Hope. "Ms. Burk. People going through life-changing ordeals feel any fighting amongst the people they love is their fault, whether it's true or not. They pick up on the tension and, like anyone, react to it. Your mother is going to feel as if she's a burden on the ones taking care of her. She will feel responsible. Cancer is not just something that must be dealt with physically. It must be dealt with emotionally as well. There are support groups you can join that meet here at the hospital. Some even meet at people's homes." He turned to Serena to include her in the conversation. "You can go online and talk to people. Also, there's call lines open twenty-four hours. Both of you must realize that your mother is not the only one going through this, you are too." With their heads hung, both women were rightfully scolded "Go see your mother. She's probably sleeping, but it will be good just the same. She needs you both, as you need her. Look into the support groups, go to the library and take out some books. The more you educate yourself, the easier it will be to understand, deal with, and make the right decisions." Dr. Kinney then stood, signaling their meeting had come to an end. They shook hands with him, said thank you, and silently walked out the door.

"I need a drink," Serena thought, aloud.

"Yeah, a strong one."

Serena snickered at her sister. "That's actually not what I originally had in mind, but I'm game."

"After we visit mom, let's get us one. We deserve it."

Serena nodded her head and gave a murmured agreement as they walked down the hall. It sounded very good to her.

Chapter 6

Their mother's room was quiet and dark. Someone had closed the shades so Katherine could sleep without being disturbed by the light. The room smelled of flowers and antiseptic. The quiet was only disturbed by the consistent hum of machines and her breathing. Sleep was deep and necessary to her health now.

As Serena and Hope entered the room, a feeling of dread came over them. They each took a chair on either side of their mother's bed and silently began to pray. Serena felt her eyes fill with tears when a hand began to stroke her hair.

Hope leaned forward. "Hi. How are you feeling?"

"You know, Mom," Serena said with a chuckle, "if you wanted me to come home you could have just asked. There are easier ways of getting me here than getting sick."

Katherine tried to give a half-hearted laugh but instead winced in pain. "I'm sorry," she whispered. "I'm a little tender in the middle."

"I shouldn't have tried to make you laugh. I'm sorry." Serena took her mother's hand and kissed her fingers. Guilt overwhelmed her.

"Hey," Hope interjected, trying to lighten the mood, "the doctor said you should be able to go home in a week. Isn't that great? Then you can be in your own bed with your own pillow. And guess what? I went out and bought you one of your favorite books and some crosswords so you won't be bored when you're here or at home." Hope took the books out of her bag and placed them on the table beside the bed. "And when you get home you'll have Serena and me to help with everything."

"Yeah, I figured I've been away too long and home is where I want to be." Serena gave her mother a big smile, and a look of deep affection.

Katherine snorted. "You're full of crap."

"Mom!" Serena exclaimed. "Since when have you developed this trash mouth?"

"Since I don't give a damn what anybody thinks."

"Thatta girl!" Hope proclaimed.

The visit was short but sweet and when they left Katherine was asleep once again. Surfacing from the hospital, Serena found it only fitting that the sky had opened up and rain had come. It seemed an appropriate conclusion to a very stressful day. They ran through the storm with lightning flashing and the sky shaking with the sounds of rumbling thunder. Drenched by the time they got into the car, they both agreed that drink would have to wait.

The ride home was solemn. The only sound they heard was the constant rhythmic drumming of the rain. By the time Hope pulled into the driveway, it had come to a slow drizzle. Not caring if she was dry or wet, Serena slowly walked toward the house with an overpowering feeling that things would never be the same again.

All Serena wanted was a nap. She was mentally and physically exhausted when she crawled across her bed and burrowed deep into her pillow. A few hours later she woke to find a now clear sky. The storm was over, the sun low. Serena's stomach was feeling a little too queasy and her body too tired to make the effort to cook so she decided supper just wasn't going to happen. She peered out the kitchen window as the sun began to set. Serena watched as the sky took on an array of color: vivid reds, sunny yellows, and magnificent oranges. Realizing she wanted to be outside with the damp fresh air, Serena grabbed a towel, something to drink and headed out to the old bench swing, a perfect place to think or not think. With her eyes closed and her head tipped back to the quiet breeze, Serena's thoughts wandered in and out of a half-dream.

* * * *

That's how Brian found her, with the setting sun casting shadows on her face. Though it's been a tough day, she's still got a beautiful face. Brian, you should… No, she probably wants to be alone. You don't even know this woman. Why on earth do you need to talk to her, to be close to her, and want to just look at her? Because you want her, you idiot! Brian tried to convince himself she wouldn't want him there but his feet never wavered from their desired destination.

Brian plopped down next to Serena and threw an arm over the back of the bench. "Tough day, babe?" Brian wrapped his arm tightly around her when she rested her head in the crook of his shoulder.

"Yeah, Mom said to tell you 'hi' and to make sure you eat." Serena turned to Brian and attempted to smile.

"Well then, I guess you're going to have to come back to the house with me, so I can make us a meal." He tweaked her chin and kissed her forehead.

"Thank you, but I'm not that hungry. Hope tried to get me to go over to her house for a bite, but I'm not in the mood to eat."

"When's the last time you ate?" Brian laughed when Serena narrowed her eyes at him. "Don't give me that look. It won't work with me."

"You know, Brian, I'm too tired to fight with you about this. My mind has completely shut off."

"Good," he said standing up. "Let's go. I know this great little pizza place in town."

"Brian," Serena said wryly, "it's the only pizza place in town."

"All the same, I'm springing. Let's go." He grabbed her hand and pulled her to her feet. "We'll use my car. You'll love it."

Brian was right. He could tell by the way Serena ran her hand along the smooth dashboard that she did love it. It was an old Nova he'd restored himself, a pastime Brian had loved every dirty minute of. The car was fast and loud, with a drive-until-you-can't-drive-anymore feeling about it.

"I wish we could drive till we didn't know where we were and then take our time trying to find our way back." Serena was smiling out the window.

"You know, that's why I bought this car," Brian told her. "It's sweet and it's a chick magnet."

"It's just nice to be in a real car for a change. Mine makes all sorts of noises and I definitely need to get the air fixed."

"Well, I might be able to help you with that, darling. I'd love to lube your engine sometime, too."

"Oh, don't give me that innocent grin. I'm onto your type! You lube our engines and then ruin our transmissions." Serena laughed easily as they pulled into the pizza shop.

"Honey," he said putting an arm around her shoulder, "the only transmission I've ever ruined was my own. You're safe with me."

* * * *

The pizza was good, better than she remembered. The service was still excellent, and the place was clean and had been recently remodeled. They'd gone with an old Roman theme. Pretty murals decorated the walls, while plaster statues of the gods stood watch in their corners. Brian and Serena talked and joked effortlessly through the meal. Somewhere along the way, they slipped into feeling more for each other than friends. It was exciting and scary.

"All right! All right!" Serena rolled her eyes to the ceiling. "This man is impossible." She took her time pouring them both more soda out of the pitcher.

"Serena, come on, tell me! I would never get away with this." Unconsciously, Brian held one of Serena's hands and played with her fingers.

She laughed at him. "So, after the cop checked to make sure my license and registration was up-to-date, he came back and let me go. That's it. Nothing else to tell."

"You honestly expect me to believe that?" Brian brought their hands up palm to palm on the table then laced their fingers together.

Serena wiggled her eyebrows and drank her soda.

Brian's tone was mildly amused. "I wasn't born yesterday. What happened from the time he went to check it to the time he came back?"

"What are you trying to say, Brian? That I would use my female wiles to coerce an officer of the law out of giving me a ticket?"

Breaking their touch, he sat back. "I think," he told her while chewing his bottom lip, "if I was an attractive woman pulled over for doing twice the speed limit." He leaned forward and flicked a finger down her nose. "Yeah, I'd do what I could to get out of the ticket."

"Brian, you would make an attractive woman." When his eyes showed delight in her statement Serena's heart did a somersault. "Anyway, I did nothing to change his mind about the ticket."

"Nothing?"

"Okay, so my skirt did move a little higher when I reached for the registration. But I didn't do it on purpose."

Amused, Brian teased her, "Oh, to be a woman. I bet you can get yourself out of anything."

"Never had a problem before." Serena watched the way his eyes lit with humor. He was too cute for words. The way he'd run his hands through his hair, the lopsided smile he'd give her before saying something devilish. Yes, Serena decided, I'm going to get to know Brian Allen better.

"So, you going to the fair?" Brian took a large bite of his combination pizza.

"Yeah." She smiled at him, then laughed.

He wiped at his cheek and chin with a napkin. "What?"

Serena rested an elbow on the table and her chin in her hand. "Lizzy didn't like the girl you brought last year."

"Really?" Brian tried to act shocked. "You think that's why she tried to bite her?"

"One day she's going to take a chunk out of the wrong person." Serena took another piece of pizza and flopped it on her plate.

"She's never bit me."

"She bit me. And if she tries it again… I'm going to have to bite her back."

"You think she'd be upset if we went together?"

"To the fair?"

Brian nodded his head and motioned with his pizza. "Yeah."

"I assumed you were already coming."

"I am, but I thought I'd ask anyway."

CHAPTER 7

The rest of the week passed in a blur. Serena was too busy between visiting her mother and preparing to bring her home to even think about Brian. Or at least dream about him as much as she wanted to.

When Sunday arrived, Serena was thankful. She had plans to join Hope's family in going to the town fair and eat lots of foods high in fat and calories. They'd play some games that no one usually wins, and then watch the fireworks while sitting on a blanket in the giant field. The fireworks were always her favorite part of the fair. She could sit on the ground as the air cooled after the hot day, and relax. She'd sip some ice-cold beverage, talk and rest while her niece played on the playscape near by.

When the knock came on the screen door, Serena happily yelled an enthusiastic, "Come in! I'm down the hall!" Given she'd spent the morning making sure the yard was in the best shape possible for her mother's arrival the next afternoon, she was running a little late and still getting dressed after her shower. Serena was just pulling on her shirt when she heard Brian's voice.

"Hey, babe. I've come to join you, Hope and Will." Brian walked right into Serena's room, since the door had been left open.

Serena caught a glimpse of the heat rising in Brian's cheeks before he turned his back to her. God, he's cute was her first thought.

"Knocking's nice, sweetie."

"I did knock. You told me to come in, remember?"

He was embarrassed, Serena realized. And this wasn't a man that would embarrass easily.

"Sorry," Brian said in more of an accusing tone than an apologetic one.

"It's nothing you haven't seen before. Hey," she said putting a hand on his shoulder, "it's okay."

"Sorry," he said again.

He was watching her so intently, Serena felt heat rise from her toes to wake every nerve in her body. "Really... It's o...okay."

"No, it's not."

Before she knew what was happening, one of his hands was in her hair, while the other wrapped around her waist, pulling her close. His mouth was savage on hers, and his tongue demanded hers to play. It only took Serena a second to register what was happening. She was becoming a prisoner to Brian's desires. Without thought, her hands went possessively into his hair and her body responded to his in a violent need.

The world spun away from them. Brian's lips were full and soft with a mouth teeming of potent flavors. When his hand streaked up Serena's back, her breath hitched and her hands began to roam, creating a hurricane of sensations that rushed through the both of them. She could feel the tight muscles under his shirt, and whimpered at the thought of feeling them without any barriers. When Serena pressed her nails into Brian's shoulders, he trembled. This is quickly going to get out of hand, she realized, if I don't do something.

Brian stepped back at the same time she did. His eyes were glued to her mouth, which was still slightly parted and swollen. He cupped her face and looked intently into her eyes. "My God, Serena, you're driving me crazy."

Serena tried to say something, but nothing came out. They both stepped farther away from one another when they heard the rap on the door. Hope's voice carried through the house as Serena emerged from the hallway trying not to appear like she'd just gotten done doing something naughty.

"You seem a bit pale, Rena. Are you feeling all right?" Whatever she would have said next was lost when Hope saw Brian also emerging from the hall. "Oh! Did I interrupt something?" She gave Serena an accusing look, as if to say 'I can't leave you alone for more than a minute without you getting into trouble'. "You're still planning to come with us, right? You did promise Lizzy."

"Of course I'm still coming. I don't know what's going through that head of yours, but I'm pale because I spent the morning doing the lawn and I'm a little tired." She gave Hope an insolent glare. "We'll meet you in the car. I have to find my sandals."

"Well, make it quick." With that, Hope tromped out the door.

"That girl could use a vacation and some good ole lusty sex." Brian nodded his head in agreement with himself.

"She makes me feel like I just got done doing something sinful and got caught by my mother. Damn her!" Serena said in a raised voice.

"Yeah!" Brian said, shaking a fist. "Let's get her."

Serena couldn't help but laugh. It was as if Brian knew exactly what would melt away all the tension. "Come on, Bri," she said, looping her arm through his after grabbing her sandals. "If we take too long, she'll think we're having a quickie."

Brian raised his eyebrow mischievously. "She has a dirty mind, eh? How about you?"

Serena winked at him. "It runs in the family."

"I'd like to see what your mind could come up with sometime."

"I bet you would."

CHAPTER 8

The short ride to the park was delayed by all the traffic. Lizzy kept up a constant chatter while seated between Serena and Brian. The pitch of her voice got higher the closer they got to the park. And, despite all of Hope's efforts, the girl was too excited to quiet down. Brian helped by carrying on conversations with both Lizzy and Willie. Serena watched as he listened intently to Lizzy's chatter, his mischievous eyes always coming back to the little girl's so she'd know he was listening. Serena felt her heart do a little flip and tried to justify it by telling herself, whose wouldn't? Then he stared directly into her eyes. Serena's breath caught in her lungs. He's beautiful, was all she could think, and not just on the outside. Damn I'm sunk. Something passed between them, something no one else in the car could see. They became the only two there, and when the hand that was draped on the back of the seat touched her cheek, Serena leaned into it and smiled. At that point, for that day, she decided the hell with everything. She was going to enjoy herself with a man, one who obviously enjoyed being with her.

The fair was everything she remembered; the crowd of cars in the field and the constant tug of exhilaration to get involved in the fun. In the background, Serena could hear her sister giving instructions to everyone. She, however, was someplace else, someplace she had been long ago when things were innocent and the world seemed new. When the only worry she had on a day like this was what she should wear in case she ran into her latest crush. As they walked closer to the concession stands, Serena felt a little hand tuck into hers. They looked at each other with twin grins and wicked gleams in their eyes.

"You ready to ride some rides, little one?" she asked Lizzy.

"Yeah!" the little girl exclaimed.

"Hey, don't go crazy and get her sick, or you're taking care of it."

"You know, Hope, sometime soon you're going to have to start trusting me. The last thing on my mind is getting our little angel sick. We're going to stick to the candy and spinning rides, okay?"

It was obvious Hope didn't share in Serena's humor. Nevertheless, that was okay in Serena's book; no harm in teasing Hope every now and then.

"Don't you worry, Hope. I'll keep an eye on them both." Brian swung an arm over Hope's shoulders and gave her a little shake. "How much trouble could they get into with me around?"

"Enough!" Willie chimed in. "Serena, keep this here boy away from the Bud stand and any bathroom floors." Willie was the person who always made the party, had a good comment for everything, and always a smile to go along with it. He was a fairly tall man with a biker's build, muddy brown hair and the darkest brown eyes Serena had ever seen. Sometimes it seemed impossible to Serena that he and her sister were together. But they were such polar opposites, they evened each other out.

"Why don't you guys go and have a little alone time. Brian and I promised Lizzy we'd bring her around the fair." Serena put up a hand before Hope could say anything. "And I promise not to get her sick."

"Have the time of your lives, kids." Willie gave Hope a playful grin. "Let's go see if we can find you and me a nice quiet spot in the bushes." He wiggled his eyebrows at them while steering Hope away.

"Don't do anything I wouldn't do," Brian called out to them.

"Come on girls, let's go get some ride tickets."

The day was beautiful. The powder blue sky had not a cloud. A small breeze teased the skin and kept it from getting too hot, and an overwhelming feeling of freedom made the moment seem imagined.

They walked over to the tractor pulls, and Brian deposited Lizzy on one. Then they went over to the pony ride where she squealed with delight the whole time. Hot dogs, hamburgers, French fries and fried dough, their bellies were stuffed, and their faces all smiles. They were walking to the horse corrals when they ran into Willie and Hope. Lizzy squealed when Willie swooped her up into his arms and carried her to the playscape. He wanted to give Serena and Brian some time to themselves.

"I love that kid," Brian said off-handedly. They were leaning on the fence to one of the corrals when Serena placed a hand on his shoulder and looked up at him admiringly. Brian couldn't help but wonder what was happening to them. It seemed like they had known each other all of their lives, not one short week. "What's happening here?"

Serena gave him a puzzled expression. "What do you mean?"

"Us." He wrapped his arms around her waist and pulled her close. "I don't understand. The last thing we both want right now is complications, yet I want to see you, be with you." He let out a long ragged breath and leaned his forehead on hers. "I didn't want to feel this again."

"I like you too, Brian. But we should be careful not to complicate things too much." She gave him a good smack on the shoulder and changed the subject. "So, you going to win me a stuffed animal, or will I have to do that myself?"

He kissed her once, quick on the lips. Brian knew if it wasn't quick he would probably drag her off into the woods. "Come on, sweetie," he said in his best cowboy voice. "I'll win the little lady a prize, and her heart, too." He pinched her chin and winked as Serena laughed in amusement.

The sun was going down and the air cooling when they all headed toward the pavilion under the trees. The local country band played a Garth Brooks classic and had people flocking to the dance floor.

When Serena saw Willie and Hope out there, she gave a long sigh. "They look so good together, don't they?"

Brian steered his eyes over the crowd until he found them. "They dance really well together. Do you dance?"

"Oh God, no!"

"Come ooon," he teased.

"I can't dance to this. I like it, but I can't dance to it." Before Serena could react, Brian had taken her hand and dragged her out on the floor.

"No way! I'll make a complete fool out of myself, Brian." There was no way he'd let her avoid it. He was bigger, stronger, and totally determined to get her out there.

Serena pouted.

"You're making a complete fool out of yourself by making me yank you out here. Now all you have to do is follow my lead. That was my foot, babe." He grimaced at her and pretended to be in pain so he could hear Serena laugh.

"I'm so bad at this," she pleaded. "I don't follow lead well, and I have two left feet. Please, Brian, don't make me do this. Really, I'm not kidding!"

He grinned down at her. She looked so pathetic. There was fear in her eyes and she kept glancing down at their feet. "Rena, trust me. I'm not going to let you make a fool out of me. Now just relax and enjoy."

With a voice as dry as the desert in mid-summer, she said, "Thanks for the vote of confidence. Making a fool out of you is what I was concerned about."

"I know," he told her and landed a peck on her nose.

"I can't believe you got her out here! She's got two left feet, you know." Hope's eyes were wide with enthusiasm.

"A person needs to know their limitations," Serena replied while trying to escape. Brian whirled her around and into a dip. "I think I'm going to be sick," she told him.

"Look, there's Darren and his beautifully round wife. I'll have to kill you if you tell her I said that."

"Let me go and it'll be our secret."

"Not on your life, sweetie," he said in his cowboy voice again.

* * * *

It wasn't so bad, Serena admitted to herself. He was a good lead and no one was staring at them, except Willie who kept making faces at her. She couldn't get rid of the giggles and Brian couldn't stop laughing with her. When Serena stepped on his feet with every fourth turn, he would mention something along the lines of broken toes or steel-toed boots.

When the music took a break, much to Serena's relief, they joined Willie, Hope and Lizzy, and Meg, Darren, and their daughter, Emily. All of them together were a noisy crowd, with lots of jokes, provided mostly by Willie. Every so often, someone would stop to say hello and welcome Serena back. It was always, "Are you here for a visit, or are you back to stay?" She felt as if she was under constant surveillance. There were so many people, and she didn't know if she was staying or not. However, she also didn't want to tell anyone about her mother. They would want explanations on her condition, and Serena didn't want to spoil the day and mood for everyone. But then they would say, "Oh, it's too bad New York City didn't work out," like she'd failed at something. In Serena's mind, she never failed at anything that she really wanted; besides, she had been there for almost seven years.

"Excuse me. I need to go to the ladies room." Serena walked

away quickly, overwhelmed by the need to get out. Just to breath freely for a minute without all the people crowding her.

Five minutes later, Hope found Serena washing her hands at the crowded bathroom sink. "Hey. You okay?"

"Yeah, I needed to get away from everything for a minute. Not that this is any better."

"Smells good, too."

"Oh, yeah. Like sanitation and a bad deodorizer. How's Lizzy doing? She must be getting tired." Deciding the bathroom was too crowded and not the place to have a chat, they walked to the field.

"She's getting cranky. I hope she makes this last hour before the fireworks."

"Oh, it would be such a shame if she missed them." Serena looked around the crowded fields and smiled. "It's so nice to be here. Believe it or not, I've missed it."

"We all missed you." They gave each other a quick hug and went searching for a beer stand.

* * * *

Brian had been thinking about a beer too. He was on his way back from getting one when he ran into his friend Tom. "Stranger!" he said while they gave each other the traditional male handshake.

"Brian, it's been too long, where the hell have you been?"

"Working, man. It seems that it's all I do these days."

"We've missed you down at the V.W." It was a little dive in town where everyone hung out, had their choice of drinks, and played some pool or darts.

"Yeah, I'll probably be down there this week." Both pairs of eyes were drawn to the two attractive women laughing and walking.

"Holy shit! Is that Serena O'Neal?" Tom asked.

"Yeah. Not bad as neighbors go."

Tom turned to him in disbelief. "Is she here on a visit? Or for good?"

Brian was too busy watching the two girls in line to hear the interest in Tom's voice. "Their mom is really sick, so I would say she's here for a while, at least." He turned to see Tom's eyes fixated on Serena. "The last thing she needs," he said with a warning in his voice, "is a complication right now."

"So in other words, hands off, you've already made a claim. I don't think so. I've waited a long time to see what music she and I could make together. Plus, I know better than to fall for someone like her."

"What the hell is that supposed to mean?" Brian could feel his anger revving up. He downed his beer and tossed the red cup in the trash. Careful buddy, I will punch your lights out.

"Well, Brian, Serena's not the type of girl who does relationships. And the guy, unfortunately, tends to fall harder than she ever does."

Brian looked from Tom to Serena and back with suspicious eyes. "You sound like a jilted lover. Is there something else I need to know?"

"Like I said, try all you want, but that girl will never be serious with one man. And getting any action…" he scoffed. "It'll take smooth talk and a lot of patience."

"So that's why you've been waiting years?" Brian's temper was ready to flare. He couldn't even say exactly why. It's not like he and Serena had something going. Yeah, they were attracted to one another, they both liked one another, but he was feeling defensive and territorial. He had the urge to go over and pee on her.

"I haven't been waiting, just biding my time." Tom wiggled his eyebrows at Brian and grinned. "Let's see how she feels about me."

Brian looked over to see both girls heading their way. He saw Serena's eyes grow wide when she spotted them.

* * * *

"Oh, shit!" Serena said under her breath.

"What? Oh!" Hope said when she spotted Tom. "This will be fun with Brian there. He doesn't seem happy."

"That's because Tom probably told him how he's going to be getting in my pants."

"He never gives up, does he? Come on," Hope said, putting her arm through Serena's, "let's have some fun."

"You're so bad, Hope. That's why I love you." The girls were smiling when they approached the two men.

"Serena, it's been way too long!" Tom grabbed her around the waist and brought her in for a very tight hug. Over his shoulder, she rolled her eyes at Brian, who tried not to snicker.

"Tom, that's a little too tight, dear."

"So, when are we going to be able to get together?" To Serena's annoyance, Tom left his arms around her waist. "I'd love to take you out some time," he told her.

Always to the point, Serena thought, as she wiggled out of his arms.

"And don't you tell me you're too busy." Tom ran a finger down her nose.

Serena checked her patience. "You know right now really isn't a good time."

"Yeah, Brian here—" Tom smacked Brian in the chest. "—was just telling me your mom is sick. I'm sorry to hear that." He glanced from Serena to Hope with a most concerned face. "You're looking beautiful as usual, Hope. And how is that wonderful daughter of yours?" The thought of how she sank her teeth into him once made his smile waver for a second.

"She is wonderful, isn't she? I really am sorry that she's with Willie, I'm sure Lizzy would have wanted to say hello." Hope then turned to Serena and grinned. "You see, Lizzy had this problem with biting, usually it's only when a stranger tries to get in the house, but for some reason, every time she sees Tom, she feels the need to take a chunk out of him. But I assure you," Hope said turning back to Tom, "she really is out of that stage."

What a wonderful charming smile she gave him, Serena thought. God, she's good.

"That's funny, she's never bitten me." Brian gave a nonchalant shrug and put an arm around Serena's shoulders. "We should probably be getting back to everyone."

"Yeah, you're right. It was nice running into you, Tom. I'm sure I'll see you around town."

"Yeah," Tom said, on a sour note, "take it easy."

Brian slipped his other arm around Hope's shoulders and steered them away. "He's a pompous ass."

Serena wanted to explode with laughter. "Oh God, Bri. Thanks for being such a good sport about all that. He just doesn't know when to give up."

"He's been trying to get into Rena's pants since high school. I don't know why you don't let him."

Both girls' bodies were jerked backward when Brian stopped abruptly to stare at Hope with disbelief. "You've got to be kidding."

"I am, Brian."

"Good, I would have to hurt you." Then on impulse, Brian turned, wrapped his arms around Serena's waist, and gave her a smacker on the lips. "He bothers you, let me know."

"I can take care of myself, Brian." Serena's eyes narrowed and started spitting fire. "And don't play the macho thing with me."

"You know what, I'm gonna see what Will's up to," Hope told them with leeriness in her voice toward the apparent temper on Serena's face.

"He's a jerk," Brian stated in his defense. "And from the way he was talking, he'll be sniffing around your door a lot."

With her hands on her hips, Serena asked, "And what are you going to do, mark your territory?"

"Thought about it."

"Well, don't." She pushed him away. "I don't need any man watching out for me. I can take care of myself, and do a fine job of it."

"If you're thinking I'm going to get in the way of your independence, don't worry about it." He started walking away from her. "I have my own to protect."

"Good. Then we're in agreement." She angled her chin, and had him laughing.

"You know, Serena," Brian said turning back to her, "I'm really going to enjoy you." He swung an arm around her shoulders again and led her back to everyone else.

And that's it? she thought, end of discussion, no rules to be made, no limitations on either of them, and no pressure? "You know," she said looking up at him, "I think this is going to be fun."

The fireworks were spectacular. They lay on a blanket and watched a great show. Well, as great as a small town fireworks display gets. Lizzy fell asleep halfway through with her head on Willie's lap. Serena couldn't help but be happy for them. It was a family unit, one that she hoped one day to have for herself. When it came time to leave, Brian and Serena opted to walk home.

"I've had way too much food today to not think about getting some kind of exercise," Serena said while holding her stomach.

"You're sure?" Willie asked while closing the door to his car. "Because there are some crazy drivers out tonight, and I don't want to be getting a phone call that you're dead on the side of the road."

"I'll protect her," Brian said in his macho voice.

Serena rolled her eyes. "Oh, for God's sake, do you ever give up?"

"Okay, Rena." Hope leaned forward and hugged her sister. "I'll give you a call in the morning before I come to pick you up."

"It's a beautiful night, isn't it, Hope?" Serena stared up from the parking lot at the star-studded sky, where she could still see the reflection of flashing carnival lights.

"Yeah it is. And don't do anything that I wouldn't do," Willie warned.

"Well, that leaves things pretty open." Serena laughed.

"You're such an ass, Will," Hope said. "But I love you." With that said they got into their car and started the very slow process of trying to get out.

"Guess it's you and me kid." Brian put Serena's hand in his own and together they started walking toward the other entrance to the park. The crowd was thinning and the carnies were packing things up. Serena didn't envy them, or the clean up crew.

"I wish you were able to bring Bart."

"Me, too. He gets too jittery around big crowds like this, though." Brian smiled. "Not to mention people tend to be scared of him."

Serena let out a soft laugh. "Well, I've got to say the first time I saw him I was scared shitless. He's as big as me."

"No. I think he's bigger," he teased and kissed the top of her head.

Brian and Serena were halfway home when they discovered how tired they really were. Their feet began to drag and their bodies began to slouch. At Serena's door there was a simple but seductive kiss goodnight that left the promise of an inevitable romance embossed in their brains.

CHAPTER 9

Katherine stirred in her bed and attempted to open her eyes. Her body felt heavy and her mind drugged.

"Hey, Mom." Hope bent over the bed to give her mother a kiss on the forehead. "How are you feeling?"

"Better."

"Have you been eating?" Serena glanced down at the full tray of breakfast and frowned. "You're not going to be getting away with that at home."

"Don't start giving her a hard time, Rena." A warning look followed Hope's words.

"It's all she understands. Isn't that true, Katherine?"

Katherine smiled at the nurse that had just walked in. "This is my drill sergeant, girls. If there was anything I shouldn't be doing, believe me, she'd let all of us know."

"That's right." The nurse nodded in agreement. "I've been your mother's nurse for only a few days, but we came to an agreement almost immediately. Right, dear?" She flashed a smile at Katherine and went about taking her vitals. "I'm Nurse Shelly," she told them.

"And a big pain in the butt. She wakes me at all hours, makes me walk when I'm too tired to. Tells me that if I don't start eating like a regular human being they'll keep me here longer, and then she'll have to make my life a living hell." Katherine's hands flew up in the air just to fall with a pop on her lap. “Like she hasn’t been doing that already?”

Serena smirked at Hope, who grinned at her. Their mother was stubborn and it was a relief she’d finally met her match.

“Good morning girls.” Dr. Kinney entered the room with clipboard in hand. He explained what warning signs they should look for in case of an infection, and when to call him. He gave them more pamphlets to read and a schedule for Katherine’s radiation treatments. It only took a few hours to get her out of there, but it felt like an eternity.

* * * *

A flood of relief filled Serena when her sister parked the car in their mother’s driveway. The hospital was over, her mother was home and now the healing could begin. Then Serena looked to the passenger seat and saw that her mother had fallen asleep—her head was resting on the window, while her left arm was wrapped around her lower abdomen. Now, the hard part began.

Gingerly, Serena and Hope helped Katherine out of the car and put her to bed. Silently, they kissed her goodnight and drew the shades.

“She’s so pale,” Serena said more to herself than her sister.

“You know she’s probably not going to want to eat when she gets up.” Hope watched Serena chop up lettuce with a vengeance.

“Yeah. None of us really want to eat, but if we don’t she’s not even going to try.”

“You’re going to use the guilt trip on her?” Hope frowned. “I guess if it works…”

“Could you get the chicken going? I’m not sure what I’m going to do with it yet, but at least it’s cooking.” Serena scowled down at the salad. “You know, I really wish I’d taken some kind of cooking class. You were lucky to be born with a natural talent for it.” Serena considered the dressings in the refrigerator. “Rob was a great cook, and liked to do it.” Serena looked up and smiled at Hope. “He was a great guy, I miss him so much. We talked the other day. He'll be coming up with more of my stuff. I never realized how much crap I have."

"We all have a lot of crap." Both girls' heads shot up to see Brian standing in the doorway to the kitchen. He was holding a large bouquet of flowers and a small scowl on his face. Serena noticed his frown but didn't understand what was wrong.

"Oh, they're lovely," Hope told him while taking the gentle blooms from Brian. "Let me get a vase and put them in some water."

"My mother is going to love them." Serena focused on the salad she was preparing. "Mom was asking me on the way home if you were going to be stopping by. She's going to be so happy to see you. It's too bad she's sleeping right now. Mom was saying how Bart was probably missing the snacks she usually gives him." Serena was rambling, but couldn't stop herself, and when Brian came to her and enfolded her in his arms, she sighed.

"Tough day, eh?" he asked.

"Yup. I don't even know what the hell I'm making to eat. I'm throwing stuff together and hoping for the best." Serena closed her eyes and wished Brian would never let her go. He was strong, secure, and at that moment, what she needed. She turned her head to look up into those steel gray eyes and time froze for them both. Home, she felt it and welcomed it as Brian brought his lips slowly down to meet hers. The kiss was light and over almost before it even began, but it was the underlining feelings of understanding and support that threw them both into emotional turmoil. They stared at one another, bewildered. Then Brian cleared his throat.

"Why don't you let me help out? I have magic hands, you know." He wiggled his fingers at her, which brought out a small giggle. "Someday, if you're a good girl, I'll treat you to one of my back rubs."

"Does that line work on every girl?"

"My hands," he said while tending to the chicken on the stove, "are famous for their incredible tenderness… when needed. And, my dear." He leaned over and flicked the tip of her nose. "For their ability to be firm and demanding… when needed."

"Well then," she answered playfully, "if your hands are that fondly known and that exploited, I don't know if I want them on my body." She stepped a little closer and put some allure into her voice. "I don't know where they've been last."

"Yes you do. They were on you yesterday."

Serena felt the familiar pull in her middle. Then guilt slipped through the playful interaction to show on her face.

"Perhaps now isn't the time for us to be doing this," Brian said. "But you can't feel guilty about having a little fun. I'm a patient man, Serena. We'll have our time." He gave her a smile and started ordering her around the kitchen while he cooked for the four of them.

Long after Brian and Hope left, Serena fell on to her bed. Her body was exhausted and fully clothed. The day had been draining, and she knew more of them were coming. As she drifted into sleep, visions of a man holding her close played in her mind. She smiled at his jokes and welcomed his comfort. She felt safe in his arms, and when the deep darkness of sleep finally overcame her, she dreamed of midnight walks and stolen kisses.

* * * *

The following week blurred by for Serena. She hardly managed a breath between finding a new part-time job and trips to her mother's treatments. Then Rob called to say he'd be up the following weekend with all her stuff. She wondered where the heck she was going to put all of it. She didn't have the money for a storage unit and her mother's cellar was already full with her junk. She didn't know how or where her furniture was going to go. After much debate, Serena resigned herself to the fact she'd have to get rid of most of it, a decision that left her feeling more than a little depressed.

The highlight of her week was when Darren called to tell her Meg had a boy that was ten pounds and two ounces. They called him John after Darren's father, and he came into the world kicking and screaming, ready for a fight.

"He's just like his daddy." Megan was saying, as everyone stood around the hospital room adoring the new life. "Stubborn." She peered down at her new arrival and caressed his pink cheek. "He was happy where he was, but there was no way I was letting him stay there. He'll have to learn, it's always my way."

"That's right, honey. Anything you want." The glance exchanged between Darren and Meg was a look only new parents could have. It was full of wonder and joy, fulfillment and love.

"Our mother sends her best." Hope took the baby away from Meg so she could get a better peek at him. "She says she can't wait to see the baby, and it had better be soon. He looks so much like a little man, doesn't he, Willie?"

"Yeah. When are you going to make me a little man? This little guy is going to need someone to get into trouble with."

"As soon as you buy me that new car." Hope batted her eyes and blew her husband a kiss.

"See! Blackmail," Willie proclaimed. "Brian, don't ever get married again. Everything comes down to blackmail and what you haven't done or haven't finished."

Brian smirked then rocked back on his heels. "Been there, done that, all set."

"Good for you," Serena agreed. "Who wants a life of slavery and submission?"

"It's not so bad," Willie declared. "You only have to give up your soul."

"And your freedom," Darren piped in.

"Don't forget half your money."

"Sweetie," Hope said, while placing a sympathetic hand on Willie's shoulder. "Half of nothing is nothing."

They were all still laughing and feeling good when Meg finally kicked everyone out so she could rest. In a few days she'd be home and enjoying all the wonderful things that go along with having a newborn, Darren by her side.

"I give him three days." Brian pressed the down button on the elevator. "He'll be over at my house and sipping down a cold one looking for some peace and quiet."

"You think so?" Serena leaned against the back wall of the elevator.

"Oh, yeah. He did that last time. So did Willie," Brian said matter-of-fact like. "The nature of the beast, babe." He swung an arm around Serena's shoulders as they walked out together. "How about some supper?"

"Sorry, I've got to get home. Hope wasn't happy I left Mom alone." She let out a long tired sigh. "She's been doing so great. She's eating well, walking, and not overdoing it. But I think she needs some time to herself. I know I wouldn't want people hovering over me all the time."

"You're doing a great job, Serena. She's only been out of the hospital a short while. And Hope's only frustrated that she can't be there as much as she'd like to." He opened the car door and let her inside. As he made his way around to the other side of the car, Serena reached over and unlocked his door. It was such an innocent and cliché gesture, yet Brian couldn't help but be moved. Her actions for others with no need for returned favors or words of appreciation had his heart somersaulting and his mind rethinking his planned future alone.

Brian got in the car then cupped her face with his hands. The act of tenderness had a wide-eyed Serena looking surprised at him. "We need to find some time together. I don't want to rush things, and I really don't know what I want. Okay, I know what I want. But, the funny thing is…" He released a slow breath. "For the first time in a long time, I'd like to spend time with someone I find not only attractive but…" Words absolutely eluded him. How was he supposed to explain what he felt and thought if he didn't even know himself? Brian threw himself back on his seat and swore. "You know what I mean," he said hoping for an easy way out. Serena's eyebrows creased together in a strained baffled look.

"Are you trying to tell me that you like me?" she asked in amusement.

Oh, she's good at playing the innocent card. "Well, yeah, I guess." This whole thing with Rob had been eating at Brian for days. He knew it wasn't fair, he knew it wasn't any of his business, but he had to know. "Is there someone else I should know about? I mean, someone that could just come and stop any chance for us?"

"Is that what you want, Brian? There to be an 'us'?"

"No. Yes. What I mean is." He was starting to sweat, damn her. "Did you leave anyone important behind in New York?"

"Yes, I did. But not in the way you think."

"So there is no guy waiting in the shadows ready to jump out at any time and claim you?" Brian was bewildered when Serena laughed. "I'm serious here, Serena, and would appreciate you not laughing in my face." Brian started the car with a jerk.

"Wait a minute." She turned the car off and put herself between him and the steering wheel, by getting on his lap. "There is no guy waiting for me, unless you count Tom." Brian narrowed his eyes at her. "I have not been in any kind of relationship with anyone in a very long time. I don't sleep around." When Brian went to open his mouth, Serena covered it with her hand. "I will stand for nothing less than honesty. In the past all I've gotten is hypocrites, and it's made me a bit leery." Taking a deep breath, Serena forged on. "You asked if I left anyone of importance behind. Yes I did. His name is Rob, and he was my roommate. We were very close, and he was a very good friend."

"But you were never involved with him, right?" Brian felt a guilty satisfaction at the fire he ignited in Serena's eyes. The woman was irresistible when in a temper.

Serena cocked her head in defiance. "No, Brian. We were never involved. You don't believe me?"

It's a challenge and a test, tread water carefully, Brian advised himself. "It's not that I don't believe you—" he started to say. When Serena let out a huff and shifted to get off his lap, Brian stopped her. "Tell me how in the world could a man in his right mind not try something with a smart, beautiful woman?"

"You're lucky you said smart first." Serena swung her hair back behind her shoulders, smiling devilishly. "You, my dear, are more Rob's type than I will ever be." It took a second, maybe two, but Brian's wheels began turning. "How the hell do you think being roommates for almost seven years worked out so well?"

"I didn't know... I just thought that... Well, I don't know what I thought... And don't give me that look!" When a self-indulgent smile crossed her face, Brian wiped it off by cupping the back of her head with his hand and crushing their mouths together. She let out a little chuckle, which had him returning his own. "We're out of our minds," he said against her mouth.

"Mmm… Who cares?" Her eyes were dreamy when she looked into his. Brian felt her smile form against his mouth before going back for another taste. This time the kiss was gentle, sweet and more arousing than ever. Brian shifted her body closer against his, with no thought to where they were or to the time of day.

Smoldering heat threatened to burst into flames as hands began to seek new discoveries. The wonder of territory yet to be traveled caused roaming hands to seize and explore boundaries. Brian's only thought was how he needed to feel the silk of Serena's skin again. Roughly, he pulled the front of her bra down and took the fullness of her breasts in his hands. At first he cupped and massaged but then his thumbs and forefingers pinched her taut nipples and Serena's body jolted.

Serena's hands pushed into Brian's hair. She tightened her grip when the feel of his hardness pushed against her. Serena drove the kiss deeper; tongues danced to the rhythm of their rapidly beating hearts, while she pushed and moved against his hands.

"Jesus, Serena. I don't have any blood left in my head," Brian said in almost a plea. He could feel the warmth that had risen in the car, hear both of them panting and the distracting beep of a passing motorist.

"Right," she said while taking a deep breath, "just let me move."

"Thank you." Brian adjusted himself, triggering Serena's laughter. "Trust me, babe," he told her, "there is nothing funny about this."

"Come on! Here we are, in the middle of the day." She motioned with a large sweep of her hands. "In the middle of a hospital parking lot, getting beeped at, and we're practically mauling each other." Serena went into hysterics. "We're like a couple of teenagers!"

Brian was laughing along now, too. "Oh, man. I haven't done anything like this in years!" He turned and gave her a cocky grin.

Serena put up a hand in retort. "Don't even think about it."

"Too late," Brian said and dove on top of her.

CHAPTER 10

When the weekend came, so did Rob with Serena's furniture, pulled behind his Toyota Echo. He arrived on Friday afternoon in a cloud of over-exaggerated hubbub about the ride and the rude New England drivers. Rob was a flamboyant character with long dark hair that he liked to pull back in a ponytail; he felt this made him appear mysterious with his sharp facial features. He always wore loud colorful shirts with snug pants to show off his 'finest assets,' he would say. Serena was never quite sure if Rob was referring to his front or his back end, because from her standpoint, both seemed excellent. Rob worked hard to stay in shape. He and Serena went religiously to the gym, four times a week, to sweat off the extra pounds. They would cheer each other on and compete to see who could do the most push-ups. Serena had wondered what she was going to do now that she lost such a great workout partner.

Over the past seven years their arrangement for living together had worked out well because their bedrooms were on opposite sides of the apartment. It was never a surprise to Serena to see Rob cooking breakfast with someone on a Saturday morning. Being generous, Rob always made sure there was enough food for her, too.

But on the personal front, Rob would continuously complain that Serena never dated anyone, and that she needed to get out more and have some fun. Even so, men weren't what was important to Serena.

She liked to watch them in their manly rituals, admire their different body types. But in the end, they were only after one thing from her. Occasionally, when she was in the need for a man's touch, Serena would give in.

"I've missed you so much!" Serena smiled across the picnic table at Rob.

"My dear, it is very mutual. The house is not the same without your loud mouth."

"You're always full of compliments." She had a wonderful feeling of nostalgia with Rob sitting across from her. "I have to tell you, I miss being in New York. I miss seeing your exquisite physique walking around in the morning."

"My sweet. You don't know how many times I thought I ruined you for other men." He sighed heavily at her. "You really need to find someone to spend some time with, someone that will treat that body of yours right."

Serena tried to conceal the smile on her face so Rob wouldn't see it.

"Do tell. I'm dying to hear." He leaned forward as if a deep dark secret was about to be told.

"Have I told you how much I miss you?" Serena said, wanting to torture Rob just a little longer.

He waved her off with his hand. "Get to the good stuff."

"He's tall," she told him with a sheepish smile.

"You always liked them that way."

Serena bit her lower lip. "He has dark blond hair."

Rob's brows winged up. "That's not your normal."

God, this is fun, she thought, I miss this. "His eyes are gray."

"Like steel?"

"Yeah!" Her eyes took on a faraway look, and she placed her chin on both her folded hands. "They're hypnotizing."

"The body, Serena, I need to know about his body." Rob saw the shiver run through hers. "Well, my dear. I guess that says it all."

"He must work out. Although there isn't a place around here, so I'll have to find out where."

"Stalking him?"

"No." She picked up her drink and took a long sip. "I can't let everything I worked for turn to jelly. If he can suggest a place," she added slyly, "that he just happens to go to, it could be fun. Watching him, of course." She felt a warm tingling sensation spread through her body.

"It's nice to see I taught you properly. Is he easily accessible?"

"He's the man next door," Serena whispered.

"Very convenient." Rob let his gaze slide to the house adjacent to them. "All by himself? Does he come from money?"

"I don't know," Serena told him with a puzzled look. "He's a mechanic. There's not much else I can tell you, except he's divorced. Apparently, she turned out not to be a very nice person."

"Bitch," he whispered venomously. "Well, I hope to meet him before I go tomorrow."

"Oh, I'm sure you will. He's very curious about you."

Rob picked up his glass and saluted her. "I promise not to steal him away."

"You'll have a hell of a fight on your hands. Come on," Serena told him while rising, "we'll watch that movie you brought."

"You know," Rob commented on the way in the house, "your mom is doing so good, you'd never know she's sick."

Serena glanced down the hallway that led to her mother's room. "No, you wouldn't. She sleeps a lot, though."

Serena was putting the DVD in the player when they heard a knock on the door. With a twinkle in her eyes Serena giggled. "I wonder who that could be."

Rob winked at Serena. "Please, let me get it."

This is going to be funny, she thought, and heard the door open to Rob's sound of appreciation.

* * * *

"Is, uh, Serena, here?" Who the hell is this guy with his bright yellow shirt and, what the hell are those, leather pants? Brian thought.

"Of course she is. She lives here." The stranger took a step closer while licking his lips.

Brian made it very clear, with the warning in his eyes, any more than that one step forward and he'd have to pop the guy. He now knew what a piece of candy felt like before it was licked and he wasn't entirely comfortable with the feeling.

"Rob, leave the poor guy alone."

Rob gave one last look of admiration and stepped back.

"Sorry," Serena said, while grabbing Brian's hand and pulling him in. "Rob's a little protective of me."

"Nothing wrong with that." Brian put out a hand. "Brian."

"Rob. Nice pool."

"I had it put in a few years back. It's like my own little lagoon." And indeed, it was. Rock walls and wild flowers surrounded it. There was a waterfall on the opposite side of the whirlpool. Plus, it was heated. The ideal in-ground pool, in Brian's mind. "If you have time before you leave, have Serena bring you over and try it out."

"Beer?" Serena asked nervously.

"Love one," both men said in unison, ending the tension.

Serena found it amusing to have a man on either side of her when they sat on the couch. The night turned into a beer-and-snack fest for all. A little more than halfway through the movie, with buttery fingers, Rob yawned and excused himself.

"It was a long ride up. And to tell you the truth, if I hadn't missed you so much, I would have been in bed hours ago." He kissed Serena and shook Brian's hand. "Till tomorrow," Rob told him.

"I hope he didn't leave because of me. I kinda like the guy." Brian put his arm around Serena's shoulders and pulled her close. "But then again, being alone with you I kinda like, too," he said, nuzzling her neck.

"I'm sure he just thought we wanted some time alone." Her mind was starting to cloud, her hands searched out his chest. "To watch the rest of the movie." She turned her head and met his lips. Oh, those wonderful lips.

"You're right," Brian said pulling away quickly. "We should watch the rest of the movie." He was rewarded with the look of disappointment on Serena's face. "Don't worry, I'll maul you again sometime soon."

"You're a shit." Serena crossed her arms over her chest and pouted. It didn't last long. Soon they were snuggled close watching intently as the night melted away.

* * * *

The heat of summer was in full swing before Serena realized how many weeks had flown by. She had become too busy with her mother and her new hairdressing job to think about herself and a certain sexy neighbor. The new job was at a great little place in the next town over. She found when she was there, her mind could relax and she could laugh; laughing seemed to be harder these days as she witnessed the torture her mother was enduring from treatment. The hours at the shop were perfect. Plus, the people at her new job never made her feel she wasn't pulling her weight when she needed to come in late or leave early. Her co-workers saw firsthand that Serena was worn down and out of sorts, and they offered any help they could give.

Serena's mind wandered as she clipped and snipped at her client's hair. She felt bad about not having enough time or energy to have Brian in her life. The poor guy probably thinks I'm trying to ignore him.

Serena rolled her shoulders back and tried to concentrate on what the gentleman in her chair was saying to her. She smiled widely at him, and then went through the files of her brain for his name. But her mind kept slipping.

"Okay." She told the man in her chair. "All done." In the mirror, Serena could see the dark circles that makeup couldn't cover around her eyes. She also looked as if in the past few weeks she might have lost some weight.

Serena handed her client his change then turned. "Ashley, can I take a break? Just five."

"Why don't you make it ten, we're not that busy." Serena walked through the break room, then out the back door. Taking a big breath of fresh air, Serena wished she had enough energy to go out that night. Just to go, and not have to worry about what was going on the next day. What happened to her life? She didn't even recognize it anymore. She no longer recognized herself, she realized with a frown.

A blissful thought slipped in from her subconscious, to cheer her up. The Fourth of July was coming, which meant she could stay home and sleep. Hope had informed Serena that she was taking their mother for the day; this meant Serena had no responsibilities.

"Serena!" The sound of her name had her head snapping up. "There is a beautiful piece of eye candy waiting for you out there. If you're too tired I wouldn't mind stroking my hands through his hair and checking out more of his ass." Ashley licked her lips. "He looks great in jeans and a t-shirt."

Serena couldn't help but smile then lick her lips in return. "Maybe I can talk him into a shampoo, stroke a little, and get an extra tip."

"Work it girl," Ashley called after her, while following with curiosity.

He was standing in front of the big window with his back to her. Serena tilted her head for a better view of his bottom just as he turned.

A devilish grin crossed his face as Serena's went beet red.

"Thought I'd come by and see how the job was going." As Brian walked over to her, his demeanor got cockier. He took a look around the shop, which was empty except for the employees who were trying to cover their interest in him, and smiled. "You seem to be a little busy. I was hoping for a wash and trim." He ran his hand through his thick blond hair, and then looked Serena up and down. "If," he said, coming close, "you don't mind putting your hands on me."

Serena swallowed hard at the suggestive statement. "I'd have to put my hands on you. How else could I get the job done properly?"

"I miss you." In an intimate gesture, he took her hands and kissed her knuckles. "Are you trying to ignore me, or are you bent on Tom?" he joked.

"I'm so sorry."

"Don't be sorry."

"I am. It's just life has been so crazy. And my car keeps acting funny, and I..."

"If your car is acting up, all you have to do is say something." He moved a little closer. "I told you I'd love to lube your engine."

Serena rolled her eyes at him. "I don't have any defenses against you," she told him in defeat. "What a dangerous thing."

"Good. Wash and cut me. Then tonight I'll take you out." Serena gave him a weary smile. "Don't even say you're too tired. We're not going to paint the town or anything like that."

"A movie?"

"A movie it is, and dinner. Your mom will be fine," he said before she could protest. "She has both of our cell numbers, and Hope doesn't live that far away." He was sick of Hope. All she ever did was complain about everything, and she wasn't even the person who was there most of the time. In Brian's mind, Serena turned her life upside down and was treated like shit. He'd been trying to stay away whenever

Hope was there, because he didn't want to say anything and make it all worse.

Serena turned to walk him toward the sinks and everyone shifted to pretend they had been doing something other than listening.

"So," Brian began, "you think you could break out that leather number of yours?"

Serena gave out something close to a choking noise.

"You know how I love that one." He smiled and winked at Ashley.

"Only if you wear it this time." Serena patted his cheek and gestured him to sit down.

"You know how uncomfortable I get in a thong." He gave her an anguished look.

Serena tried to cover a giggle. "But honey, it's so naughty on you."

"I know. But it hurts."

"I thought you liked it that way?"

"Jesus!" Ashley shrieked. "Look at the man." She indicated to Brian. "He doesn't need to wear anything at all. And it's quite obvious that we all want to know everything... after he leaves, of course."

"Oh, you can talk now." He grinned up at Serena, hoping she wouldn't spray him with the hose. "I'd love to know what she thinks and wants from me." Big smile. Big, big one, he told himself.

"If you don't know what I think and want from you by now, then there isn't any point in breaking out the leather."

With Serena bent over him to rinse and her breasts strategically placed, a nice little fantasy danced in Brian's head. He would have preferred getting drenched with her sprayer than to endure this type of female torture. His loins told him to reach up and take a bite. They screamed for him to touch and... He swore loudly.

"What's wrong, honey?" Serena's voice was velvet smooth. "Do you need to cool down?"

"You are an evil woman, Serena, and someday, someday soon…" Brian shook his head, and let out a long breath. That was all he could say. She scored her points and looked very self-righteous about it.

* * * *

Twilight tinted the sky, summoning street lights to turn on and buzz their golden glow. The air smelled sweet and sultry from the light drizzle that dampened the road. Brian cleared his throat as the summer smells permeated the interior of the car.

"Pretty good movie."

"Yeah." Serena looked out the window so the wind coming from it could play with her hair. "Better than I thought it would be."

"I'm having a party for the Fourth. It would be great if you'd come." He grabbed Serena's hand and gave it a quick kiss before letting it go again.

She turned toward him and smiled. "I was planning on staying home and getting some sleep. But I guess I could take time out of my busy schedule and attend for a few hours. Darren's not cooking, is he?"

"Yeah," Brian replied in a longing voice. "You can't stop the guy. He really thinks he can cook."

"We'll just have to make sure Meg's watching." Serena frowned out the window. Brian was exactly what she wanted in a man and exactly what she didn't want. He's perfect, and if we're not careful we'll end up in a full-fledged relationship. Not what you need or want, Serena, she reminded herself. Okay, he is what I want, she admitted grudgingly. But there are going to be complications…

"Where did you go?" Brian parked the car in his driveway and, placing one arm over the back of the seat, faced Serena.

"You know me." She shrugged. "I'm always somewhere I shouldn't be."

He picked up one of her stray curls and wrapped it around his finger. "Where were you?" he repeated.

"Thinking you should be complicating things, not making them easier for me."

"Good. Because that's what I'm out to do, make things easier." He kissed her quick and was out of the car and opening her door when he said, "You don't need someone to complicate things right now. But I have to be honest. I want to."

"And I can't help hoping that you would, even if I don't want you to." She took a step closer so their bodies would brush. "Some day soon," she whispered when his hand cupped the back of her head.

"You'd better get going." Brian rested his forehead on hers and his other hand on her bottom. "I can't be responsible for my actions if you stay much longer."

"Me either." She gave a hum of pleasure when he brought her closer.

"I'll take a peek at your car this weekend." Brian moved his lips to the soft curve of her neck.

"She's really not that bad," Serena said with heavy eyes. "She's just got a couple quirks."

Brian tugged on her earlobe with his teeth. "Is that what you call that noise?"

"Yes. Now kiss me goodbye, Brian."

Serena couldn't wipe the smile from her face. It wasn't only the session of necking in his driveway that she had enjoyed, although that made her feel wonderful and wanted. It was the fact he could please her on so many different levels and he always smelled so good. She was actually looking forward to the Fourth of July now. There would be the smell of burgers and dogs on the grill. Burnt ones, if Darren had anything to do with them. There would be potato salad and baked beans, green salad and chips. Soda and beer, maybe some wine. There would be loud laughter and quiet gossip. No doubt, she and Brian would be featured in a lot of those little conversations.

Serena's mind shifted back to the movie when she entered her room. She could still smell the butter from the large popcorn. When she thought she heard something, Serena stopped changing, and then dismissed it as a figment of her imagination, a consequence of how loud the sound had been in the theater. As she climbed into bed, she heard the noise again. No, this wasn't her imagination. Serena made her way out to the hallway where she stood for a minute waiting to hear it again. Her heart stopped. Her mother's room, she registered with alarm. Slowly and quietly, Serena cracked the door. She's crying. Why's Mom crying? Serena gently opened the door all the way and stepped inside.

"Mom?" she asked, while sitting on the edge of her bed.

"I'm sorry, Serena. I didn't mean to alarm you." Katherine took a breath and flicked on the small lamp on the side of the bed. "I guess I'm feeling a little down."

"Mom, you have a right to feel down if you want to." Putting a comforting arm around her, Serena kissed the top of her head and reached for the tissues. "We all feel like that every now and again."

"You poor thing. You moved all the way back here, from a life you loved, and now you're stuck playing nursemaid." The tears that had flowed soft and slow now came swiftly while Katherine's body began to shake.

"Oh, Mom. I didn't do anything I didn't want to do. Yes, I loved my life there, but that's over. And if it makes you feel any better, I really am happy to be back." Serena felt tears start to run down her own face. Her head began to hurt from the conversation that had taken place too many times. She knew her mother felt guilty about her coming back, but Serena also suspected it had a lot to do with the treatments that were sending her mother on an emotional rollercoaster. Serena decided next time she saw the doctor she would ask him about it. She had mentioned something to Hope but it seemed to be taken with a grain of salt.

Katherine stood up suddenly and began to tidy up her room, mumbling to herself.

“Mom. What are you doing?” Serena asked cautiously.

“You can’t be the only one doing things around here.” Katherine’s voice was sharp and precise.

“Mom, I’m not the only one doing things around here.” Serena tried taking a quiet deep breath. “As I’ve told you before, when you’re all better you can do everything and anything that you want to around the house. I promise I’ll be as lazy as possible.” Serena got to her feet and went to her mom. Shock and hurt stabbed through her heart when Katherine shrugged her off.

“You can go back to your room now. I don’t need someone watching over me twenty-four-seven.” The contemptuous look on Katherine’s face made Serena back up.

“If you want to be alone, that’s fine.” Serena put up both hands and started to walk out, then stopped and faced her mother. “I can’t pretend to know how hard this has been on you. And I can only hope that I have never made you feel like an invalid.” Serena took a deep cleansing breath. “I came back because I love you, not because I had to. I have never made a decision that I have come to regret, so get used to me being around, because I’m here for good.”

“I don’t need you here anymore,” Katherine shouted. “This is my house, and damn it, I’ll clean it.”

“Fine.” Serena’s palms grew sweaty, her head slightly dizzy from all the adrenaline. “Tomorrow you can do what you want, no questions asked. And when you’ve exhausted yourself I’m still going to be here.” Serena’s body was trembling so much it felt as if she’d shatter into pieces at any moment.

“You’ve always come and gone as you pleased.” Katherine’s eyes were vicious as she scolded her daughter. “What’s going to assure me that you're going to stay this time? What makes you think I want you to?"

She's sick, Serena kept reminding herself. Her hormones are out of whack and she doesn't mean what she's saying, she only wants someone to blame. Serena looked at her pale mother and wanted to cry for her, for all of them.

"Tomorrow morning is going to be better," Serena said in a soothing voice.

"How the hell do you know? I want you out." Katherine came at her and shoved. It took Serena by such complete surprise that she lost her balance and on the way down was struck by the doorknob on the side of her head. Even seeing stars, Serena got right back up.

"I'll leave tonight. But," she said still trying to find some clear focus in her vision, "I will be back tomorrow."

With that, Serena walked out the bedroom door. She could still hear her mother yelling about every mistake Serena had ever made in her life. How she was making a fool out of herself with the boy next door, and how he wouldn't go for a girl like her if he knew. Knew what? Serena wondered.

Serena closed the outside door on her raving mother. It occurred to her then that all she had on was her nightgown and robe. She stood in the driveway for a full two seconds before she headed to Brian's. God, she hated to do this, but what choice did she have? Pride would just have to be put aside for one evening.

To her relief, there was still a light on in one of Brian's rooms. She gave a little knock and Bart came racing to the door. When Serena saw his paws on the window she took a step back.

The kitchen light came on, followed by a sharp order to be quiet. Bart stopped barking, but he was still staring at her through the window with his big dopey tongue lolloping out of his mouth. Brian flipped on the outside light and had Serena covering her eyes and swearing.

* * * *

"Get down, Bart!" Brian opened up the door and saw the blood that had trickled down Serena's face. "Jesus!" he said, pulling her in. "You're bleeding!" He could see the dazed expression on her face and the shadows under her eyes. This wasn't the woman he'd left a little under an hour ago. This one was stressed and obviously in need of some medical attention. He dragged her in the house and all but threw her in a chair.

"Brian, I'm fine. I just hit my head." Serena sounded tired. He put his hand under her chin and lifted until she looked at him. "That's not why I'm here, anyway."

"Well, that's a relief. Because I'm a mechanic and if you had needed stitches I couldn't guarantee my work." He examined the wound and decided it wasn't that bad. Then he was up and out of the room before she could say another word.

She scared the hell out of him. At least I have the good sense not to jump to any conclusions, Brian congratulated himself. If there had been some kind of emergency, she would have said so, right? Of course, you really didn't give her much of a chance, he scolded himself. Brian burned himself on the hot water and swore. Damn woman. It wasn't enough that he had a hard time sleeping at night, she had to come over and scare the shit out of him, too. And why did she come over? He never even asked what happened, just hauled her in to the house and tossed her in a chair. He swore again and headed back to the kitchen.

"What the hell are you doing?" Brian asked with some heat.

Serena had been trying to get by Bart who had parked himself in front of the door. "I'm trying to leave. I'm sorry I disturbed you. And I'm really not up to any more fighting." Serena held both hands up and let them drop back to her sides in defeat. "I didn't think I had anywhere else to go."

Brian walked to her with the face cloth and started cleaning the blood from her face. “This is exactly where you should have come.” He connected his eyes with hers. “You’re tired and worn down. Do you have to work tomorrow?”

“No. All I have to do is bring my mom for treatment at two.” She let out a sigh and leaned into the hand that was cleaning her face. “I think I’ll call Hope and have her take Mom. She doesn’t seem to want me around right now.”

“She’s having a tough time?”

“Yeah,” Serena whispered.

Brian could see that at any moment Serena would slide to the floor from exhaustion. He remembered what it was like. The words said out of anger, not supposed to be aimed at any of them directly. How hard it had been not to take it personally, while trying to find an outlet for his own anger and resentment. Brian simply picked Serena up in his arms and started walking toward the bedroom.

“Tonight, you’ll stay here. Hope, for once, can pick up a little more slack. And you…” he said, looking at her and letting out a sigh. She was half asleep. “You will sleep.” He laid her on the bed and started taking off her robe. Any other time he would have appreciated the little pink slip that she had on under the big puffy lime-green robe. “You are full of surprises. I have to work tomorrow. But I’ll call and check on you,” he whispered. Brian bent over to give her a kiss on the head and she snuggled up to him.

“Don’t go,” she said and was deep into slumber.

He brought the covers up over the both of them and wrapped an arm around her. What the hell are we doing? was the last thought that went through his head.

CHAPTER 11

Brian blindly smacked at the shrilling alarm. When he put a hand to the weight on his chest, his eyes opened wide. Usually it was a 120 pound dog's head on his chest, not a 120 pound redhead's. When she shifted closer and wrapped an arm and a leg around him, he had a bad moment. Get out quick was Brian's first thought. He circled his arms around her, gave her a kiss on the forehead, and slipped out, a cold shower the only thing in his mind. He looked down at her when he was ready to go. She was still sound asleep, and he hoped she would be for hours. On the way out Brian taped a note to the door and said goodbye to Bart.

* * * *

Serena woke slowly. She nestled in deeper, enjoying the comfort and warmth. I'm just going to stay here a little while longer. An hour had passed when her mind came around again. Serena could tell it was light out even though her eyelids were still shut. The smells of the pillow made her think of Brian. Maybe I'll go back to sleep, and dream of him. She opened her eyes leisurely when her brain registered the happenings of the night before. The sun was high, the room was neat, and Brian was gone. She sat up wanting to stretch when pain shot through her head. Bringing her hand up, Serena gingerly touched the knot that had formed overnight. "What a mess," she told Bart, who replied with a groan.

Serena jumped when the phone beside her began to ring. It sent small searing shots of hurt into her eyes. She gave the phone a murderous stare, while trying to decide if she should answer it or not.

* * * *

"Damn it! Answer the phone!" Why wasn't she answering the phone? He told her he was going to call, she should answer. The morning had dragged for Brian. He had waited until eleven to call so he wouldn't wake her up. She couldn't be still sleeping, he thought, and glanced up at the clock. If she didn't answer the phone, he was going to find her and kill her for doing this to him. He had already dropped a coffee on himself that morning. Then he knocked a bunch of paperwork off his desk, and on top of it all, he had left the house without his wallet, which meant no money and no lunch. "Damn woman!"

"If you're going to swear at me, I am not going to talk to you," she said after picking up the receiver.

"What took you so long to answer?" Brian was a little put off.

"I was busy staring at the phone deciding if I should answer it."

He huffed. "I told you I would be calling to check up on you."

"Did I keep you up last night?"

"No."

"Did you not sleep well?"

"I actually slept great." His eyebrows creased together in concentration. "Why?"

"Because you're grouchier than all hell."

"Sorry. It's been a tough morning and nothing seems to be going right." He groaned. "I spilt coffee on myself, dropped paperwork everywhere, and have no money, because I forgot my wallet this morning. How are you feeling?"

"Wow. You can change a subject quick."

"If need be. How's the head?"

"Throbbing."

"I have some aspirin in the bathroom, help yourself. I also left some clothes out for you." Now Brian smiled. "I didn't think you'd want to walk home in your slip and robe."

"I appreciate that. You haven't asked."

"I figure if you want to talk about it, then we will, tonight. Not on the phone."

"Boss! Hey boss!" Brian tried to wave off his fellow worker, Mike, who just wasn't getting it.

"Boss? I thought you were a mechanic?"

"I am. Hold on a minute." She listened as he gave the man instructions and told him to beat it. "Hi, sorry."

"Do you talk to all your employees that way?" she teased.

"We're a bunch of guys."

"Oh! So you're admitting that you're lower in the chain because all you do is stand around swapping girl stories, scratching, spitting, and sniffing foul things?"

"Yeah. Wait a minute! No!"

"You really are having a rough day, aren't you?"

"I really am. But the sound of your voice has made it so much better."

"Well, I hope your day does get better. I need to go and jump in the shower." She smiled wickedly. "Wish you were here."

"Jesus, Serena, I do too. Call your sister, and stay out of trouble."

Serena showered and dressed quickly. His soap smelled of mint, his shampoo, apples. An interesting combination that left her feeling refreshed. The drawstring shorts he'd left her were a bit big, but the old college shirt was great. It was so comfortable Serena decided when she went home to change she would keep it on.

She was about to walk out of Brian's door when she accepted that calling her sister and facing the music sooner rather than later was the right thing to do. Hope didn't sound very happy.

"I can't talk to you right now. I have Mom here, and I'll be taking her to the appointment today."

She's pissed, went through Serena's head, and what else is new?

"Thank you. That's why I was calling." Serena took the deep breath she always needed when dealing with her sister. "I think we need to talk to her and the doctor about her mood swings."

"She's fine."

"If she was fine, she wouldn't have come after me last night."

"I can't talk to you right now, and I don't know what you're talking about."

"Hope, this is not a game. The doctor needs to know how bad her moods are getting. I'll call him myself if I have too. I'm the person who's with her the most. I would know."

"Well, you weren't with her last night."

There's that condemning voice she's so fond of using, Serena thought while rolling her eyes. "Do you know why?"

"Because you were too busy running around with your new boyfriend."

"Is that what she told you?" Serena couldn't believe it. How could her sister think she'd do such a thing? "She was crying last night when I went into her room, and then she started snapping at me about being in her house, watching over her twenty-four-seven. Then she pushed me. I lost my balance and hit my head on something. Want to see the lump? It's not pretty." Serena refused to let Hope interrupt. For once, she was holding her ground. "She was screaming like a banshee about me getting out of the house and a lot of other ugly things." Serena counted to three, slowly, and made sure Hope was still on the line. "The only place I had to go was Brian's. I was in a nightgown and robe, for God's sake. Along with blood dripping down my face. I thought Bri was going to have a heart attack."

"Oh God. I didn't know it was that bad."

"I figured if anything was wrong, she would call you or Brian. I didn't want to go back for my car keys. I'm sure you can understand that."

"I'll speak to him, and I think sometime this afternoon you should call." Her mother was in the room, Serena now realized.

Guilt swarmed over her. "Is everything okay? She's not hurt, or anything?"

"No, everything's fine. We just had a tough morning here."

Serena let out a mirthless laugh. "It's going around. Please call me after the doctor's."

"Not a problem."

When Serena hung up the phone, Bart came over and rested his giant head on her lap. "I guess it's you and me." He gave out a groan in reply. "Come on. We'll go get you a snack, and I'll change."

* * * *

Serena knew what dealership Brian worked at. But from the conversation on the phone, she figured he was a little more than a mechanic. Walking into the parts and repair department was going to be fun. She had picked up his wallet and some lunch for the both of them; well technically, it was brunch for her. The bell sounded when she walked in and the man at the desk took a long appreciative glance at her.

"Can I help you?" he asked.

"Maybe. I was looking for Brian Allen." She gave her best imitation of innocence.

"He's locked up in his office right now. Is there anything I can do for you?" Mike was trying not to look her over, again. She wasn't a woman the eye passed over without a glance or thought.

"He'll want to see me. I have food." Serena batted her eyes at him.

"Don't say I didn't warn you, he's not in the best of moods." Then he leaned on the counter and said, "We'll worship the ground you walk on if you can change that."

"Where's his office?"

* * * *

The knock on the door was too annoying to even look up. "Go away!" He roared. Mike gestured Serena to take a step in. She slammed Brian's office door at her back.

"What the hell!"

"I brought you some lunch." She held up the bag and winked at him. "So I hear that you've been quite the bear today. Have all those poor employees shaking in their boots." She pulled out the chicken and mashed potatoes. Brian just stared. "They're making bets right now on if I'm going to make it out of here alive." Out came the coleslaw. "Oh, and you forgot this, this morning." She threw his wallet at him and smiled some more.

Brian simply got up and came around his desk. He framed her face with his hands and kissed her gently on the lips. "Thank you." He wrapped his arms around Serena and brought her close. "I'm glad to see you're okay."

"Besides a good knot on the noggin, I'm fine." Her arms fastened tight around him before she demanded, "Let's eat!"

They had a good half hour together and no one dared interrupt them. She's still wearing my shirt, Brian thought, and she looks delicious in it. He sat back in his chair and watched her. He had no idea when the last time someone brought him lunch was, or why his heart kept tripping over itself every time her eyes met his.

"You look rested."

"Your bed is the most comfortable thing I have ever slept on. It took everything to get out of it." She shoveled more coleslaw into her mouth. "I haven't had a decent night's sleep since I've gotten back." Serena took a big swig of soda and made a noise of pleasure. "I love fast food. I know it isn't good for you, but it's so much better than my own cooking."

"You could come over and I could cook sometime."

"Who taught you how to cook?"

"My mother was a great cook, and when she wasn't showing my brother, sister, and me, Rosa was."

Serena asked nonchalantly, "Who's Rosa?"

"She was our nanny slash maid." Brian glanced up half expecting some kind of reaction, but didn't get one. Serena made a face and shrugged her shoulders like it was no big deal and went on eating.

"So you hounded your mother and Rosa to show you how to cook? Wish I had done that, maybe I would be a big-time chef at a fancy restaurant." Brian gave out a snort. "Hey, you never know." She gestured with her fork.

"Yeah, you never know." Brian rocked back in his chair. "I always thought that's what I would be. Then I discovered girls, and how much they liked food and cars." He leaned forward on his desk. "I decided I liked cars better."

"So you wine and dine your women, then take them out in that chick magnet of yours."

"I haven't wined and dined you, yet."

"And do you plan on it?" Serena asked with fun in her eyes.

"Maybe." Brian got up and walked around his desk and, taking her hand, pulled her to her feet. "Would you like that? 'Cause I was thinking dinner at my house with lots of food, candles, and music." Gracefully, Brian led Serena into a dance. "You smell so good. I like the way my shirt looks on you." He nibbled at her neck and sent tingles through her body. "We need to find some time alone, Serena. I've been having a very hard time concentrating on anything since you've walked into my life."

"I know the feeling." Serena replied in a sultry voice. "I just need a little more time."

"Not a problem. But I still want that supper." His patient lips found hers, trustful and welcoming.

"You still haven't asked about last night," she said quietly.

"I told you, it can hold till I get home." He pulled back and searched her face. "Unless you want to talk about it?"

"No. It can hold." Serena tried to smile and was rewarded with a bear hug that brought her feet off the ground. "It's time you got back to work."

"Then kiss me goodbye."

When Serena walked out the service door, Mike gave out a whistle. The heavy hand that landed on his shoulder stopped any other thought from escaping.

"I have to agree with you, Mike," Brian said. "She sure does make your day." Brian shook his head, as if he couldn't believe something.

"Feel like a second chance?" The surprised but confused expression on Brian's face said it all. "Hadn't thought of that yet, had ya?" Mike gave Brian a knowing look. "Take it from a guy that's been married for a while. She may not know it yet, and you may not know it yet. But it's written all over your faces. The two of you may think you're playing, but one morning you're going to wake up and her face will be the first thing you see and you'll hope it'll be the last thing you see at night. You're so sunk." Mike left Brian with that to chew on.

* * * *

"Babe," Brian was saying, "you need your belts changed."

Serena glanced under the hood and smiled. "I thought you were going to lube my engine?"

"Maybe some other time." He shook his head at the car. "How did you make it back with this thing?"

"I made a deal with it. She survives the trip. I do what I can to make the rest of her life comfortable." Serena looked down again at the engine. "Will it be expensive?"

"Don't worry about it. The belts are going to be the least of your worries come winter. What the hell are you doing in a piece of shit car like this?" Brian wanted to know.

"I love this car," she moaned. "We've been through so much together."

Brian smirked down at the little Escort. "Only you would get attached to a car this awful. Or is it just pity?"

"Shh! She'll take it personally and won't run tomorrow."

Brian's eyebrows shot up. His gaze went from Serena to the car. "She'll run if I have something to say about it." He bent over and started taking things apart.

Serena stood back and realized a man working on a car could be quite stimulating. Long muscular legs in shorts that were fitted just right and a dirty old t-shirt with holes. She had a little fantasy about grabbing one of those well-placed holes and ripping the shirt right off him.

"Stop it, Rena. I can't concentrate with you leering at me."

"How do you know I'm leering?" Serena purred.

"My ass was getting hot. Now if you're going to help, go get me something to drink."

"Testy, aren't we?"

"Damn woman," he muttered.

"I heard that!"

Brian smiled. She was enough of a pain in the ass to make it interesting.

Serena came back with some lemonade for the both of them. She watched as Brian drank his in one big gulp.

"Thirsty?"

"Yeah," he said breathlessly. "Sooo." Brian strained with one of the belts under the hood. "You've cleared things with Mom? Is Hope still pissed that you stayed over at my house the other night?" One belt out.

"Mom's getting help for her depression. Her spirits have been better the last couple of days." Serena peered over at her house, she felt stronger today. Not just because her mother was doing better, but because her outlook on life was different. She couldn't help but think it might have something to do with the man in front of her. "I don't care what Hope says, a support group and the medication is what she needs. That and a little independence." Serena gazed back down at Brian's butt and tilted her head.

"Cut. It. Out."

"She still thinks we slept together that night. She even asked how it was."

Brian rapped his head on the underside of the hood. "Shit!"

"Are you okay? Hey, now we'll have matching lumps!"

"Don't change the subject." He rubbed his head as fast as he could.

"Here, take the rest of my lemonade."

Brian drank it, eyeing her the whole time.

"Stop damning me. I can see you doing it." Serena's eyes narrowed. "It's not my fault you hit your head."

"It's your fault for everything, get used to it."

Serena let out a huff and crossed her arms.

"What did you tell your sister?"

"I don't know what you mean." She pouted.

"How it was!"

"How what was? Nothing happened!" She fisted her hands on her hips. "I was practically asleep before you got me to bed."

"I'm not stupid, you know." Brian went back under the hood. "I know girls talk to each other, especially sisters. I have one with a lot of friends."

"That I'm sure you tried to impress with your cooking abilities."

He grinned down at the engine. "An older sister did come in handy sometimes. But that's beside the point. What did you tell her?"

She came up behind him and ran her hands up the back of his shirt and her nails back down it. If he could have stretched like a cat, he would have.

"I told her I don't kiss and tell."

She's smooth. "Get away from me or these belts aren't going to get done."

"Boy, you're testy today." Serena began to back up when Brian nipped her around the waist and laid a smacking kiss on her lips.

"Lack of sleep. Now go away for an hour, at least. Then maybe I can get something done."

Serena was back an hour later, just as Brian was turning on the car.

"Oh!" she said clapping her hands together. "She's not making that horrible sound."

"No." Brian glared at the car. "She makes other horrible sounds."

"But that was the worst one." She bounced over and kissed him on the cheek.

Brian started picking up his tools and bringing them into the garage. When he came back, Serena was still grinning ear to ear at her car. He just shook his head.

"It'll have to go soon."

"Stop being so negative about everything. She only needs some TLC. And the AC fixed."

"You want to fix the AC on this?" He gestured toward the car. "It'll cost more than it's worth. I won't do it."

"Then I'll find someone who will."

"You can be as stubborn as you want. But there is no way this car is going to make it through a winter out here."

"Out here? Where the hell are you from that we live 'out here'?"

"Everywhere." He started picking up tools and headed to the garage again.

Serena picked up some stuff and headed the same way. "What is that supposed to mean?"

He mumbled something but then noticed Serena was too busy staring at the other car in the garage to hear him.

"What is that?" She walked around things and ran a finger down its hood.

"It's a car."

"No. It's a toy. A very expensive toy." Serena determined.

Uncomfortable, Brian shifted from foot to foot. "It's a Mercedes SLK convertible, midnight black with cream interior."

"Very nice," she said. "Why don't you ever take it out?"

"It was my mother's." He may have said it simply, but his actions spoke louder than his words. Brian turned and started organizing his tools, banging them around a bit. When Serena placed her hand on his shoulder, he stiffened.

"You loved her very much."

"And miss her every goddamn day."

"What happened?"

"She lost her battle with breast cancer about seven years ago. Not all the money in the world could save her." Brian turned so fast he saw Serena take a step back. "All the money my family has made for all those years and it still couldn't stop her from hurting." With his hands shoved in his pockets, he tilted his head up. "My dad had people flown in from all over to try and save her. It just wasn't enough."

"Do you think she would want you to hurt this way still? Brian," she said, placing her hands on his face.

"I don't think I want to talk about it right now."

"Okay," Serena said stepping back. "But you really should think about that car. It does have feelings, you know." She glanced over at it. All polished up, with tons of stuff surrounding it. "Why don't you go and get cleaned up and I'll treat you to the best pizza place in town."

Her smile in return for his was its own reward. "All right. But we're driving my car."

"Betsy's going to start taking this personally."

"You would name your car."

Chapter 12

Brian was busy swearing at the pool when Darren and his family arrived. They had promised to come over early and help with the preparations for the party.

"Darren, go see what Brian's already swearing about. I'm telling you the guy just can't do anything without getting irritable." Meg was getting what they now referred to affectionately as 'the cretins' out of the car when they heard the loud and heated profanities. As soon as she set Emily free, the little girl went running to see what Bart was up to, while Meg discovered she had to change John's clothes, again.

Meg sliced cheese for platters and organized chips with dip while Darren made sure the coolers had ice, and were packed full. By the time people began arriving, the grill was already starting to get warm, and the pool filter that Brian had been swearing at was working.

"Brian!" Darren was yelling over the small crowd and music. "Should I start the burgers soon?"

Brian tried not to cringe. "Why don't we wait a little bit?" The woman next to Brian moved herself a little closer. Brian gave her a passing glance.

"I'm so glad you invited me. I love a good party." She batted her eyelashes at him affectionately.

"I hope you enjoy yourself." Brian looked over the ever-growing crowd, searching. "Do you want a beer or something?" he asked absently when she pulled on his shirt ever so lightly to get his attention back.

"I'd love one." She followed him into the kitchen. He reminded himself that he was going to have to bring the coolers out as soon as he took care of... shit, what was her name?

"Here you go, Mandy." When he stood up and turned around, Brian ran smack dab into her. "Sorry."

"No need to be," Mandy said, closing the gap between them. "What do you say we get together some time?" She got on her toes, and brought her face close. "We could make our own party."

Brian put his hands on her shoulders and gently backed her up. "You know, it's very tempting."

"But?" she said narrowing her eyes.

"I'm involved with someone." Am I? Brian asked himself. Did I just say that? Mandy was not someone to balk at. He'd even engaged in a little fantasy or two about her the first time they met.

She took a step back. "I hadn't heard that." She looked suspiciously at him.

"I am. We've been seeing each other almost a month now." Jesus, had it really been that long?

"So, you're only dating?"

Brian took a deep breath; he couldn't believe he was coming to this realization because one of his buddies' younger sisters was hitting on him. "I would like to keep it exclusive between her and I. Messing it up would suck."

"You really are quite a man, Brian." She kissed his cheek. "I hope she feels the same way."

"I think she does." At least I hope she does. What if she doesn't? Brian felt a bit of panic.

"Good for you. No hard feelings?" Mandy took the beer from him.

"No. How could there be?" He smiled charmingly.

"If she hurts you, I'll kick her ass." When Mandy gave him a warning look, he laughed.

"I'm a big boy. Now go join the party." As she left, Brian picked up a cooler to bring out. What if he was wrong? What if she wasn't serious? She had so much going on right now that them getting serious would only make things more complicated. He swore at himself. When the hell had he last thought about having a serious relationship with anyone, anyway?

Brian was just picking up another cooler when Meg walked into the house. "Is everything okay?"

"What?" He'd been too busy with his own tangled thoughts to hear her.

"You okay, Brian? You seem to be a little touchy today."

"Oh, I'm fine. I haven't been getting a lot of sleep lately." He brought the cooler out and came back in for the next.

"Does the lack of sleep have to do with a certain redhead?" Brian hated when Meg smiled at him like that. She only did it when she was right.

"I don't know what you're talking about." He put his hands on his hips and a guilt-free expression on his face.

"I'm sure you don't." Meg patted his cheek and breezed back out the door.

Damn women, they should all burn in hell.

* * * *

Serena brought her mother over to Hope's instead of her sister coming to get her. Serena's car was on the skids again, and she didn't want to tell Brian. She needed to do some shopping, and since the Fourth of July wasn't until the next day, stores were open.

Therefore, Serena dropped her mother off and headed to the supermarket and the liquor store. She was standing in line when she caught a glimpse of herself in the convex mirror mounted high on the wall. Slightly uncomfortable with what she decided to wear that morning, Serena pulled down on the hem of her skirt. She still wasn't sure about the bikini she had on underneath, either. She'd never been self-conscious about it before, but now she felt half-naked and vulnerable.

"Stupid," she said aloud to herself. "I'm acting like a teenager." Looking up, she saw the woman standing next to her staring at her.

"Don't stop your conversation on my account," the woman said. "I talk to myself all the time."

"Great. Everyone's going to think I'm going crazy," Serena mumbled to herself. Maybe she was, she pondered.

* * * *

Where the hell was she? Her car was there, so she must be home. Her mother's was gone and he knew Katherine should be at Hope's most of the day. So where the hell was she?

"Darren, you had better go and stop Brian from prowling around before he scares everyone away. He's in a bad way, and it serves him right for thinking love was never going to nip him in the ass if he didn't want it to."

Darren kissed his wife gently on the lips. "Serena's driving him crazy. I wonder if he's having the same effect on her. Hey Brian! Why don't you come and help me with the burgers?" Darren called out.

"Why? You don't feel like having any fires this year?"

"Very funny. Now get your ass over here and help me."

* * * *

Serena couldn't believe the line of cars. What did he do, invite the whole town? She had to squeeze into her driveway because two cars were almost blocking it. She started hefting the goods in and thought to herself that this was intended to be a relaxing day. She could hear the music playing, smell the food cooking, and was reminded just how hungry she really was. Serena didn't even put the non-perishables away. She wanted to go see Brian and stop her nerves from dancing. Should I go up and kiss him? Crap, I don't want him to think I'm taking claim of him because we're in front of all his friends. He has the right to see whoever he wants. Maybe I should let him make the first move. Yeah, that's what I'll do, she decided on the way over. When a very obnoxious looking man holding a beer greeted Serena in Brian's driveway, she rolled her eyes to the sky. Just what she wanted, to be tagged by a drunk.

* * * *

Brian should have been happy. The party was going great, and Darren wasn't burning anything yet. So what was his problem?

"Damn it, where the hell is she?"

"Who?" Darren grinned.

"No one," he said, sharply and a little too fast.

"Of course not. You're always in a bad mood when you throw a party. That's why everyone comes. We love your sparkling personality, good food, and," he said, glancing around and expelling a large sigh of appreciation, "half-naked women."

"You're a dog." Looking around, Brian couldn't help but grin. "I like the way you think. If she doesn't show, I won't..." The sight of a redhead cut off his words. She was wearing a blue mini skirt and a white tank top. "Shit," he said aloud. There was no way he was going to be able to keep his hands off her. But he'd make damn sure every other man did. "Excuse me for a minute." Brian didn't even wait for an answer.

"Go get her, boy," Darren said under his breath.

"Hey!" Brian yelled to Serena.

Serena put on her biggest smile and practically leapt into his arms for a hug. "Brian. Sorry I'm late."

Brian's ego inflated when she stayed beside him with her arms around his waist.

"I see you've met Mark," he remarked with hidden laughter in his voice.

"Yeah, I found this damsel walking out front. She seemed in need of some friendly company." Mark flashed what he felt was his million-dollar smile.

"Brian, could you bring me to get a burger? I'm starving." She looked up at him with pleading eyes.

Brian choked on a chuckle. "Sure. Hopefully Darren hasn't burned them by now." He put an arm around her waist and nodded to Mark. "If you have any trouble with him," he whispered in her ear, "any, you let me know. I would take pride in hurting him."

Serena let out a giggle. "You really are sadistic, aren't you?"

"No, I just enjoy beating annoying drunks."

"I thought you were friends? Didn't you invite him?"

"I did." Brian tightened his grip and turned into her, knowing full well it would have people talking. "He's never given me a reason to smash him, but…" he said, letting his gaze wander down to her lips and linger.

"But?"

His gaze came back to hers and locked. "He just has to give me one, only one reason." Brian was staking claim on her. He would have to think about why all of a sudden he had this macho persona when he'd always detested men who acted that way.

* * * *

The day was beautiful with blue skies and small puffy white clouds. The temperature was high but a small breeze helped keep it bearable. Serena had been enjoying the constant chatter of the women both Brian and Meg had introduced her to when she spotted the striking woman that was talking to Brian. It occurred to her there was something very personal about the way they touched. It wasn't intimate. It was the type of affection that comes with knowing someone well. The woman was tall and slim with dark brown hair. There was a polish about her that could only come with money. The instant they hugged Serena knew the woman was his sister. He talked to her as if she was the only one around. When Brian turned his head and caught Serena's eye, he waved her over.

"Excuse me," she said, getting up from the table.

From across the lawn, Serena could feel the woman taking a quick survey of her; so she kept her eyes only on Brian. Not once did she sway. People, men, tried to stop her and chat but she just excused herself and stayed focused on her path. When she made it over to them, she didn't drape herself over Brian, like many women would have.

"Serena," Brian proclaimed, putting an arm around her shoulders, "this is my older sister, Jacqueline. Jac, this is Serena." They both put out hands for a shake.

"It's so nice to meet you, Jacqueline. Brian hasn't told me much, except that 'Torture' was always a fun game."

Jacqueline gave out a hearty laugh and the two women smiled at one another. "Oh yes! Brian and Gabe were masters at the game."

A large cloud of black smoke escaped the Bar-B-Q.

"I thought you knew better than to leave the grill for too long. I can't imagine him feeding a family…" Serena gestured toward Darren. "Anything Darren's cooked, he's burned."

"I hope you've become a vegetarian," Brian said to his sister. "I better go help." He turned to Serena. "I can trust you with her, right?" Brian kissed Serena quickly and ran off.

"Sure," she said calling after him. "She probably knows more about these people than I do." Serena gave Jac a nod. "Let's go get a beer."

"Sounds great." They headed to the coolers, dodging people as they went. "So how long have you been seeing my brother?"

"I'd say about a month. Since we met he seems to be everywhere." Serena smiled. "Look, he's giving Darren hell over at the grill."

"So, my brother is stalking you?" Jacqueline asked jokingly and popped the top on her can.

"I don't mind. Although he does keep damning me." The expression of puzzlement on Serena's face made Jacqueline laugh.

"He damns anyone he cares about. You should hear our father. He was always damning our mom and me. It's a sign of Allen affection."

"So it's a family trait." Serena peered over at him and laughed. "He can be such a grouchy soul, but he's so damn cute."

* * * *

Brian had been watching Serena all day with the dozens of people. She mingled with the crowd, keeping the conversations light and friendly. He noticed how she was always open and cheerful, yet reserved and cautious at the same time. He wanted all of her, all those things that she held back. He could feel the heat rising as his system started going into overload. Oh, he wanted all right; to feel the soft pillow of her lips, the curve of her body against his, all that heat and sexual tension that would be released when she finally surrendered. He saw her walk inside his home. "Fuck it," he said aloud and flung the spatula at Darren before stomping into the house determined to loosen the tight ball in his gut.

Serena had headed into the bathroom, Brian discovered. Well, I'll just wait till she comes out. "What the hell is she doing in there?"

"Probably going to the bathroom," he heard a voice behind him. He ignored the voice and placed his hands on either side of the doorway.

When Serena opened the door, he took her by such surprise that she jumped back with one hand to her chest. Brian didn't have a particularly friendly look on his face when he stepped into the bathroom.

"Brian... umm. If you needed to... umm."

He kicked the door shut behind him and with one arm crushed her body to his. He hadn't said a word, he simply removed the hair from her neck with his free hand and proceeded to slowly, gently taste and torture that long slender column. Brian's head began to swim from the fury of emotions running through his body; lust, heat, passion, and the driving need to control what was happening between them. He sought total and complete surrender. It was what he wanted, and it was what he would have. Brian worked his way up to her jaw line as she tipped her head back. Running his hands, strong and firm, up silky legs, Brian cupped her bottom and hiked her up on the sink. This is what he needed from her. No more dreaming about it, no more fantasizing about it, and by God, no more aching for it. He wanted, and he wanted now. His hands took possession of her breasts. He squeezed and molded as moans escaped her to heighten his throbbing need. He bit one of the hard peaks that strained against her tank top. She whimpered from the poignant assault. A fury of torrid emotions and repressed desires, kept too long in hiding, needing to be released, surfaced and demanded Brian capture her.

Later Serena would think back and not remember how she got on the vanity, but she couldn't think of that now—or anything else, for that matter, because he'd taken her breath away along with all reasonable thoughts of defense. The cold smooth surface was an erotic contrast to the heat and roughness of Brian's hands. His lips assaulted her neck and ravaged her mouth. His hands were everywhere—fisted in her hair, squeezing her breasts, grasping her thighs to pull her forward so she could feel his pulsing need. Heat streaked through her body and the last of her sanity snapped. If surrender was what Brian wanted, then she'd give in to his needs, but only on her terms. She turned her face into his. With the eyes of a temptress, she sucked out his bottom lip.

Serena wanted Brian's body and loins to plead for her to pleasure him. She licked her upper lip and fisted her hands in his hair. Crushing her mouth to his, Serena wrapped her legs around his waist and moved furiously against him. With hips grinding together in desperate need to mate, they both lost recognition of where they were. Need swept over them, a fiery inferno of sensations too hot, too out of control to handle. Hands tugged on shirts for a touch of flesh against flesh. With one hand gripping the back of her head, Brian's other hand groped for Serena's blazing heat. She gasped when he cupped her. The room filled with the thick sweet smell of sex.

Serena's own hand sought Brian out. He moaned when she clasped her hand around him. He was long and deliciously hard. Beads of salty sweat rolled down his neck and Serena sampled them with pleasure. Sight and hearing became secondary senses to touch and taste.

Brian was going to take her there, and she had no problem with it, Serena welcomed it. Their blind madness for one another was explosive, it was a wonder the room didn't ignite—

"Oh! Shit! Sorry!" Serena heard the words and the door close quickly. Still, Serena wasn't ready to let Brian step away from her.

"Guess I should have locked it." His breath was still coming fast, but he pulled her shirt back down and kissed her forehead. "Sorry."

"Don't be. I've never been ravaged in a bathroom before. Come to think of it," she said while adjusting her bikini top, "or anywhere." She combed her hands through his hair in an attempt to fix it and normalize her system. "Brian, I can't find it in me to feel ashamed about this. Embarrassed someone walked in, but in no way ashamed."

"You know, Serena," Brian told her while still nestled tight between her legs, "I just have a really hard time resisting you."

"Then don't do it so much."

The rest of the night was exactly what it was meant to be, one big party. All the neighbors were there laughing, smiling, and swimming in the pool. Bart kept the grounds clean by eating up anything that fell. And as the sun went down, the fireworks went up. The only thing out of place was Serena's own feelings when she saw Tom arrive.

"Don't worry," Brian assured her. "If he gets out of line there are plenty of us who'll take care of him."

"He gives me the creeps," she replied with a shudder. Brian pulled her close and kissed her lips.

"That's because he is a creep."

* * * *

Mark had watched Tom carefully through the night. He may have liked his women but he never was one to make trouble with somebody else's. She was Brian's girl, and that meant hands off. Mark had seen Tom stare at the couple and personally witnessed how his face had become red when Brian kissed her. Mark didn't like the whole mess Tom was starting with Serena. There was still old business between the two men that needed to be resolved from another woman Tom had tried and failed to woo because of his chauvinistic ways. Mark knew, sooner or later, Tom would mess up and Mark really hoped he was there to straighten the slime-bag out.

"Great party, man. Serena, I hope you can forgive me for being such an ass earlier." A smile spread across Mark's lips as he gazed into her eyes.

"There is nothing to forgive."

"You have a good woman here, Brian." Mark turned giving Brian a very serious look. "Tom's on the prowl. If you need anything, just ask."

"Appreciate it." They shook hands and he was gone.

"What was that about?" Serena asked with her hands on her hips and suspicion in her eyes.

"A little guy talk, that's all." Brian shrugged it off, and went to talk to some of the other guests that were leaving.

Serena glared at his back. "Guy talk," she repeated sarcastically, and went to talk to Jacqueline.

CHAPTER 13

"I don't get it." Serena's jaw went slack. "What do you mean we should now start thinking about chemotherapy?" Her mother had been looking better, acting better and doing more things than she probably should have been. It never seemed like she was getting worse.

"Things aren't progressing the way I would like them to." Dr. Kinney folded his hands on the desk then took a small deep breath. "Her counts are not where I would like them to be at this time. I feel this would work to everyone's benefit."

"Then why didn't we start with the chemo right from the beginning? This is insane." Hope was furious. She got up and started stalking around the room.

"I believe you will have to ask your mother that question."

Hope stopped pacing. Serena turned and stared at her mother.

"Well!" Hope yelled at her mother with a face beet red.

"Sweetheart," Katherine spoke softly. "I didn't want to go through that if I didn't have to. You must understand although you and Serena are with me every step of the way, in the end," she said with eyes pleading for understanding, "it is my decision."

"Mom." Serena took her mother's hand in hers and pleaded with her to understand what she was trying to say. "We can't pretend that we understand what you're going through, but we do have a right to be upset about this." She glanced up at Hope, who had tears streaming down her face. “We have all tried to do what we feel is right for you and ourselves, but keeping things like this is not a way to help us.”

Smiling at her now, Katherine nodded and put her other hand out for Hope. “I just didn’t want the two of you fighting any more than you already were about all this.” Tears began to roll slowly and silently down Katherine’s pale cheeks. “I know you only want what’s right for me. I didn’t want to disrupt your lives any more than I already have.”

“You don’t get it,” Hope said, and squatted in front of her mother. “We’re here because we love you so much. Disrupting our lives isn’t what we’re thinking about. We’re thinking about you.”

Serena had to take a deep breath. “Hope and I will always disagree on just about everything. But, when it comes to you, we know where we stand. We’re big girls, and you can’t put your health in jeopardy because you’re afraid we’re going to fight. We like to fight.”

“If chemo is what it’s going to take to beat this, then let’s do it.” Hope sounded so sure of everything, while Serena’s mind was full of doubts. Doubts that she refused to let show. She wanted her mother to live. She wanted her to be able to grow old with lots of grandchildren at her feet. Nevertheless, from the reading she had done, Serena knew her mother’s condition wasn’t a very good one. It was keeping Serena up at night, and affecting her thought process with everything. She was getting forgetful with things that were so simple. The day before, she forgot her ATM pin number and couldn’t get any money out of the bank. She had finally remembered it before she went to bed, and then proceeded to cry herself to sleep. She knew everything was taking its toll on Hope, too. It could be seen in the way she looked these days, hollow-eyed and weary. Emotionally, the two of them were drained.

“I feel we should start the chemo right away,” Dr. Kinney told the three women. “It’s very important your mother gets her rest. We will be doing some of the treatments here at the hospital and she’ll be receiving some drugs that will be taken at home.” With concerned eyes, he turned his attention to Katherine. “Some of the side effects will seem worse than the disease, a loss of hair, fatigue, emotional strain. But it will help make you better.”

It just wasn’t fair. The crushing sense of helplessness kept all of them quiet on the way home. It wasn’t raining, but it sure felt like it should be. People were everywhere, some walking their children, some their dogs, some jogging, some biking. But none were aware that the world was crashing around the O’Neal women. This isn’t good, Serena kept thinking. Things aren’t supposed to happen to us like this. It was as if all hope had been stripped from her, and she couldn’t breathe, she couldn’t feel.

When they got home, Serena went right for the kitchen. “I’m going to make supper.”

“I have to go home. Mom, I’ll see you tomorrow.” Hope kissed Katherine goodbye and left before the tears began to fall.

Supper was a flop. Just looking at the food had both their stomachs aching. Katherine excused herself and went to bed; she had a big day tomorrow. Serena grabbed some beers and headed out to the back swing. She didn’t like to drink alone, but sometimes the moment called for it.

She was well into her third beer when Bart came running over. She had been just sitting and dreaming about nothing in particular. “God, you’re cute,” she said while scratching the top of his enormous head. Bart let out a groan and plopped his head on her lap.

“If you keep telling him things like that he’s going to get an ego.”

Serena tried to smile. She hadn’t realized that she’d wanted to see Brian, but she was sure glad he was there now. Bending down, she grabbed another beer and handed it to him.

* * * *

Things aren’t good, he thought while sitting down. Still he waited. She would talk when the mood struck her. They sat there for a few minutes gazing up at the stars and petting Bart.

"She has to start chemo tomorrow." She turned to look at Brian. "You don't seem surprised."

"I'm not." He took her hand in his and squeezed. "I was surprised they hadn't started it right away."

"I guess my mom didn't want it." Serena concentrated on the beer in her hand.

"She's a stubborn woman when she wants to be." Brian gave her a little smile. "Not like anyone else I know."

It made her smile, too. "What was your mom like, Brian?"

Brian took a deep breath. "Well…" He adjusted in his seat and put an arm around her shoulders. Serena nestled into him and closed her eyes. He thought about how strange it was that he was willing to share his mother with her. He'd known there would come a time when he would have to talk about her. It was just so hard.

"She and I looked a lot alike. My sister, as you saw, has more of my father in her. So does my brother Gabriel." This isn't so hard, he thought while taking a slug of beer. "Man, Serena. She was so full of life," he said almost breathlessly. "You couldn't help but feel it when you were around her. She was always getting into something, and Dad would just say, 'Damn woman! She's always doing something she shouldn't be!'" Brian laughed at the impression he had made of his father. "There was this one time. I don't remember how old I was, probably eleven or twelve. She was showing my sister how to drive, and I said I wanted to learn, too. She had Jac pull the car over and let me in the front. I did pretty good." He laughed. "Until she had me go in reverse. I went right into the rose garden. Oh, man, Dad was pissed! He ranted, raved, and threw his hands up in the air as if he was through with the lot of us. All she did was laugh and keep us behind her. Not that my father would have hit us," he explained, "but because she wanted him to know that it was all her idea. Dad stormed into the house and you could hear him saying something about bodywork needing to be done and paint. Then he started asking himself questions like, 'do you know how much it's going to be to replace those roses?' and 'what about the safety of the children, no one thinks of the children.'" Brian let out a long sigh. "He loved her so much. We thought it would destroy him when she got sick." He fell silent for a minute. Serena brought her hand up to Brian's cheek. "It almost destroyed us all." He took a big swig of beer, and found it tasted bitter.

"Is there anything you would've done differently?" She needed to know. Regrets weren't something she took lightly.

"Not a thing. After she died, I kept thinking there was so much more that I could have done. But in the end you realize you can only do what you're capable of." He leaned his head on hers. "I miss her every damn day. We all do. I know I haven't dealt with it in the best way, but it's my way."

Serena let out a small sigh. "Oh, I know what you mean."

* * * *

July might have been hot, but August was scorching. Brian had helped with her car so many times, Serena lost count. Their nightly walks had become less regular because Serena found it hard to leave her mother, even for a short amount of time. Katherine had become so sick it was heartbreaking. She was weak and losing so much weight. The doctor had tried to prepare them for this. However, Serena just hadn't realized how unprepared she really was. For weeks now, Serena could feel the walls slowly closing in. The vertigo that plagued her was now a motion she'd become accustomed to. Instead of the revolving movement she experienced bouts of nausea and lightheadedness. Brian brought over soups and meals to make it easier on her. He's been so sweet, Serena sighed into the dishwater. She wondered if their relationship would ever go any farther. She wondered if he had started dating anyone else. He could. It wasn't as if she was his girlfriend.

They'd hardly spent any time together lately.

She broke a glass in the sink and cut herself. "Damn it!" Serena picked the shards of glass out of the sink, one by one; the repetitive action calmed her nerves. "I really have to get out of this house for a little while." She thought about calling Meg and Mandy and heading down to the Legion. Just for a couple of hours. Hopefully Darren wasn't working so he could watch the kids. The very idea made Serena smile and feel better as she put the bandage on her hand.

As it turned out, Darren wasn't working and Meg was thrilled. Mandy had been bugging Serena to go out since they'd met at Brian's party a month before. The Legion wasn't what Mandy had had in mind, but she understood why Serena wanted to stay close to home.

When Serena arrived, she wasn't fazed by the fact it hadn't changed much. The outside still looked a little run down. She could hear music emerging from within, and smell the stale smoke lingering in the air. It wasn't much different on the inside. There never were a lot of people, but everyone was always friendly enough. The girls were already there with drinks in hand. They saluted Serena when she walked over and pointed to the drink they had already ordered.

"You guys are the best," Serena said, taking a seat. "Boy, this place hasn't changed much." She spotted Tom over in the corner making his moves on some colorfully dressed woman. "Oh wonderful."

"Yeah." Mandy smirked. "Thought you'd like that. At least he's got his hands full with the new chick in town."

Meg rolled her eyes and lowered her voice as if there was someone other than them to hear. "Thank God! He's one of the most obnoxious people I have ever met."

"Him and Mark are something else," Serena said before taking a swig of her beer.

"Now don't go talking about Mark."

"That's right, Serena." Meg gave a nod. "Mandy here has a thing for him."

"Now that's not true."

"How could you? He's so…" Serena screwed up her face. "Oh, I don't know. He's nice to look at but he seems just as obnoxious as Tom."

"He really is a great guy. You have to get to know him."

"Which is something she'd like to do." Meg raised her glass to her mouth to sip and then almost spit it out everywhere.

"Good evening, ladies."

"Tom," Serena and Mandy said in unison.

"I thought I'd come over and say hello to the most beautiful women in the place."

And there was the grin, right on cue.

"Is that the line you used on the woman with the very high skirt?" Mandy fluttered her lashes at him and taunted.

"Now as we all know, there is nothing wrong with showing your best assets." There was a sneer under the exchange, and the temperature in the room dropped twenty degrees.

"Yes," Serena said with a smile. "You're absolutely right. You show yours all the time."

"Well you have good taste, and know when you see something good." He turned to Meg. "Don't you agree?"

"Of course I do. Serena is a very conscious woman. As is Mandy." Meg mocked, without being too obvious. "Now at the risk of being rude, we're having a girls' night out."

Tom smiled. If he was going to score any points with Serena tonight, it would be by backing out quietly. "In that case, I hope you girls have a good time." He kissed Serena's hand and went back to the bar where some of his friends had been watching.

Serena tried not to wipe her hand on her shorts. He gave her the heebie-jeebies. "That was fun." She took a slug of her drink. "I take it you and Tom don't get along."

Mandy snarled. "You could say that. He wanted to do some dancing between the sheets. I wasn't willing. He took it personally."

Meg snorted into her beer. "That's an understatement. He was so pissed off that he would go out of his way just to be a jerk to you."

"No way!"

"Oh, yeah! He would show up at bars and clubs I was at and start trouble by saying that I was being a bitch to him, when I hadn't said a thing. Then he would try to get me kicked out of the joint. People were not happy. They knew he was only doing it because I wouldn't sleep with him. But you know, to this day, there are bars I can't go into because of him."

Serena turned and gave Tom's back a glare. "What an asshole."

"Darren finally told him if he didn't lay off, he was going to charge him with harassment." Meg gave a wistful smile. "I love that man."

"I owe that man."

"I can't believe Tom is so much more of a jerk than I thought," Serena said awestruck.

"That's how I got to know Mark so well," Mandy explained. "He was always there when I needed him. One time, I was walking to my car and Tom was following me saying all sorts of not nice things. Mark came over and told him if he ever caught him doing anything like that again he was going to correct his temperament toward women."

Serena leaned on the table and rested her chin on her hand. "And here I thought Mark was just like him."

This time Meg chimed in. "He likes his women, don't get us wrong. But once you get to know him, he's not so annoying."

"I don't think Brian likes him very much."

Both girls laughed as they looked at Serena, who was shocked. "He didn't particularly like him at the party." Meg flagged a waitress to order another round of beers.

"I know. He told me he was more than willing to put him in his place." Serena paused with her beer halfway to her lips. "What?" she asked when Meg and Mandy began laughing at her.

"Are you blind?" Mandy exclaimed. "Now I'm going to tell you something, and I don't want you getting mad or acting differently toward me afterward, okay?"

"Yeah, sure." Serena took a swig of beer, for some reason thinking she might need it.

Meg leaned forward in anticipation. "Oh, I can't wait to hear this. It's something new, isn't it?"

"Yes. It's something new." Mandy took a swig of beer to build the tension. "I came to the party a little early, thinking I could help out. Brian was in his usual adorable mood." Serena smiled dreamingly and no one at the table missed it. "He offered me a drink and I followed him into the kitchen. I then proceeded to put the moves on him."

Serena sat back in her chair. She wasn't sure what she was feeling, but she knew it was something new, something she didn't like.

Being pleased with Serena's reaction, Mandy continued. "You can only imagine how surprised I was when he told me that he was involved with someone. You look a little surprised at the involvement thing, Serena."

"Well I didn't realize he was."

"My God, you really are dense." Meg smacked the top of Serena's head. "He meant you!"

Serena glanced over at Mandy who was nodding her head. "He said he wanted it to be exclusive between him and this person."

"No shit?" Meg's jaw had gone slack and her eyes had grown huge.

"And he was talking about me?" Serena pointed at herself.

"I love you, Serena," Meg said while patting her friend on the back, "but you are slow."

"It's only that we just met, Meg. He's not the type of man that usually attaches to one woman. I figured he was sticking around because of my mom."

"Is that why you haven't slept with him?"

"What!" Now the shock registered on Mandy's face. "You haven't slept with him yet?"

"There hasn't been time. It's not as if I don't want to. How do you know?" Serena said, turning to Meg.

"He and Darren tell each other everything, and Darren tells me. If he knows what's good for him."

"Okay. So why haven't you just walked over to his house, knocked on the door, and when he answers started tearing his clothes off?"

"You know, Mandy, that's something that's crossed my mind. Along with a dozen other things. It never seems to be the right time."

"You need a right time? Hell, Darren and I did it for the first time in the back of his squad car."

Both Serena and Mandy turned their attention to Meg.

"Oh, yeah! He was pissed off at me for being at this little party that was busted up. He was yelling at me and wouldn't stop. Finally, we argued so much that he pulled the car over and when he went to pull me out I pulled him in. Not intentionally, mind you." She gestured with her beer. "I just wasn't about to be dragged out of the car I was dragged into in the first place. Next thing we know we're like two dogs in heat. Never had better sex before. And let me tell you." Meg leaned forward again. "It just keeps getting better."

"I think I need another drink." Serena got up and went to the bar.

"Boy, she's chewing on this."

"It's good for her. Mandy, did you really put the moves on Bri?"

"Yup. And he wouldn't even let me touch him."

"Darren's going to love this."

"Love what?"

"Mark!" Meg piped out. "You here with your cronies?"

He smiled wishfully at Mandy. "Yeah. I see our buddy Tom is in the house."

"Pay him no bother," Mandy told him coyly.

"I haven't seen this many people here on a Friday in I don't know how long. We should get a game of darts going." Mark's eyes never left Mandy's. Electrical charges bounced from one to the other.

Serena was nearly struck by one of those sexually charged bolts on her way back from getting her drink. "Well why don't you two go ahead. Meg and I will catch up."

Mark simply grabbed Mandy's beer and told her to come on.

"But we're having a girls' night out," she protested.

"And we'll play teams. Right, Meg?" Serena asked.

"Right."

"I just have to go to the ladies room. And you know I can't go alone." She batted her eyes at Mandy and grabbed Meg's hand. "Okay," Serena said once they were in the girls' room, "are those two dancing around each other or is it me?"

"No. I think you've got that right." They grinned at each other and decided maybe their girls' night out wouldn't be ruined if it included some of the guys.

* * * *

"So where's Brian tonight?" Mark glanced at Serena before aiming to take a shot.

"He's at his dad's for the weekend. Something about them all getting called in." Serena shrugged her shoulders and tried not to think about what Mandy had told her.

"His dad is a trip." He missed his shot. "Shit! Have you met him yet?"

"No." Serena knew she'd miss this shot. She'd missed them all so far. "From what he tells me, they're a lot alike. Even if he doesn't want to admit to it." She hit the wall. "Damn."

Meg gave out a good hearty laugh. "All the two of them do is get grouchy about everything. It's quite comical."

"Why do they do that?"

"Because they like to," Meg said as she and Serena watched Mandy set up for her shot. They both grinned when Mark came up behind her, and held Mandy close so he could adjust her aim.

"Aren't the boys going to get mad that you blew them off to play with us?" Mandy's body visibly stiffened with Mark's behind her.

"No. They understand." Mark took a step back from the passion they brought to each other. "I need another drink. Anybody else?"

"I'm good," Serena said. "I'll have to get going soon anyway."

"Me, too." Meg sighed.

"If you don't mind, I'd like another one."

"Coming up." He walked away from Mandy a little fast and had Serena and Meg snickering.

"What?"

"And you said I was blind? Honey, that man is head over heels, tripping on himself. If I didn't see it I wouldn't have believed it."

"Me either," Meg said, shaking her head. "Girl… that man wants to kiss you so much, he's nervous around you."

"Give me a break. He backs off whenever I get too close in the slightest way." Serena saw the light bulb in Mandy's head come on. "Are you telling me we've been torturing ourselves for nothing?"

"If you feel the same way he does." Serena nodded.

"Well, if you don't mind, I might have to hang out a little longer than the two of you. You wouldn't mind leaving one at a time so it doesn't seem too suspicious, would you?"

"Only if you call and tell us all about it tomorrow."

"Serena, dear, I love the way you think." Meg put an arm around her shoulders and they grinned at one another. "I'm so glad we came out."

An hour and a few sodas later, Meg excused herself to leave. She needed to get home to her family. About half an hour later, Serena got up to go. She was tired and worried about being away from her mother for too long.

None of the girls had noticed throughout the night someone had been watching them, like a hawk waiting to swoop down for its prey, but Mark had. He knew he needed to be prepared in case the observer tried anything.

"I'm so ready for bed," Serena said. "I can't believe I made it this far." She hugged Mandy and then Mark, said goodbye to Mark's 'cronies,' and headed out the door. Mark just watched and waited. When Tom got up and headed out, Mark decided to give him a minute, or less.

"Serena!"

"Tom. What's up?" She'd been about to open her car door.

"Serena," he said, coming close and trapping her against the car. "I think we've been avoiding this a little too long." She could smell the alcohol on his breath.

"Tom," she said firmly. "Back off. I wasn't interested then, and I'm not now."

He brought his face closer, as she averted to get farther away. When she tried to shift and knee him in the groin, he blocked it and pinned her hard on the car door. She was trying to bring her hands up to push or scratch, anything to defend herself, when to her surprise Tom went flying through the air.

"Son of a bitch! I knew I couldn't trust you." Mark picked up Tom and laid a fist in his face. "I've been waiting to do this for a long time," he said, throwing another punch.

Tom's speech slurred as he stumbled to his feet. "I'm really sick of you putting your nose where it doesn't belong." Tom tried to swing and ended up striking air. "Now I'm going to break it."

Mark made a sound of disgust, and when Tom attacked, he grabbed him by the arm and threw him to the ground. "You're lucky it's me and not Brian. But I can guarantee he'll be gunning for you when he gets back." He turned to Serena. "You okay?"

"Yeah," she said, still stunned by all that had happened. Mark and Serena looked down at Tom as he tried to get up. She rubbed her hands up and down her arms as if to ward off a chill. "Thank you. I don't know what would have happened."

"Do you want me to call the police? You can charge him, you know."

Serena breathed a sigh of relief. "I think once morning comes, and he remembers what happened, he'll be sorry."

"Once Brian gets a hold of him, he'll really be sorry. Are you sure you're all right to drive home?"

"Oh, yeah," she said, waving him off. "I've been through worse."

"Well, if you're sure. I don't want you playing the strong woman thing, and then getting yourself into an accident."

They watched as Tom staggered to his feet and to the bar door. "I'm fine," she said patting him on the shoulder. "And thanks again."

"Anytime." Mark smiled down at her and opened the car door.

"Can I give you a little advice? If you don't mind."

"Sure."

"She's been waiting for you to make the first move. I think tonight would be the perfect time."

"She's not interested, trust me," he told her, and then Serena saw the wheels turning.

"You men can be so stupid." She closed her door and headed out.

Mark pensively walked back to the bar. As he reached for the door, it flew open.

"Mark. My God, are you okay? What happened?" Mandy had her hands cupped around his face, inspecting it. "He's such an asshole. When I saw him come in and you didn't, it got me worried."

"Come on. You know I can take care of myself."

"So that means I can't be worried?"

"Only if you're willing to kiss it and make it all better." Oh, what the hell. If there was any truth to what Serena just said, he was going to find out.

"Okay. So where's it hurt?" Mandy had her hands on her hips and was looking all too delicious to Mark.

"Here," he said, pointing to his chin.

She got on her toes and, while eyeing him suspiciously, gently kissed his chin. When she went to step away, she found his arms had encircled her waist, and he was holding on tight.

"I don't think we can be friends anymore." His voice was low, their eyes were locked and their mouths a whisper apart. Slowly he closed the gap between them. When their lips touched, her hands moved slowly up his arms. It was gradual and patient, as if sampling a fine wine. Smooth, sweet, intoxicating. He lost himself in her. When she closed her eyes and sighed, all bets were off. They held onto one another as if their very lives depended on it. Drinking each other in, everything the other had to offer, so their parched palates could be sated.

Slowly they pulled away from each other, words absent for both of them. A smile spread across Mark's face, and when he pushed the hair back from Mandy's eyes, he saw she was smiling too.

"I guess I don't have to ask if you minded that."

"Mark, I won't mind if you ever want to do that again."

"Good. Because I plan on doing it more and more." He bent down and kissed her again. "I need to get inside," he said against her mouth.

"Make sure that Tom gets home all right." Mark tried to pull away from her, again. "Really, I need to go inside."

"Okay." Mandy's eyes were dreamy and her lips were so soft and warm. Mark had no choice; he went back for more. This time she let out a giggle when he pulled her back into his arms. He laughed with her when their mouths met. Yes, he was definitely going to be doing this more.

* * * *

When Serena arrived home, she slid her key in the door lock and realized for the first time her vision was blurry and she was shaking. There was no question why. Tom had scared her. Serena's mind was whirling; she placed a hand to her head where her eyes were pounding. She knew it was late, but the idea of a bath was so appealing. She needed to scrub him off of her. His body had been pressed against hers. She had felt his arousal, smelled the stench of alcohol on his breath. Serena's stomach turned and its contents threatened to come up, making the ache in her head pound more.

The water was warm and relaxing. Getting in she realized her back was a bit achy. Must have been when Mark grabbed Tom while Tom was holding her. Serena rubbed at the sore spot and thanked the good Lord her mother was sleeping soundly. Countless times in the past few weeks Serena had awakened to the sounds of her mother being ill. The latest session of chemo would be over soon and then she'd have some time off, at least until the next one.

Serena's mind drifted until she figured it was time to dry off. Her bed felt like a miracle, a welcoming nirvana. Her last thoughts were of Brian and of him coming home.

CHAPTER 14

"What do you mean you're going home early?" Daniel Allen's voice echoed through the house.

"Dad, I have a job to get to."

"Well then, you should have taken the day off."

Brian rolled his eyes at his sister.

"Daddy," Jacqueline said lovingly, "Brian needs to get back tonight. You'll still have us here." She was doing what she could. Brian and Daniel tended to butt heads quite a bit, but it was all love, and done with affection.

"You're going to the dinner next month. And for once, will you please bring a date?" They had the same conversation year after year. They would sponsor a benefit supper for the American Breast Cancer Society, and in the last four years Brian was always solo.

"Yes, Dad. I'm going." He had a strained tone to his voice that didn't get past Daniel.

"Don't take that tone with me boy! And your sister here tells me that you have a new lady in your life."

"Dad!"

"Now hush." Daniel waved Jacqueline off. Brian gave her an evil stare. "If this boy is getting involved with someone then I want to know about it."

"Yeah," said Gabe, raising his drink. "Love to know what you're bringing home this time."

"From what my wife says, she's quite a looker," Donald added cheerfully, earning a swat off the shoulder from Jacqueline.

"You know, Jac, you have a big mouth."

Daniel set the trap. "Now don't go sassing your sister, Brian. She's just happy you've finally found someone to have some fun with."

"Have some fun with?" Brian said with a sneer to his sister. "I thought you liked her."

"I did. She was very nice."

"Nice?" Daniel questioned. "Is that how you would describe her? It sounds boring."

"She's not boring. And she's more than 'nice.'" Brian set his jaw tight.

"Well, I guess we'll have to be the judge of that," Gabe replied.

"You'll like her!" Brian's patience was gone and he didn't care for how his family was acting. "Just because I made one bad judgment doesn't mean that I haven't learned from it."

"Of course you have," Jacqueline added and patted Brian's hand.

"Don't use that tone with me." Brian pointed at his sister. Her laughter filled the room as he scowled at her.

"She's only trying to help. Now tell us what is so special about this lass." Daniel sat back in his chair satisfied they'd all outmaneuvered his youngest son.

"Fine." Brian threw himself into one of the large chairs in the room and took a swig of his brandy. "She's my next door neighbor."

"I thought your neighbor was in her late fifties?"

"Gabe," Brian said dryly, "it's her daughter."

"I thought she was married with a kid?" Donald asked with amusement.

Brian let out an impatient breath. "This is her other daughter."

"Well why didn't you say so, boy!" Daniel crossed the vast room and grabbed the brandy decanter to fill everyone's drinks.

Roping in his patience one last time Brian prepared himself to speak, again. "She's been living in New York for the last seven years. She's a hairdresser, and a pretty good one at that. Her name is Serena and she moved back to help take care of her mother who is ill."

"Now that's a good girl," Daniel boomed.

"What does she look like?"

Jacqueline, appalled, glared at her older brother. "Does it really matter, Gabe?"

"Yes!"

Brian glanced from his sister to his brother. "She's a redhead. Not too tall, but quite shapely." He wiggled his eyebrows at Gabe and Donald.

"Just the way we like them," Gabe announced.

"At least he didn't say she has a great personality."

"You know, Donald, you're as bad as the rest. I can't believe after all these years I'm still surrounded by all men!" And with that, Jacqueline left the room.

"Damn women," Daniel said. "The only thing they're good for is a headache."

* * * *

Brian left a lot later than he had planned. It was only a few hours back, but the ride seemed to take forever. His mind kept wandering back to Serena and how his family had bullied him into talking about her. They were good, he acknowledged. Usually he was the one getting things out of people, but they definitely scored some points tonight. Then his thoughts wandered to how happy he had been over the summer. How he seemed to get out of bed easier, go to work a little happier, and look forward to spending his evenings, no matter if it was five minutes or five hours, with a certain redhead. He smiled in disbelief. "Nope. Never saw that one coming, did you, Brian?" he asked himself and laughed.

It may have been mid-evening when Brian parked in his driveway, but the sun was still giving off some light and the sky was an explosion of color. He wondered what Serena had done all weekend and thought about how a trip would be good for them. Something close and something fun. There was an amusement park not too far away. A day at the park and water world would be exciting. Maybe the beach; they could go north and do some shopping at the same time. They could always go south, he mused. Connecticut had a lot of interesting places—and his family. Bart let out a bark.

"Yeah, boy. It's nice to be home." He peered over at Serena's house and wondered if he should call her. It was around nine in the evening and he knew she'd still be up. He just didn't want to seem too pushy, or like a puppy dog begging for attention.

Brian was grabbing his bags in the back of the car when Bart went running for Serena's house. She was bringing out the trash and Brian couldn't help but wonder how a woman could look so damn attractive doing something so typical.

* * * *

It wasn't that she'd been waiting for him to get home. It was merely that she really didn't have that much to do. So what if she waited on bringing the trash out? So what if she decided to bring it out as he drove in? She missed his dog, she rationalized, trying to satisfy her conscience. She missed him, too. Serena looked up and smiled when she heard Bart barking and running toward her. She had enough time to put the bag of trash down when Bart knocked her off her feet. He put one large paw on her chest to keep her down, and furiously licked her face.

She could hear Brian yelling over her laughter. "Bart! Get off of her!" The dog put his head down and made some kind of groaning noise. "Are you okay? I don't know what it is about you." Brian shot

Bart an angry stare as he helped Serena up. She was a little off balance and teetered right into him. “Wow! Maybe you should sit down.” Brian had his hands cupping her elbows to hold her up while he gently brought her back down to the ground. “Don’t even think about it,” he said, glaring at Bart.

“Really, I’m fine. I think I got up a little too fast.” She brought a hand to her spinning head. “I don’t think I’ve ever had anyone so happy to see me.”

“I’m happy to see you.” He cupped her chin and lowered his mouth to hers. Just a taste, she thought, that’s all I need, a small taste. Next thing they knew he was on top of her. She could feel the softness of the grass under her and the warmth of his body above. He pulled away but kept their faces close. “I didn’t mean to maul you on the grass like my dog did.”

“Oh, somehow when you do it, it doesn’t seem so bad.” She stroked her hands up and down his back, and had him stretching like a cat. The sky above them showed only a few rays of sunlight, and the air was dry and cool.

“I have a question, actually, more of a favor to ask you.”

“Serena?” Both Brian and Serena’s head whipped toward the house where her mother was standing. “I’m sorry. I didn’t mean to interrupt.” Brian was already to his feet and looking rather awkward. He ran a shaky hand through his hair. When Serena tried to get up he helped by grabbing her arm, hoisting her to her feet, and then taking a very large step away.

“How are you feeling?” he said quickly. “I just got back, and Bart came running over and knocked Serena down on the ground. Then when I went to help her up she wasn’t quite steady on her feet so I helped her back down and then...” he trailed off, not sure if he should explain what happened next. Serena figured he probably ran out of air. “I really should be getting home. I’ve been away for a couple of days and have to unpack and get myself set for work in the morning." Brian turned as if he was going to kiss Serena goodbye, then decided to simply wave and dashed to his house.

Brian hurried to his house with dog in tow, while Serena walked to her mother and smiled. "I think you made him a little nervous." Serena was trying to suppress the laughter but she could see her mother's face cracking under the pressure of holding back. They both fell into hysterics.

"He looked like he just got caught with his hand in the cookie jar." Katherine was holding her stomach. "I haven't had a good laugh like this in a long time. Do you realize the last time I caught you making out with a boy?" There were tears running down their faces. "I'm so sorry," Katherine barely got out. "I... Oh my! That poor boy!" Her laughter took over again and she wheezed. Serena put her arm around her mother's shoulders and guided her back into the house.

"You need to calm down." However, the harder Serena tried to suppress her laughter, the more she giggled.

"Did you see the way he darted back to his house? My God! It was so damn cute!" Katherine continued to chuckle as her daughter helped her take a seat on the couch.

Serena flopped beside her, and they both let out a long and satisfying breath. "We needed that." They leaned against each other for support. It was exactly what they needed.

Later, Serena tried calling Bri, but no one answered. She had to wonder just how embarrassed he really was. As she put the phone down, she could hear her mother in the bathroom. Sometimes Katherine tried to cover up the fact she was getting sick. However, tonight things weren't agreeing with her stomach and there was no covering it up. Brian was all but forgotten as Serena dashed down the hallway to the bathroom. This time her mother hadn't had time to lock the door. Thank God, Serena thought, as she opened it.

Her mother seemed so frail and ghost-like, lying there on the floor. The only thing that was keeping her up was the bowl. Serena went to grab a washcloth when she realized her mother hadn't quite made it in time. She was going to need to get her into the tub, and then clean up the bathroom. She grabbed the washcloth and rinsed it in some cold water. When she placed it on the back of her mother's neck, Katherine let out a moan of pleasure. She was burning up again. Serena could feel how hot her mother was through the cloth. She gently pushed back her sweat-soaked hair to feel her forehead. Shit! Her mother had been running a fever on and off for a few days; it was definitely time to call the doctor again. Serena reached over and started the tub.

"I don't want to take a bath," Katherine said weakly.

"Well, that's just too bad. You're not going to stink up the sheets with that body odor of yours."

"You're the one who stinks."

"Maybe so. But I'll take care of myself after we take care of you." She closed the lid on the toilet and helped her mother sit on top. Trying not to think about what she was stepping in, and slipping on, Serena helped her mother take her clothes off. She tried to think of roses and daffodils. Fresh cut grass and sea air. Anything so she wouldn't dry heave from the awful stench that permeated the tiny bathroom. As Serena helped lower her mother into the tub, she found herself turning the other way as not to see what the radiation had been doing to her mother's body. She knew her mother had burns; she had seen them, tended to them. However, now with the chemo added on to her treatment, Serena sometimes felt things were out of control. She wasn't trained for this, and neither was her sister. Serena took her shoes off before she left the bathroom. When she went to throw them out the door, she almost threw them at Brian.

"I'm sorry, honey. It's really not a good time." She saw the pot of soup in his hands and longed for a quiet evening with it.

Brian smelled the vomit. "You go get a candle and I'll start filling up a bucket." He walked right past her and put the pot on the stove.

She didn't ask how he knew what had happened, she was just glad that he was there. Serena grabbed a candle and some rags for the floor and headed into the mess. She wiped it up the best she could, then washed her mother. Getting Katherine out of the tub was becoming more of a feat every day. Katherine may have been getting lighter, but she was certainly getting weaker. Serena dressed her mother carefully and when she opened the door, Brian was there. He simply picked Katherine up and headed for her bedroom.

"You know I hope this can help you to forgive me for attacking your daughter on the front lawn."

Katherine gave out a small weak laugh. "There's nothing to forgive you for."

He laid her on the bed, took off her robe, and then covered her up.

"Get some sleep," he said kissing her forehead.

Brian turned out the light and closed the door softly. He found Serena cleaning the toilet. The floor was wet from her mopping, and so was she. Waiting patiently, his thoughts wandered to the free spirited woman he had met only a short time ago. He understood what it was like to feel as if you were two people. One was the everyday person who laughed and dreamed. The other was a robot, doing things in a mechanical way as if they were supposed to be part of your everyday life. He grabbed the bucket and brought it to the kitchen to empty. When he felt her rest her head against his back, he turned and wrapped his arms around her.

"You know, it's times like these I remember how short you are." Brian heard her try to muffle a sniffle and stroked her head. "You know it's okay to let go sometimes."

"Just not in the presence of a man, right?" She was sniffling in his shirt and wiping her eyes on it.

"I really don't mind as long as you don't blow your nose on me." He was grinning down at her when Serena lifted her head.

"Does it get worse?" He knew what she was asking. He just wasn't sure how he should answer it.

"Well, I think it's probably different for everyone."

"You're right." She buried her head back in his chest and wrapped her arms around him.

"Okay, sweetie. Or should I say smelly." He picked her up and brought her back into the bathroom. "Strip and get in the shower." Her eyebrows shot up. "I'm not going to join you. However, I am going to rifle through your things to find some sleepwear. Go on," he said, smacking her on the ass. "You'll feel a lot better."

He closed the door and heard the shower start as he headed into her room. Wondering what treasures he would find, Brian was disappointed when her gown and robe were on the back of her desk chair. "So, you're sneaky." He glared toward the direction of the bathroom. "No wonder you didn't object." He picked the garments up to his face for a whiff. They smelled of summer flowers, fresh and clean. He remembered what it was like when they had slept side by side. The smell of her hair as it tickled his face in the night, the touch of her skin when he took the robe from her, and the sight of her snuggled in his bed like she belonged there. Damn woman, she was driving him crazy. This was not the night for a teenage boy's fantasy, he told himself. Yet here he was in her bedroom dreaming about the woman he had yet to have. Brian stomped out of the room, opened the bathroom door, and threw the clothing in.

"Your mom is sound asleep," he told her when she came out refreshed and smelling all too alluring. He shoved a bowl of soup into her hands. "I checked on her a minute ago."

"Thank you."

"You're welcome." Why was he so pissed off? Brian's mood had become bitter and he couldn't figure out why. He watched as Serena put the bowl down and wrapped her arms around his neck. He gave her a puzzled expression and she gave him a small understanding smile.

"You know, Brian. You are in need of a little attention." When she came a little closer, his system wasn't sure if it should overload or loosen up. She brought his face down as she looked into his eyes. At the last minute, Serena brought her cheek to his and squeezed him tight. His response was automatic. He squeezed her back, and let out a long slow breath.

"You're going to kill me, Serena."

"Why?" she whispered into his ear. He rolled his eyes when he felt her breath on it.

"Because it takes every ounce of control not to drag you to the floor and make mad passionate love to you. " Brian lazily started kissing and nuzzling her neck. "But it's the wrong time. It always seems to be the wrong time."

"We have to find the right time, and soon." She stretched her body up against him.

"I know." He took a step back, a very large step back. "But right now you need to eat your soup and get some sleep." Picking up her bowl, Brian handed it back to her. "And I, my dear, am going to go home before we do something stupid."

"Earlier, you said you had a question to ask me. Then you ran away." Serena smirked at him.

Feeling his cheeks heat up, Brian responded, "I did not run away."

"No. You sprinted."

"No. I just felt it was time to take leave."

"Right." She nodded her head slowly.

"Anyway," Brian said, feeling a little impatient. "You know what? It can wait till tomorrow."

"Don't you dare." Serena poked a finger into Brian's chest.

"You've been through enough tonight. Don't you think?" He couldn't suppress the sarcasm in his voice.

Serena glared at him and gripped her soup bowl harder. Brian saw what she was thinking and put his hands up. "All right. All right." He put the bowl aside and wrapped his arms around her waist. She cocked one eyebrow and tilted her head.

"My dad puts on this big shindig every year for Breast Cancer Awareness Month. Which is in October." One of his hands started brushing through her hair. Man, he loved the color and feel of it.

"And?"

"Sorry. I lost track for a minute. Well…" He brought his eyes back to hers; he hadn't even realized they had wandered. "It's not a whole lot of fun. And you'll have to get all dressed up. It's black tie. Not that I would mind seeing everyone in the place absolutely jealous of me. Because," he said, pulling her closer and kissing her lips softly, "I will be with the most beautiful woman in the room. If." He kissed her lips again. "You agree to come with me."

"Yes. You're killing me, Brian," Serena whispered before his lips found hers again.

They melted into each other with a slow, easy pace. It was warm and smooth, not hot and edgy. The sensation journeyed from the tips of his toes to the crown of his head, and left him with a content but confused feeling.

Something was different, something had changed. They pulled away slowly from each other with this knowledge, but without any understanding of it.

"I should go."

Serena only nodded at him.

He gave her a quick kiss on the nose. "I'll call you tomorrow."

"Okay."

Brian was dazed and confused, fuzzy-headed and numb. He'd

walked out and sensed there was something else he was supposed to say; the problem was he just couldn't think of what it was. His heart felt as if it had grown ten sizes. He rubbed at it as he headed toward his home. How did he always end up in this dream-like state when she was around? Did she feel it too? She must. There was no way she didn't. He thought about all the cute little things she did. All the times she made him laugh without even trying. He adored her, he discovered. He adored everything she was.

CHAPTER 15

Every time Serena started the engine there was a new noise. If the car wasn't coughing, it was moaning in a plea for rest. It hesitated when she pressed the accelerator, and sometimes when she turned it off, it would try to start up again. She was beginning to think the car was possessed. She tried to take her mother's car whenever she could, but that would always make her feel guilty. What if her mother had to go somewhere and Serena's car broke down? She'd never forgive herself. Serena recalled the girls at work called it "the Beast" and how she'd laugh and smile while cringing inside. Serena knew she was going to have to think about a new car, and soon.

She got home a little after six on Friday night. When she drove past Brian's, she could see Mark's car in the drive. Getting out of the car, Serena thought about how she'd talked to Mandy the previous night. How Mandy talked about her and Mark spending every moment they could together. And how there was so much more to learn about each other than they'd thought. It was as if they were completely new people. Serena was brought back from her daydream by the calling of her name. She looked up to see Mark waving for her to come over to Brian's. Dropping her gear, she headed over. As she approached, she smiled at Brian, who kept his arms folded across his chest and a very unhappy expression on his face. He seemed to be standing in a fighting stance and wasn't saying anything as she came closer.

"Mark." She gave him a weary smile and a hug. "What's going on?"

"I was just filling Brian in on some things."

The light came on in her head, and she turned to Brian who cocked one eyebrow at her.

"It was nice seeing you, but I think I better go." Mark turned to go to his car and stopped. "By the way, Serena, thanks for the advice."

That also took her a second to register. She had been too busy watching Brian glare at her. Serena was about to say something to Mark when Brian went to walk away.

"Hey! Where are you going?" She began to move quickly after him when he turned suddenly, causing her to ram right into him.

"I really don't want to talk to you right now." His gray eyes were as cold as steel. "I don't think it was Mark's place to have to tell me about what happened Friday night at the Legion." His hands were now on his hips and he seemed so much taller than Serena remembered. She saw his muscles quivering from anger and her heart did a quick flip from panic.

"No, you're right. And it was probably not a very comfortable thing for him to do." She could feel her temper rising as Brian only stood there and glared at her. "So when do you think it would've been a good time for me to tell you? Since I've seen sooo much of you lately?" Brian went to say something and Serena mowed right over him. "Perhaps when we were cleaning up vomit? On the other hand, how about when I got back from the doctor's with my mother, and Hope and I were fighting about how I wasn't doing a good enough job keeping her in a cleaner environment. Because I'll tell you," she said jamming a finger into his chest, "it wasn't Tom I was thinking about when I was on the phone with God knows how many people this week at the insurance company trying to find out why we are getting these very big bills."

"Why isn't the insurance company covering it?"

"Does it matter?" she yelled. "They don't give a crap we can't dish out thousands. Most people in this world can't! They said, 'well, why don't you sell the house?' And where, I ask you, are we supposed to live? If you want to know what happened, he followed me out. I didn't even know he was there until he said my name and had me pinned up against the car. I tried to knee him in the balls and he blocked it. Before I could gouge his eyes out, Mark had him flying through the air. I don't remember what words were exchanged between us and I really don't care as long as he stays the hell away from me." Serena now stood there with her hands on her hips and death in her eyes.

"God," Brian told her, "you're beautiful when you're riled up."

She pushed at Brian with both her hands and all her body weight. By the time he found his balance, she was halfway across the yard.

"Oh, no you don't. I'm not finished with you yet." Brian sprinted after her and tried to get in front. She cvaded him. He tried to grab her arm and she yanked away. "Fine, you want to do this the hard way, then we will." He picked her up over one shoulder and headed back to his house. She was kicking, punching, and swearing all the way. "You have some mouth on you when you're mad. If you would just calm down."

"Calm down! You expect me to calm down after a comment like that. You weren't even listening to me. Just those damn hormones of yours!" She tried to wiggle out of his grip again but he was too strong.

"Serena, calm down. I was listening. And if you don't stop fighting me…"

"If I don't stop fighting you what?" Serena went flying through the air and landed with a splash. "Son of a bitch!" she cried when she came to the surface.

"Now will you please calm down and listen?" Brian squatted at the edge of the pool and looked at her with a hard edge. "How the hell is someone supposed to apologize, if you don't let them get a word in? I'm not sorry that I was pissed off about what happened with Tom. I have a right to be. As for my comment." He took a deep breath and prepared to eat crow. "It went through my mind, it wasn't supposed to come out of my mouth. I'm sorry that you're so appealing when you're angry."

Serena treaded water in the middle of the pool. "I don't think that sounded much like an apology, but that wasn't what I wanted anyway." She swam over to the side of the pool and reached her hand up so he could pull her out. Brian scrutinized her hand suspiciously as he stood. She just smiled.

"Do you trust me?" Serena batted her eyes.

"Should I?"

"You shouldn't, with most women." This was something he already knew, but he grabbed her hand anyway.

"You're not like most women," he said pulling her out. "And you're very wet."

"Thanks to you."

"If you would have simply calmed down, you wouldn't have ended up in the pool."

"If you weren't such a pain in the ass, I wouldn't have reacted that way."

"But you like me, don't you?"

"Maybe." Serena wrapped her arms around his waist and came close to make sure he got good and wet.

"What are you doing tomorrow?"

"Nothing out of the ordinary. I don't have to work."

"Good, call your sister. We're going on a road trip."

"What about my mother? I can't leave her, Brian."

"Yes, Serena." He cupped her chin to make sure she looked at him. "You can for a day. She'll be fine. We have our phones, Hope's close, and I'm sure your mother is getting sick of seeing your face by now."

"You have the nicest way of saying things."

He gave her a cocky grin. "Bring your swimsuit and a change of clothes." He ran his hand through her wet hair. "You'll want something to tie this back. A hat would be best."

"And where exactly are you taking me?"

"Away. But not too far." He gave her a kiss and smacked her on the ass. "Now go home and dry off. I've got some things I have to take care of." She reached up and kissed him goodbye, a habit they both had gotten into.

"What time tomorrow?"

"Morning, eight o'clock." When Serena moaned, he continued, "I'd prefer seven, but I figured you'd complain."

"Damn straight I would have." She headed across the yard toward her house.

"And my sister will be calling tonight to get together for dress shopping," he called after her. "My father said this one's on him."

She stopped and turned.

"Don't start that pride crap with me. The old man pays for the whole thing every year, for everyone. It makes him happy. When you meet him you'll understand."

"Fine. But I'm not going to like it."

"You don't have to." Brian smiled, waved, and went into his house. That was easy. Now he simply had to make sure she didn't run into Susan. Just what he needed, his girlfriend and ex-wife in the same room together. Why did she insist on going every year? To remind him of what a fool he was, that's why.

Brian went into his room to change. Serena was able to take care of herself. She didn't need him doting over her every second. If Serena ran into Susan and didn't like what she had to say, Serena would simply put her in her place and walk away. Brian pulled a dry shirt over his head. There was nothing to worry about. He caught his reflection in the mirror and sighed. Except, maybe, what was happening to his heart.

* * * *

"You know Hope, I have a right to a life as much as the next person." Serena was trying to keep her voice down so that her mother wouldn't hear. "I only called so you'd know I was going to be gone all day tomorrow."

"You mean gallivanting around, right?"

Serena stuck her tongue in her cheek; she was not going to fight with her about this. "Mom doesn't have a problem with me going."

"Of course she doesn't!" Hope interrupted. "She feels guilty for everything that's going on."

"And she doesn't have to. I have my phone if anything happens. And you live close by."

"And I live close by," Hope mocked. "I knew sooner or later all the responsibility would turn to me. It's just like you to take off when things get tough."

"It's one day, and you're being completely unreasonable!"

"And how about her meals?"

"She's not an invalid, Hope." Serena's voice went very low. "And you're not the one who's here almost twenty-four-seven making sure everything's okay. Yet you feel you have a right to judge and convict me on everything. I'm going and that's all there is to it. She's a grown woman who needs to feel some independence right now and I'm going to give it to her whether you like it or not!"

"Well, I don't like it."

"Well, I don't care."

"You never do when it comes to what anyone else thinks."

"Why should I when they already have their minds made up on

who I am? It's obvious they don't know me." Serena knew she was talking about her sister. Hope probably knew it, too. Serena also knew there was no getting through. They had grown apart from each other a long time ago.

"Serena, if anything happens, it's on your head." The good old guilt trip, Hope always knew how to play her cards right.

"You know Hope. You really are a bitch. How the hell do you make it through the day being you?" Fuck it. Hope wants to play hardball, then I'll play too.

"That's a very childish way to handle things. I'm not swearing at you," Hope said with a smart prissy tone.

"I call it like I see it. And right now, that's exactly what you're being. So tonight, when you get off the phone with me and you go to bitch to Will about what an ungrateful selfish person I am, don't get too mad at him when he says that you made more of this than you needed to." Serena was feeling smug. She knew she'd backed her sister into a corner that Hope couldn't worm her way out of.

"Screw you!" Hope yelled, and hung up.

Serena glanced at the receiver and shrugged. It wasn't that it didn't bother her. But just if she let the guilt overwhelm her, then Hope would succeed in convincing her to stay. Serena had learned a long time ago that she didn't want to be the puppet Hope wanted her to be. Sometimes the battle was easy, sometimes the battle was lost, but she knew in the end she won the war if she did what she felt was right. Not what Hope felt was right.

The phone rang again when Serena placed it back in its cradle. Looking at it, Serena closed her eyes and hoped to God it wasn't her sister calling back. If she didn't answer she was a coward. If she did answer, she knew the battle would start all over again. Suddenly, Serena was feeling very tired.

"Serena," her mother called out, "it's for you."

Serena lifted the cordless and pressed 'talk'.

"No, she didn't tell me that she was going," Serena heard her mother say.

"I can't believe Brian is bringing someone. I can't wait to go shopping together!" It was Jacqueline, and Serena let out a sigh of relief.

"Hey, lady. What's up?" Serena plastered a smile on her face and tried not to think of her sister.

"I'm calling... Oh, bye, Kathy! We have to make an appointment with my dressmaker for the party next month. So, what's a good day for you?" Serena could hear it, Jacqueline was all smiles.

"Where is she?"

"Down here in Connecticut. She'll open for us on a Sunday, if that's more convenient." She made this sound so natural. They have a different way of life, she reminded herself, and felt a little sliver of fear race up through her.

"I don't know. How soon do we have to get in?"

"It depends on whether you're going to have something made or something off the rack. You'll love her selection!"

"You sound way too used to this." Serena laughed.

"You'll be fine. I'll be there. Brian will be there. And wait till you meet Dad! You're going to love one another." Jacqueline was so enthusiastic that Serena couldn't help but believe her. "The best thing about it is that I'm not the only woman in this family any more. Thank the Lord above! You have no idea the torture I go through."

'Part of the family'? Serena thought. She was part of the family? "Well, Jac. I'm glad I can help with the torture in any way I can. It's too bad we can't do it tomorrow. Brian made some sort of plans and he won't tell me what."

"Brian likes his surprises. We'll just have to surprise him with some hot sexy dress that'll knock him off his feet."

Serena made a sound of agreement. “I wouldn’t mind driving him as crazy as he drives me.”

“You and I are going to drive all the men crazy that night. I can’t wait!” They talked a little longer and made plans for the following weekend. Serena was feeling a whole lot better about things when they hung up. She didn’t know if it had been the woman on the other end, or the fact that she had something to look forward to now. Either way she was glad that she had said yes.

Deciding to take a walk after her mother went to sleep was another thing Serena felt good about; it cleared her head some more and brightened her spirits. The air was heavy with humidity, but that didn’t seem to matter. Everything had a sheen of dampness to it, and she could smell the freshly cut grass.

“I wonder where Brian went?” She turned and looked in the direction of his house and his empty driveway. As she walked by his home, she stopped abruptly. “That shithead!” she said aloud. He’d been really mad about Tom and she knew exactly where he went. Her first thought was to go after him. Her second thought was that she hoped he pounded Tom’s face in a little more than Mark had. “Serves him right,” she said with a wicked grin.

CHAPTER 16

"Honey, it's not that big of a deal. I can take care of things for one day while you're gone." Katherine watched as her daughter busied herself making sure her mother had everything she needed for the day. Serena had even gone so far as to make lunch and supper for her. They were wrapped in foil and waiting in the fridge.

"Mom. I simply want to make sure you're going to be okay. I know you can take care of yourself, it's just that I worry."

"Now you're starting to sound like me."

Serena stopped in the middle of making breakfast and stared at her mother. "I don't think there's any reason to insult me," she said with a smile.

"Oh, I would never want to do that. It's just you're acting like a little mother hen, and I think it's very sweet." Katherine walked over and gave her daughter a hug.

"Stop that!" Serena said pushing her mother away. "If you make me cry, I won't stop until the sun goes down."

"And you want to look your best for Brian." Katherine wiggled her eyebrows and laughed at her daughter's stunned expression. "That man has a physique like a Greek god." She gave a sound of approval. "If I was twenty years younger, I'd rock his world!"

Serena put her hands over her ears. "I'm not hearing this. I'm not hearing this," she kept repeating.

"Oh, honey. You have a fine catch there. Have you seen him without his shirt on?" Katherine let out a whistle. "Of course you have! Probably have seen more, too, right?"

"I will not talk about this with you. Or discuss my sex life, or lack thereof." Serena went back to the pancakes she was making.

"Sweetheart. I didn't mean to sound as if I was prying. It's just now I understand why you've been so uptight. One day alone with Brian is going to do wonders. Especially if you're able to find one of those secluded rest stops. Or maybe one of those rent-by-the-hour motels. Oh those were the days." Katherine remembered what it was like having to rent one of those a time or two. Being new lovers, needing to touch each other all the time.

"Stop! Please! I can't believe what I'm hearing. My mother has a filthy mind, and is obviously feeling very well to be trying to talk about sex with me." Serena was shaking her head and scooping the pancakes onto plates. She was also talking to herself, to Katherine's pleasure. She always got more out of her that way. "I don't even remember what it is, for goodness' sake! And here I am in the kitchen waiting for one of the most appealing men I've ever met to pick me up, and she wants to talk about what base I've gotten to with him."

"Have you gotten to a base?" When Serena turned to look at her mother, Katherine was grinning ear to ear.

"You dirty dog. A very clever way to pump me for information, and it worked!" Serena brought the plates to the table and sat down. "And no, I haven't gotten to any multiple bases yet."

"Now there is nothing wrong with taking your time." Katherine patted Serena's hand. "No one's going to buy the cow if you give the milk for free. How long have you been dating now?"

"Mom, eat that pancake before I dump them over your head."

"Testy." Katherine put the piece in her mouth.

"Two or three months." Serena scowled into her breakfast.

With wide eyes and surprise on her face, Katherine proclaimed, "Oh, dear! It's about time you give that man something."

Serena's eyes shot up to her mother's. "I can't believe you just said that."

"Well, I thought for sure you had something going on after you stayed the night at his house."

"Mom? What're you trying to find out?"

"If you've slept with him or not. And how serious you are about him."

"Brian and I really haven't discussed it."

"Oh!" Katherine exclaimed, and waved it off with a hand. "This is not something that you discuss," she said leaning forward in her seat. "It is something that you feel. Well, this is obviously not just lust. Otherwise you two would be like rabbits over at his house, or in his pool… he has a gym in the cellar, you know."

"Mom, this is really embarrassing. I would appreciate it if you would… if we could… talk about something else."

"Okay." Katherine plopped her chin on her fists. "Are you still on the pill?"

"Oh my God! You don't give up! Yes, I'm still on the pill! Unbelievable. My mom has lost her mind. It's the only explanation for it." Serena rose from her seat, visibly too wound up to eat any more. "I need to finish getting ready. And you!" she said pointing at her mother, "need to get your mind out of the gutter and finish eating." With that, Serena walked into the bathroom to get the extra stuff she would need. She didn't see her mother throw away the rest of the meal, or the expression of pain on her face. Katherine had gotten very good at covering up what was ailing her. She didn't know if she should be proud of herself, or ashamed. Either way she was not going to spoil this day for her daughter. When Serena left, she would simply go back to bed, and stay there. It was the only place she wanted to be, anyway.

"Serena! I think I heard Brian's car start. He'll be here any minute." Serena came out with her baseball cap on and her bag slung over her shoulder.

"Now you have both mine and Brian's cell numbers next to the refrigerator. Don't feel guilty about calling unless it's because you have no money to buy ice cream. I don't know what time I'll be back but there is plenty of stuff in the house to eat. And don't stay in the sun too long if you go out." Katherine was pushing Serena toward the door. "And stop pushing me or I'll think that you want me to go, and I'll end up staying." They stopped in front of the door and gave each other a big hug.

"Serena, please go and have fun. And for God's sake! Run some bases!" Serena rolled her eyes and gave her mother a peck on the cheek. Katherine released a sigh of relief when she closed the door behind her. She thought she was going to fall on the floor at any moment. Damn girl. She always was the one who could wear you out. Katherine collapsed on the bed and fell into a deep sleep. She wouldn't wake again for hours.

* * * *

Brian took a deep breath when he saw Serena come out of the house. She had a cap on her head, a simple pair of blue shorts and a bright yellow t-shirt. She was worth taking the risk on second chances. Not only for the way she looked, but also for the way she made him feel.

Serena had quite a shock when she walked out the door. Brian knew she wouldn't be expecting to see a Mercedes with its top down. To his pleasure, her smile grew wide when Brian got out of the car to open the passenger side door for her.

"I thought about what you said. And I think she probably was getting very lonely in the garage." He grinned and bent to give her a good morning kiss. Serena answered him by grabbing the back of his neck and throwing herself into it.

"Very nice," she said in almost a purr.

"Glad you like her. She's fast, too." Brian tried to wiggle his eyebrows and instead ended up grimacing in some pain.

"The car is nice. But," she said taking off his sunglasses, "I was talking about that." Serena gently touched the black and blue by Brian's left eye. "I hope it doesn't hurt too much."

Brian put his head down as if he'd been a bad boy. "You're not mad?" He slowly lifted his eyes to hers and put on his most pitiful face.

"I haven't decided what I am. But it does make me feel good to have some big, strong, tough hulk of a man watching out for me." Serena rose to her toes and kissed his bruise. "So what's the other guy look like?" she said sweetly and seductively.

Brian was waiting for the trap. No woman likes her guy to go and protect her honor without her say-so.

"Pretty bad," Brian said with caution. "You're not mad?" he asked again.

"What I am really doesn't matter. We're going to have a wonderful day, and I'm going to harass you about that shiner all day long." She slid her hands up his chest and Brian brought his lips, once again, to hers.

Minutes later, they were on the road to an unknown destination. It was a warm morning with the sun high in the sky. They could see it was going to be another humid day, for the air was getting thick and the sky was starting to get hazy. They were heading south on the highway with the radio on and the conversation loud. If someone asked Brian later what they had talked about, he couldn't have answered. Nothing was rushed, the conversation fun and light. And when they fell into silence just listening to the radio, it was okay. For the first time, Brian experienced the feeling of complete contentment with the person he was involved with.

* * * *

They were cruising along on the highway when Serena noticed they were holding hands. She wondered how such a simple gesture could make her heart swell. When he turned and smiled at her, she knew it was over. Her heart was completely lost to him. No woman would have the defenses to fight what he stirred inside of her. I'm falling in love with him, she realized. What the hell was she thinking? She swore under her breath and shifted in her seat.

"Is something wrong? Brian squeezed her hand unconsciously.

"No, I was just thinking about something." She scowled. "I can't seem to decide if it's a good thing or not."

"With things like that, I always wait. Sooner or later they work themselves out." He grinned at her and squeezed her hand one more time before reaching for his sunglasses.

"I don't know if I have the patience for it. But I guess we'll have to see."

"Is it something I can help you with?"

Damn it, there he goes again. Always ready to help with patient understanding. Serena saw Brian take a quick peek over at her. She smiled at him and then heard a series of swears come out of his mouth. Before she could register what he was doing, Brian had yanked the car over to the shoulder.

"Brian! What the hell are you doing?" Serena was holding on to the dashboard as he brought the car to a stop. "You could have caused an accident, for God's sake!"

He shut the car off, threw his sunglasses on the dash, and turned to her. Serena couldn't help but shift to the far corner of her seat. There was a heat in his eyes that she'd never seen before. Whatever was on his mind, it was obviously making him crazy.

"Is this for real?" he demanded.

Exasperated, Serena said, "I don't know what you mean, Brian. Is what for real?"

"You and me!" he yelled above the traffic.

"I sure hope so. I've never put my heart on the line before." She was now sitting erect in her seat, and had thrown her sunglasses to accompany his on the dash.

"Well, I have put my heart on the line and got it shredded apart. I'm not interested in playing games with you, Serena. It's been a very long time since someone has made me want to take a risk. And I can honestly say that no one has made me feel the way you do. I want to know if you feel the same."

"If I didn't, I wouldn't be here." Why was her temper up? Were they actually arguing with one another about their feelings? Or are we arguing with ourselves? she wondered. "I don't give away my trust easily. I never have, especially when it comes to my heart. If you think you're going to walk away from me without a good fight, you had just better think again." Serena leaned forward and poked a finger into his chest.

Brian's eyes became slits. "If I walk away? Honey, don't even try that. I may not know exactly what I want out of this, but I can tell you for sure that you aren't going anywhere." He swatted her hand away from his chest and yanked her into his arms. "I'm going to be around for a long time, get used to it." When his lips touched hers, there was none of the anger and impatience that had shadowed their conversation. There was more serenity and sweetness to the kiss than either of them had ever experienced. Serena felt her system melt, as well as her heart.

"Take me away, Brian," she said against his lips. "Wherever you want to go."

"Later I want to bring you to meet my family." He was searching her eyes now for any sign of reserve.

"That should be fun," she said with a smile. "Is your dad as moody as you?"

"I'm nothing compared to him."

"Then I'll absolutely love him." She gave him a big smacking kiss and grabbed her sunglasses. "Can't wait to see what he's going to say about that eye."

Brian laughed as he grabbed his own glasses and started the car. "Oh, he'll have plenty to say." With a loud booming voice, he said, "Boy! What did you go and do that for? You're not supposed to let them get a punch in!"

"Does he really sound like that?" They were back on the road, whizzing by the other traffic.

"He has one of those voices that carry through the house. It's too bad we all learned early that his bark is worse than his bite."

Serena laughed. "It sounds like he and I are going to get along just fine."

"Yeah, he'll love that you won't mind putting him in his place. You'll give him someone new to debate with."

"So, you're only bringing me to get the pressure off of you?"

"Damn straight!"

* * * *

It was about an hour later when Brian put on his blinker to get off the highway. Serena smiled and clapped her hands together when she saw the signs for the Mystic Aquarium.

"Please! Tell me that's where we're going." She looked as happy as a child in a candy store when she grabbed his forearm and leaned toward him.

"Calm down."

"Do you know that I haven't been here in years? I used to love when my mother would bring us here." Serena took a deep breath and beamed as she reminisced. "I used to stay at the starfish tank forever. Hope would get so mad. They used to let you pick them up, they were so slimy." She wrinkled her nose at him, and Brian laughed.

"This was my mother's favorite place. She would drag us here all the time. It didn't matter how old we were. She would give us those big puppy dog eyes and that would be it." He swung into a parking place and put up the top.

"Well, I guess I know where you got it from."

He flashed a grin and got out. "I haven't been here since my mother passed. I hear they've made improvements to the place." Brian draped an arm around her shoulders as they walked to the crowded entrance.

"I just hope they still have the starfish." Serena leaned her head on his chest as they walked. He hasn't been here since his mother died. This place means something to him, and he wants to share it with me. Serena felt something warm inside of her, and she looked up at him. He glanced down and gave her a peck on the lips.

"I hope they still have the sharks," he declared enthusiastically.

"Men," Serena stated. "Always wanting the aggressive animals. What about the sea crabs or the jellyfish? And there's always the dolphins."

"How about the manta rays? They're peaceful, till you mess with them." Brian winked at Serena as they got their tickets and headed inside. "Let's go over here first." He grabbed Serena by the hand and darted to the right. There were big glass tanks with large fish and sharks inside. Serena couldn't keep her laughter of delight inside. Brian had his face pressed up against the glass and was trying to get somebody's attention.

"I don't think we're supposed to tap the glass."

Brian peeked over his shoulder at her and beamed. "Come here." He pulled her forward and put her face right up to the glass. When Brian looked over at her he could see a smile and glint in her eyes that he knew his mother had once seen in him.

"I care very deeply about you, Serena." Did he say that out loud?

No, he realized, Serena was still staring intently into the tank. Brian stood up and stared blankly at Serena's back. He knew she was chattering about the fish. However, he couldn't understand what she was saying. It was as if he had been put into a trance. His body had become warm and his chest felt heavy. He saw her turn and smile at him, then watched as the smile dissolved and she straightened her body to ask him what was wrong. He shook his head to try to clear it as she led him to a bench.

"Brian, are you okay?" Serena squatted in front of the bench he was now sitting on. "I'm going to get you something to drink."

"Serena," he finally got out. "I'm okay. I've just been..."

"Don't hand me any bullshit. I'm queen of it. And if I want to go and get you something to drink because I don't want your ass fainting on me, I will." She stood and fisted her hands on her hips.

"I wasn't going to faint," Brian grumbled.

"I forgot. Sorry! Guys don't faint. They pass out, and only when they're drunk." Serena stomped off, and left Brian to feel like an ass.

"Damn woman," Brian said to himself.

* * * *

Serena returned with the drinks and found Brian grumbling to himself. "You don't have some kind of medical condition I should know about, do you?" She shoved the soda into his hands. "Drink. I figured the sugar would be better for you. Then we'll have some water." She held up the bottle of water. "Then we're going to go inside… Drink! And we are going to wander in there for a while."

"What?" he said to her when she stared at him. "No, I don't have some kind of medical condition." He took a big swig of the soda. "And I wasn't going to pass out."

"I'm sure you weren't. If you were going to do that, you wouldn't have turned pasty white and started weaving back and forth. Then of course, there was the fact that you wouldn't, or couldn't, depending on how you look at it, say two words to me." Serena grinned at him, showing all her teeth. He showed his teeth, but it wasn't with a smile. She leaned forward and kissed him on his cheek. "It's okay, honey. Your secret is safe with me."

Brian gave her an evil glare that was returned. He couldn't help but laugh. "You're just so easy to get along with. Come on, babe," he said, standing slowly. He put out his hand to help her up. "Let's go see some starfish."

Serena placed her hand in his, and eyed him suspiciously. "Don't go doing something like that again. You're the most normal guy I've ever dated. And I would be very disappointed if I had to return you."

"Same here." He bent over and gave her a kiss. "I wouldn't want to have to return you. You're not planning on getting fat, ugly and bitchy, are you?" He swung his arm around her shoulders. "Not necessarily in that order."

"Well, I don't plan on it. However, I have to tell you, I can get pretty ugly sometimes."

All was forgotten when they went inside the large building. It was dark inside, and their eyes had to take a moment to adjust. They could smell the salt in the air from the tanks, and the first thing they saw was the jellyfish. The tank went from the floor to the ceiling. They were so tranquil and mesmerizing to watch, Serena could have stayed there for hours watching them do their dance.

"It's too bad they sting," Brian said absently.

"Yeah. They would have been nice to swim with."

"Do you dive?" Brian asked. "I love to. My mother insisted that we all learn how to swim and my father insisted we learn how to dive. He said it was good serenity for the soul."

"No." Serena was watching the fish in the tank wistfully. "I've never had the time to learn. Or someone to show me." She turned and gazed up at him. "You feeling better?"

"Yeah. Don't change the subject."

"Fine," she said with a huff and crossed her arms. "I'm scared of the water, or at least being under it. A pool, I seem to be fine in. But it takes a lot to get me on a boat or under water when it's way above my head." Serena walked to the next tank, and Brian made strides to keep up with her.

"Maybe it wouldn't be so bad if you were with someone you trusted." He started rubbing her arms, and kissed the top of her head.

Serena leaned back into him. "Maybe you're right. Too bad there's no one I trust." She was grinning, sheepishly. Brian could see it in the tank's reflection.

"You're right not to trust me, I would just leave you there over your head. Then wait, not too far off, and watch the sharks come and get you." Brian gave out a small yelp when Serena elbowed him in the ribs. "You started it."

"Why does everyone say that?"

"Because you do. Now let's go see some more dangerous sea animals." He had that glint back in his eyes and put all of Serena's fears that he was ill to rest.

There was so much to see. Like the giant tanks with the coral and sea grass that had enormous eels, spanning several feet, swimming in them. They got to hold a couple starfish, to Serena's delight. Brian laughed when he saw Serena push her way through all the children so she could be next. He couldn't remember ever having such a good time with someone, and it was starting to scare the hell out of him.

"You're not very good at waiting your turn," Brian said as they headed to the dolphin show.

"With that kind of group you have to be pushy. I would have never got up there. And that little girl with the pig tails, she kept trying to push me out of the way. She's damn lucky I didn't push back."

"Yeah. That would have been a fair fight. Although…" He

scratched his chin. "She did look like she could take you."

Brian and Serena went back outside where the brightness of the sun forced them to squint. They walked along the manicured paths to see the penguins and walruses eating and lazing around. When Serena's stomach rumbled they headed to the commons for food. This turned out to be a small mistake before going to the underwater voyage, where watching a lightning quick trip from outer space to the depths of the sea on a massive screen made their stomachs revolt. Holding their stomachs, Brian and Serena knew it was time to leave the aquarium. It took about a half hour before both their stomachs settled from the visual exploration.

"Are you sure you're ready to meet my family?" Brian said while putting the top on the car back down.

"How bad can they be?" She smiled. "Do they live far away?"

"Twenty minutes, give or take." Brian maneuvered the car out of the parking lot and into the crowded neighborhood. "They live in Essex."

"I hear that's a nice town to live in." If you're rich, Serena completed the sentence in her mind. Don't be nervous Serena, they're only people.

"It is. My parents fell in love with the house as soon as they saw it. Of course, being in banking, my dad had to barter to death, and my mother hounded him till he finally gave in and paid them what they wanted for it."

"Did your mother always know what buttons to press with your dad?" Serena was thinking how romantic their relationship sounded. As if they were so in love, that despite how much they would bicker, things would still be okay come the morning.

"Oh, yeah! He would do anything for 'his girls,' as he would call my mother and sister. My dad's a real trip. We didn't always get along, but time heals all sorts of wounds."

"You're lucky to have him." Serena stared out the window as they passed house after house. She could see the ocean behind them. Its salty smell became stronger as the wind over the water picked up.

"You don't talk about your father," Brian said, as he glanced over at Serena.

"No, I guess I don't." Serena gave out a long slow breath, propped her elbow on the open window and her head on her fist. "There isn't much to tell. He's a drinker. Always was, always will be. I gave up trying, a long time ago, to be the good daughter who sent him money for food. Of course, he would spend it on booze. But to him that was beside the point. I don't think Hope will ever forgive me for 'leaving him to rot,' as she puts it. I just feel after a certain amount of time and help, it's up to you to do the rest." She gave Brian a weak smile. "In the end, we're all responsible for ourselves and our own actions. Tom learned that."

"Yes he did," Brian agreed. Reaching over he took her hand. "I hope you don't turn and run. We can be quite loud and obnoxious." Brian maneuvered into a driveway that weaved around a small forest. Through them, glimpses of the house could be seen. "My folks liked it because it was quiet and secluded. Not something you could see from the street." The drive opened up and a two-story stone-covered house stood before them. There were flowerbeds everywhere, and a building off to the left held a three-car garage. "Above the garages there's a guest house. Gabe and I used to sneak our girlfriends up there, and play board games, of course."

"The naughty kind, right?"

"We would never think of doing something so..." He gave a thought to his next words as they got out of the car. "Ordinary."

"This is beautiful. The porch must have been great to sit out on." There were a couple of comfortable-looking rockers on one side, and a swing on the other.

"My mother and father always liked things to be welcoming. Come on, let's go inside." He opened the screen door and stepped in. "I'm constantly telling him he should lock this when he leaves the door open. What if someone walks in?" Brian was tsk-tsking as he led Serena into the foyer. It was as inviting as the outside, with strong bold colors and old furnishings to soften them. The floors were hardwood with embroidered rugs placed here and there. Serena was led through to the living room where the giant windows facing the ocean took her breath away. She stopped walking and stood mesmerized by what she saw.

"Quite a view, don't you think?" Brian stuffed his hands in his pockets and looked out with her.

"That's an understatement." Serena turned and inspected the rest of the room. It was spacious with the same country feel as the foyer. The room was a rust color with big green fluffy sofas. It felt so warm and friendly that she just wanted to leap on to the seats and put her feet up. There was a large flat screen T.V. on one end and the other held a huge stone fireplace. It reached up to the cathedral ceilings, and was made of the same stone as the outside of the house.

"Why is everything so big?" Serena asked in awe.

"Because I'm a big man," a voice boomed from behind her. Serena felt herself jump right out of her skin and let out a yelp. She placed a hand over her rapidly beating heart when she whirled around. There stood a man that must have been close to six-four. His eyes were the color of a lush green forest in June. He had ebony-colored hair that was salted heavily on the sides and a beard that covered his face, giving him the appearance of Grizzly Adams.

"Dad! You practically gave Serena a heart attack. And why isn't the screen door locked?" Brian ranted at his father.

"You're just like your mother, boy. Now give me a hug." His father reached over and gave him a bear hug that lifted Brian clear off the ground. "Now who is this pretty lady?"

"Dad," Brian said, and then wiggled from under his father's arm. "This is Serena O'Neal. Serena this is my father, Daniel." Brian then moved out of the way so that his father could step closer for a better look.

"I can see why my boy is so taken with you. She stands her ground, doesn't she?" he directed to Brian.

"Yes, she does."

"Then why did you have to go and get yourself that black eye? Damn boy," Daniel said. "Never could keep him out of trouble."

"My mother would say the same for me."

Daniel let out a rolling laugh and grabbed Serena in one of his hugs. "Hope that you like roast. It's what Rosa's making for dinner."

"I'm a true lover of meat."

"Good! My biggest fear is that one of my crew will bring home a tree-hugging vegetable-eating environmentalist. Not that there's anything wrong with saving the planet, but nobody could convince me that meat is bad for you."

Just then, a middle-aged woman in an apron came through what Serena assumed was the kitchen. "Don't get him started," she said with a heavy Spanish accent.

"Don't start with me, Rosa," Daniel said waving a finger at her.

"I'll start with you if I feel like starting with you. Your father eats too much meat, Brian."

"Don't go dragging the boy into this. And we have company." He pulled Serena under his arm while smiling at Rosa.

"Leave the girl alone. She's not going to protect you." Rosa walked forward inspecting Serena as she got closer. "It is very nice to meet you. I hope this big sorry excuse for a man does not scare you away."

Serena felt Daniel take in a large amount of air and let it out slowly.

"It takes a lot to scare me away. Besides, I love meat, too." Serena and Daniel looked at one another and then gave twin grins to Rosa.

"A fine example you will be." Rosa waved her finger. "Now, I am going to start preparing the meal. Stay out of my kitchen!" she ordered to Brian.

"Not a problem." Brian walked over and gave her a kiss on the cheek. "You are the most heavenly creature in the kitchen, Rosa. This woman works magic," he said to Serena. "I could only dream of being so talented."

Rosa and Serena glanced at each other as if they had just heard the most pathetic line to come out of a man's mouth.

"He tries to be a smooth one," Rosa said and patted his cheek. "Thank the Lord above he has looks." Then she disappeared back through the door she came from.

"Well now," Daniel began, "I think it's time that you brought our guest around the house. There's still time before your brother and sister get here. Donald is back from his trip across country, and he can't wait to meet your new lady." Before Brian could reply, Daniel headed up the staircase to the second level. "Now you kids don't go getting into any more trouble." His voice boomed off the walls.

"That man is something else, don't you think?" Brian turned and smiled.

"You absolutely adore him, don't you?"

"Yeah. How can you not? He just has this thing about getting his own way."

Serena felt her heart warm. "I can't imagine that stops you from getting your way."

"No, it never did." Then he looked at her skeptically. "What are you saying? That I'm exactly like my father?"

"If the shoe fits." Serena headed to the door that led to the backyard. "Now show me the rest." Through the door, she could see the in-ground swimming pool. As they stepped out, she saw more flowerbeds and rock gardens. "Does he hire someone to take care of all this?" There was greenery everywhere she turned. Clematis climbing the pool fence, and clusters of flowers frocking the rock walls that were placed to the west of the house, where one could sit and watch the sun set over the ocean. Then there were the big pots strategically placed around the pool. They were crowded, with vines and colorful annuals spilling out of them.

"No. My father likes taking care of them. He and my mother used to do it together. When she passed I think it became a way to feel close to her again." Brian surveyed the yard. "I think he's gone a little crazy over the years. We keep telling him that there isn't going to be a backyard if he keeps it up."

"I think it's wonderful."

They walked around the spacious yard and then headed to the beach. With no shoes on, the sand felt hot and the water cool. He pointed out their boat, which appeared more like a yacht to Serena. They walked up the pier and looked on board, but Serena wouldn't get on. It certainly was big enough; she just wasn't feeling brave enough.

They walked back to the house hand in hand. The breeze was licking at their faces, the heat of the day coming down. It was still warm, but the distant clouds were promising rain.

"I'll go get our suits from the car and we can jump in the pool."

"You really are a fish. Have you always loved the water?"

"Me and my dad, when I was younger, would go out in the boat and not come back for hours. We'd go diving and snorkeling. Pretend we were sea pirates and board all his friends' boats."

"Didn't your brother want to come along?"

"Sometimes. Gabe's a die hard and likes to do his own thing. You'd never know it looking at him. He's dived everywhere and anywhere you can think of. Jac was okay with it, but she didn't like to mess up her hair." Brian leaned down and kissed her gently on the mouth. "I'll be right back."

* * * *

From the windows above, Daniel watched them. He could see from the way they moved together that there was something special there. He liked her. He considered himself a very good judge of character, and she wasn't someone that was looking at his boy for money. She was willing to joke around and be herself.

"She is very good for him."

"Yes, Rosa. I think she is."

"I do not think that you should be worried."

"She's losing her mother to cancer. I'm worried if she passes, Brian will go through all the pain again."

"Then they will help each other through it. Maybe that is what he needs. Sometimes we must relive to live again."

"You're a wise woman, Rosa." Daniel let out a long breath and turned to her.

"You are worried. Do you think they are together only because they have this in common?"

"No. I just hope she's good to him."

"I am glad to hear that you are not a jackass, Daniel." He smiled at this. "And I have no doubt her mother is thinking the same thing."

Daniel wrapped his arms around Rosa's waist and pulled her close. They were alone so she didn't resist when his lips touched hers. There had been few women in his life since his wife died. Rosa had always seemed to be a constant.

"You will eat dinner with us tonight. Don't even try to protest. The children are not blind or stupid."

"I never said I thought they were." Rosa's back straightened and her pride was in full swing.

"Please stop this." It had become an old argument between them. Daniel just figured if he chipped at her slowly, she would come around. "I am not your boss."

"You pay me, therefore you are."

"Then I'll stop paying you and we'll get married."

Rosa's eyes grew big and her mouth was in search of something to say. She tried to wiggle out of his embrace but knew it was close to impossible.

"You don't have to answer me now. You only have to let me love you. I do love you, my Rosa."

"I love you. But..." He cut her protest off with a kiss, and then swept her into his arms to lie on their bed. He had considered it their bed for a long time now. The only time they didn't sleep together was when any of the children stayed the night. He figured he was going to break her of that habit too, and soon.

CHAPTER 17

Brian thought of Serena all the way to the car. She felt so right here in his home. He always considered this his home. If he showed up, out of the blue, no one cared and no one asked any questions. He remembered once, he had shown up unannounced and had walked in on his father and Rosa in an intimate embrace. Brian had slowly backed out of the room and then proceeded to make some noise so they would know he was there. After, he had to think long and hard about what he thought of Rosa and his father together. He even mentioned it to his sister and brother. They both laughed because Brian was the last to know. They all knew why it was kept such a secret. Rosa had pride and she felt ashamed about having a relationship with her boss. She refused to speak to any of the children about her affair with their father or listen to their approval of it. Rosa was part of the family and she had been for a long time. She never tried, or would try, to take their mother's place. Rosa had too much respect for the woman who was "the lady of the house." Many women had tried to do just that. Brian felt very lucky that his father had never been blind to it.

He grabbed their bags and headed back into the house. He could see Serena standing by the rock wall staring out at the breathtaking view. But to Brian, watching Serena was staggering. Her beauty, inside and out, had everything around her paling in comparison. She'd taken off her hat and lifted her face to catch the breeze; the afternoon sun shimmered on her cheeks. Brian's whole body stiffened. He was going crazy with wanting her. He needed her, and he needed her now.

Brian stepped out of the house to where the wind and the ocean had a battle going on, much like the one inside of him. He took a deep breath of the ocean air and felt the power of it fill him. When he wrapped his arms around Serena from behind, she wrapped her arms around his.

"It's so magnificent. What was it like growing up here?" Serena nestled into his chest.

"Well, we didn't move here until I was around ten. Up until then we were in Manhattan or Europe during the school year and mostly the islands in the summer." He let out a long sigh. "It was nice to finally settle down."

"I'm not much for traveling. I like it, and it can be fun. But there's something about a place that you can call home." They stood there for several minutes listening to the soothing sounds of the ocean.

"Do you realize this is the first day we've been able to be alone?" There was mischievousness in Brian's voice, and he pulled her a little bit closer.

"We're really not alone."

"Don't be so technical," he whispered in a husky voice.

Serena turned to smile up at him and found her lips captured by his. Turning around she melted into his arms. Brian felt his system overcharge and his eyes roll.

"You should change into your suit," he said, her lips a whisper away.

"The ocean is a little chilly."

"The pool isn't, it's heated." Brian took her hand and led her to the cabana, where he went in with her and locked the door.

Inside the small room was a long couch and vanity. There were sunscreens and tanning lotions on the shelves along with big fluffy towels and moisturizers. Through the one door in the room, there was a small shower and toilet. The whole inside was made of wood, and smelled of cedar. There was a golden tone to the wood and Serena reached out to touch the smooth surface. Turning, she smiled at Brian as if she'd just found a secret room. He watched as she walked to him and Brian felt his breath catch and his heart skip. Her eyes were dark, mysterious and focused only on him, which sent a shiver through his eager body.

Brian ran his hands around her shoulders then up into her hair. "I need you, Serena," he whispered before his lips touched hers.

Running her hands up his chest, she framed his face. Her lips, a feather touch to his, were inviting and honest. "I couldn't deny you even if I wanted to. I've been lost since we met."

Brian took a deep cleansing breath and moved his hands to her face. "Maybe we've both been found." His lips cruised over hers, then to her eyes and temples. His hands molded slowly down her body to her waist where he gently pulled her shirt up. She raised her arms above her head and grinned at him. It took all of Brian's control not to throw her on the couch and take what he needed, what he wanted.

"Did you wear that lacy thing to drive me crazy?" He felt his chest starting to heave.

"I have barely anything on for bottoms." Serena had a wicked grin as she undid her shorts and let them slide to the floor.

She is right, Brian thought, those aren't panties. "I'm trying to take this slow," he announced taking a step back. He knew if he touched her now it would be over all too soon.

Serena came close and yanked his shirt over his head. "Who said I wanted it slow?"

Brian dragged her body against his and captured her mouth. They moved together in a kind of dance to the couch. His hands fumbled with her bra and he heard her give out a low seductive laugh.

"Here honey, let me get that." She took a step away from him as she let the straps slide off her shoulders one at a time, then the whole bra to the floor.

"Jesus, you're beautiful." He stepped forward, unsure if he should touch. Why did this moment seem so important? He'd been with lots of women, and yet this one, this time, just seemed so different.

She ran her hands down his arms to his hands and slowly brought them up to her breasts. "Take me Brian. I need you to take me." He ran his thumbs over her taut nipples and she let out a deep, ragged moan as her head fell back. His lips began to cruise her neck as he slowly lowered them to the couch. He whispered her name seconds before his lips found hers and the urgency that was driving them took over. He moved down to her jaw then to her breasts, where he began to suck and nibble one at a time.

"Next time... Brian… next time… we'll be thorough. Please..." Her words were cut off with a cry when his fingers plunged into her. It brought her over that first exquisite peak as she clawed at him, begging for more. He moved his face to her stomach while grabbing a hold of that tiny barrier.

"Don't you dare rip those," she stated breathlessly. He gave out a chuckle and smiled as he nuzzled into her hip.

"I sure was thinking about it." Serena laughed with him as he slid her panties down her hips and legs. Slowly Brian began his journey back up by running kisses from ankle to knee to thigh. She pleaded with him again when the next peak washed over. His mouth had found the burning core of her, and his tongue was doing all sorts of delicious things. She was feverously hot and wet. Nothing had ever prepared him for this kind of explosion from a woman. She bowed back and gave out a cry as the world around them spun.

"Serena," Brian whispered, "keep it down."

"How?" she managed to get out.

Every nerve in his body was on alert, and her touch sent shivers everywhere.

Brian hastily wrestled with his shorts to free himself. Rushing up her body, capturing her mouth again, he drove himself into her. Serena's nails dug into his back as her hips worked like pistons to keep up with him. When they rolled off the couch, neither one of them noticed. Her body arched back above him as she pushed him beyond reason. Grabbing her hips, Brian gave her no choice but to take more of the pleasure he gave. His body jerked up to feast once again on those glorious breasts. Her arms wrapped around him as their mouths sought each other's out. They rolled once again and Brian grabbed both Serena's hands with his and brought them above her head. He never wanted it to end but his body was betraying him.

"My God! You feel so good," he said before his mouth ravaged hers. She tore away from his lips in time to let out a cry of release. Their bodies went rigid together as they both sank into blissful delirium.

Brian collapsed on top of her. He wasn't sure at that point if they were still alive. Serena ran a limp hand up his sweat-slicked back, and he gave out a moan. She let out a chuckle.

"I promise I'll try to move in a minute." His voice was low and saturated with sex-fueled elation.

"If you fall asleep I'm going to have to hurt you." Serena was now stroking both of her hands up and down his back, and he let out a purring sound. They stayed like that for what seemed like an eternity. Content and happy.

"My sister, her husband, and my brother will be here soon." Brian nestled in and tried to shift closer to her.

"You're quite a snuggler, aren't you?"

"Just don't tell anyone."

"It'll be our secret." She tried to shift, but was weighed down by

Brian's body. "We need to get ourselves dressed, Brian."

"We should probably take a shower first." Brian was up and pulling her with him before she knew what was happening. He led her to the small shower stall. Serena had to admit it really did feel good to be able to wash up after such a hot and active day. She grabbed the soap and started washing his back.

"Do you think your father's wondering where we are?"

"No. I think he's probably too busy harassing Rosa into having dinner with us." Brian turned and smirked down at her. "They think none of us know what they've been up to all these years. Can I wash your front?" He wiggled his eyebrows at her.

Serena was too intrigued with the gossip to think about what he was up to when she handed him the soap. "So they're having an affair?" She felt her body begin to warm and realized that his hands had started wandering all over it.

"Like us," Brian said, trapping her against the shower wall. His mouth began to explore her neck and jaw.

"Brian, I really think we should..."

"Try that again," he finished.

Serena let out a moan. "Yes, definitely."

* * * *

Gabe looked out the living room windows and stared. His brother had brought a woman home. It had been a long time since Brian had even mentioned a woman. The funny thing was, since he had gotten there twenty minutes before, there was no sign of either of them. He turned to walk away before spotting the cabana door opening. His eyebrows lifted in interest and he brought the brandy he'd been sipping to his lips. The full-figured redhead that exited the small house wasn't a woman any man would miss. He just hoped she wasn't like the other one. When his brother walked out after her, towels in hand, Gabe let out a snort. It always was a place to have a little privacy, and no doubt, that was exactly what they had been looking for. Gabe saw his brother drop the towels and head toward the woman. He knew what was coming next. A person can't grow up with someone and not know all their tricks. Brian grabbed her around the waist and jumped into the pool. They both came up laughing. The woman was still trying to dunk Brian under when Gabe heard his father behind him.

"They do well together," Daniel was saying. "You'll like her. She's..." He trailed off, trying to find the right words.

"Into herself, only after money, needs to be taken care of."

"You really didn't like Susan, did you?" Daniel ruffled Gabriel's hair. "No, she's nothing like that. You'll just have to meet her." Daniel headed for the door when Gabe stopped him.

"And where have you been?"

"I've been taking care of business." Daniel set his chin and squared his shoulders.

"Do you think she's going to eat with us?"

"Who?" Daniel turned to Gabe who gave him an expression that said 'give me a break'. "I told her that she has to."

"There you go, Dad. Women always listen when you tell them what they have to do."

"She'll eat with us, even if I have to drag her out of that kitchen." Daniel studied his oldest son. He was tall, broad, and proud of his roots; more so now since his mother's death. Yet his thirst for adventure always worried Daniel. "How was Australia?"

"Fun." Gabe's eyes lit with mischief. "The water was clear and refreshing. Too hot for clothes."

"I'm not interested in your sexual exploits, boy. How was the diving?"

"If you'd lost that extra forty pounds, I could have taken you with me."

Daniel gave Gabe a glare of disgust. "A man shouldn't talk to his father that way."

"A man should listen to the ones who love him."

Gabe's father straightened his shoulders and tried to suck in his middle. "I'm healthy as a bull."

"Yeah, that's why your last doctor's visit—"

"We should head outside."

"Oh, absolutely," Gabe teased. "Wouldn't want you to discuss your pending heart attack." Gabe and Daniel headed outside to the pool area.

* * * *

Serena froze when she saw the two men walking toward them. "It's okay," Brian whispered in her ear. "They don't know what we've been up to."

"Please." Serena rolled her eyes at him. "Look at the grin on your brother's face. That is your brother, right?"

"It's nothing he hasn't done himself." Brian swam to the edge of the pool and proceeded to get out and greet his brother. Serena accepted it was the polite thing to do and followed. Feeling self-conscious, she wrapped a towel around herself, missing the silent message exchanged between the brothers. It wasn't so much one of admiration, but of curiosity and warning.

Serena turned and smiled up at Daniel. "Are you going in?"

"I was thinking about it."

"Serena," Brian said, "this is my brother, Gabriel."

They shook hands, and Serena instantly knew she was going to be watched for the rest of the day. Let him. She didn't care.

"It's nice to finally meet you. Bri here has told me many stories of long nights and loose women."

"Has he told you any cabana stories?" She heard Brian choke on the lemonade Rosa had brought out.

"Oh yes! You have quite a following as I hear. Is it as nice above the garage as Brian makes it sound?" She took the lemonade that Brian offered her.

Gabe's laughter rolled as well as his father's did. They were nearly the same height, which to Serena was just tall. He also had Daniel's dark hair and green eyes.

"I like her," Gabe announced. "She's not a snob."

"That's a compliment," Brian told her.

"Thanks." Serena creased her eyebrows together. "I think."

"It's one of my highest." Gabe saluted her with his drink then flopped in a chair.

"Come," Daniel demanded, "let us have a late afternoon swim." He grabbed Brian and tossed him into the pool like a rag doll.

"Is this a family thing?" Serena didn't get to hear the answer because she was tossed in, towel and all. She came up in time to see Daniel make a cannonball that splashed Gabriel, 'the innocent bystander'.

That's how Jacqueline and Donald found them, laughing and jumping around the pool.

"Well, this is a sight," she said, and cocked one hip with her fist on it. "Daddy, leave the poor girl alone, you're going to drown her."

Serena climbed out of the water looking like an exhausted wet rat. "Thanks, Jac. Now I know what you meant about being the only girl."

"You have to be tough to hang with this group. Gabe!" She and her brother exchanged a big hug. Brian and Daniel got out of the pool again to say 'hello,' but not for long. They were back at it again, only this time they tagged Gabe and threw him in, clothes and all.

"Are they always like this?" Serena asked Jacqueline.

"Pretty much. Notice Donald slipped away before I could introduce you. He knows he better get his suit on if he wants to keep his clothes dry." Jacqueline took a seat while Serena grabbed one beside her.

"Why don't you go in?"

Jacqueline's eyebrows shot up. "Are you kidding? It would be suicide." They watched as Gabriel finally made it out of the pool. He peeled off his shirt, revealing a well maintained body, and then smirked at them.

"He really thinks that he's something else," Jac said while sipping her lemonade.

"I guess he can since he looks like that." Serena turned and smiled at Jacqueline. "I prefer them shorter with dark blond hair myself. But I know plenty of girls that would stroke his ego."

Jacqueline laughed. "Yeah, that's just what he needs, someone to fawn over him."

"Over who?"

"We were discussing your brother's ego. Anything you care to add?"

Brian put a hand on each arm of Serena's chair and leaned in close to her. "I'll have to blacken his eye if he tries anything." Serena gave him a lopsided grin and stroked a finger around his bruise.

"Brian's my hero, Jac." She never took her eyes from Brian's. "Always willing to face the danger. But this time the man has quite a few inches on you."

"I'm quick." He kissed her hard and jumped back into the water. Serena watched him dreamily.

"What happened?" Jacqueline gestured toward Brian.

Serena took a big breath and told her about it. "I think he's feeling a little protective today. I'll let him." She shrugged her shoulders and beamed at Jac. "I've never had a man do something like that for me before. It's kind of romantic."

"Sweetheart. That man is head over heels for you." Jacqueline took a long swig of her drink. "Don't tell me you didn't know."

"It's not that I didn't know, necessarily. It's just that things are so complicated right now that I don't—we don't—want to start anything serious."

Jacqueline patted her knee. "Whatever you say."

"Shit. Don't confuse me." She looked into the pool, where the men were starting to wind down. He really was something special. She thought about what had happened in the cabana only hours earlier, what he'd made her feel for him. "Jacqueline?" Serena turned to face his sister. "Can I ask you something, between us?"

"Sure you can."

"Do you think I'm out of my league? I mean, do you think he's just passing time and I'm there?"

"Did he ever give you that impression?"

"No."

"Good. I'd have to slap him."

"It's just that… well." Serena glanced around her. "This really is intimidating. And I don't want him to think that I'm here for this," she said, gesturing around.

"Brian doesn't think that. Trust me. As a matter of fact," Jacqueline said with a smile, "he feels just as intimidated by you."

Serena brought a hand to her chest. "Why? I have nothing to be intimidated by."

"He's intimidated by you. And what you're making him feel. Now that's all I can say on the subject without breaking sister-brother confidentiality."

It was something else to think about and Serena decided it could wait for another day. It was time for all of them to dry off and change. Serena, who was thinking ahead, locked the door to the cabana. A short time later she heard the doorknob jiggle. She couldn't help but laugh.

"Brian?"

"Yeah, let me in."

"No."

"Why not?"

"Because I'm changing."

"So?"

"So? Everyone's here and you're just going to have to get control of your hormones." She opened the door fully dressed, to Brian's disappointment.

"Too bad." He pushed her back in and captured her lips with his. Swearing lightly under his breath he pulled away. "You better get out of here."

"I better get out of here? What kind of game are you playing? Wind me all up. Then you tell me I better get out of here," Serena said as Brian was shoving her out the door. "I do believe I was here first."

"If you don't get out of here, we're going to miss supper. And I can guarantee that my father will not be happy."

"Sure, now you want to be the good son."

"Stop giving me a hard time."

Serena smirked at him to let Brian know she'd been giving him a hard time for no reason. "If we weren't here, Serena, I'd teach you a lesson."

"And I would look forward to it." Serena smiled seductively at Brian who reached out to snatch her, but she was too quick. "Go take a cold shower, sweetheart." And Serena sashayed off.

Supper was delicious. Dessert was a chocolate cream cake, which everyone dived into with gusto. They all laughed and joked, talking about secret escapades of the past. Serena felt right at home with the boisterous group. Then when Jacqueline announced she was going to be having a baby, the crowd went wild. Daniel had tears in his eyes as everyone kissed and hugged the parents-to-be. Rosa, who had reluctantly joined them for supper, was the first on her feet to congratulate them. With tears streaking down her face she turned and bumped right into Daniel, who simply picked her up and laid a smacking kiss on her. Everyone went wild, again.

"I guess they just came out," Brian whispered into Serena's ear. He wrapped his arms around her from behind and squeezed. "I'm so glad you're here."

"Me too."

It was a short time later when Serena and Brian left in the rain. On the ride home, they were like two children, talking at the same time, and reminiscing about all the fun things they had done. She loved his family, how could she not? Everyone was their own person, yet together they forged a unit. The bond they shared was tight yet not restricting. Serena smiled over at Brian as they turned off the highway. She was happy. Happy and falling in love. But when Brian drove into her driveway, a feeling of loneliness and inevitability overcame her. She had to go back home. It was her responsibility. Brian squeezed her hand when all she did was stare at the house in front of them.

"Thank you, Brian. You gave me something wonderful today."

"So did you." He leaned over kissed her softly, then pulled her body closer to his for an embrace. "Dream of me tonight."

"How can I not?" Serena laughed and opened the car door to get out. They walked to her door together and had one more goodnight kiss before he was gone. When she closed the door behind her, Serena leaned her body against it. She wasn't supposed to fall in love with him. I'm not falling in love with him, she reassured herself.

Serena went and checked on her mother, who was sound asleep, and then proceeded to the bedroom where she found a note from her mother. It said she hoped Serena had had a good day. Serena beamed down at it and got ready for bed.

* * * *

Brian let himself in, where there was a very impatient Bart waiting for him. "Gotta go?" Bart gave out a yelp and darted past him. Brian didn't know what to do with all the energy he had. He thought about going and knocking on Serena's window, but then thought he'd appear too desperate. With Bart's prompting, Brian opted for a late night walk. He could think about what it would be like to be an uncle. That made him smile. He was going to spoil the hell out of that kid. Then he thought about what he felt for Serena, and the smile faded to worry. It wasn't the right time for this. Yet how could they stop it? They were going to have to slow it down again. Not spend so much time together. He glanced over at her house as Bart led the way down the street. His heart pulled him in that direction as his head pulled him in the other.

* * * *

As Serena climbed into bed that night, she thought about how serious things had become that day and how they should probably slow things down. Yet somehow, in the depths of her dreams, soft tranquil scenes of the day they had spent and the intimacy they had shared overpowered her doubts.

CHAPTER 18

Serena was waiting. It felt as if she was always waiting. Waiting to go to work, waiting for her turn in line, waiting in a waiting room, and waiting to be given a break. She didn't feel a break was too much to ask. She only wanted the time to be by herself, be herself. She took a big gulp of coffee and resigned to the fact that life really didn't care if you had enough time to even go to the bathroom. The Saturday she'd spent with Brian had been wonderful. However, she wondered if it had been worth all the aggravation she had endured in the days that followed. Serena had woken up the next morning to find her mother very ill. She didn't have the heart to ask why Katherine hadn't called her. She knew. Her mother was going through too many guilty feelings for Serena to get upset with her. When Hope showed up around eleven unexpectedly with her family, Serena ended up suffering through her wrath.

Serena swore softly under her breath. Screw Hope. The woman had no right to try to make her feel guilty. Hope was there for only a short time every day. Serena was there the rest of the time. If Hope wanted to go out for a day, she wouldn't have any trouble justifying it. The buzzer went off telling Serena there was a customer waiting for her to get back to work. And then there was Brian adding fuel to the fire, she thought viciously while heading out to the floor. Screw him! It had been days, and he hadn't even tried to contact her. He got what he wanted. It didn't matter that she had been going to tell him they should slow it down. What did matter was she needed someone to confide in and he was the one she wanted to talk to.

As Serena headed to the front desk, she could see Mandy sitting in the waiting room. She felt a little of the tension plaguing her lift away.

"You're a good sight to see." Serena smiled.

"Hey, I'm here to tell you that someone's a complete wreck."

"You mean besides me?"

"At least you're being civil." Mandy got up from her seat and made her way to Serena. "You look as if you could use a big hug." She wrapped her arms around Serena and squeezed. "Now cut my hair and tell me all about how awful a slime bag Brian is."

* * * *

At the moment, that was exactly what Brian was feeling like. Not only had he not called Serena in days, he was barking at anyone and everyone he could. He'd forgotten his wallet at home again, so that meant another day without lunch. They were overrun with cars and it seemed like everyone was getting the summer flu. Not that that should be an excuse for missing work. He snarled at the knock on his office door. He didn't want to be disturbed; he also didn't want to be alone. Still, he found in the last couple of days people were talking to him less and less, and avoiding him more and more.

Mike peeked his head in a little. "You have a call on the outside line." He tried to duck out quickly, but Brian wasn't going to let it happen.

"Who is it?" he growled.

"I don't know." He tried to close the door again.

"Mike! Come in here for a minute."

Mike moved very cautiously, opening the door slowly but not stepping in.

"For God's sake! I don't bite."

"That depends on who you're talking to," Mike murmured.

"What's that supposed to mean?" Brian narrowed his eyes.

"Well... You haven't been quite the mister sunshine lately." Brian quickly took care of the call then hung up and glared at Mike with a blank but stern stare.

"I think you should call her." Mike took a step back from his boss.

"Call who?" Brian leaned forward in his chair and folded his hands.

"The woman who's put you in this mood. Obviously, you did something that's eating you alive and it has something to do with her."

"Why does it have to do with a woman?" Brian wanted to know.

"You're talking to a man who's been married for ten years, Brian. When a guy is in this kind of mood, it always has something to do with a woman. Trust me." Mike advised, "If it's bothering you that bad, go see her."

"I can't. I haven't called." Brian put his head down on his desk with a thump.

Mike shook his head. "You're such an idiot."

"I know. Now what do I do?" He banged his head a couple more times on the desk.

"You need to go and talk to her."

"She's not going to talk to me. I made what was between us cheap." Brian sat back in his chair and gave out a long breath while scrubbing his face with his hands.

"Well then." Mike planted both his hands on Brian's desk and leaned over it. "If you don't want to make things any worse, I suggest you get your ass to wherever she is at this moment." The light ignited in his boss's eyes.

"All of a sudden, Mike," Brian said while rising from his chair, "I don't feel very good."

"You look a little pale, too," Mike put in with a smile.

"Do you think you can handle things from here?"

"I think the place will still be standing tomorrow."

"Thanks." Brian slapped Mike on the back and hurried out.

"You'll be married in a year," he said out loud, then smirked all the way back to his desk to call his wife.

* * * *

Brian glanced at his watch. She worked down the street, less than five miles, but it was Wednesday, her early day for leaving. He only hoped that she hadn't left yet. When he pulled into the parking lot, he saw Mandy leaving and stopped.

"You're a real ass, Brian."

"I know."

"If you hope to make this any better you better have brought flowers or something." Brian's expression showed it wasn't something that had crossed his mind to do. "You're such a man, Brian. God help her." She tsk-tsked him and began to leave.

"Wait!" Brian's yell caused Mandy to bring her car to a sudden halt. "Should I go and get some?"

"No! She's about to go home."

Brian was maneuvering his car around the parking lot when he spotted Serena. She had already started her car. He pulled up behind her and parked. He figured she'd either ram into him, or get out and yell. He was hoping for the latter.

"Look at this jackass," Serena said out loud to herself. "He's blocking me in. I should just ram right into him and crumple his pride and joy."

Brian got out of his car and ran over to hers, "Serena. I really need to talk to you."

She stared straight ahead. "Did someone die?"

"What?" Brian shook his head in confusion. "No. No one died."

"Well you obviously weren't in a detrimental accident, so get out of my way."

"You could have called, too." As soon as it was out, he regretted it.

"You have obviously been avoiding me for some reason. Why would I want to call you?"

"Get out of the car, Serena." When she didn't move he said between his grinding teeth, "Please. Get. Out. Of. The. Car." Brian's swore at his own hotheadedness when he saw the tears swimming in her eyes.

Brian reined in his patience while she slowly turned off her car, unbelted herself, and got out. When she stood before him all he could think of was holding her. Therefore, that's what he did. Reaching out he gently pulled her into his arms and buried his face in her hair.

"I'm sorry, babe. I'm so sorry." He took a deep breath of relief when her arms came around him and held tight.

"You're such an ass, Brian." Serena wiped away her tears on Brian's work shirt and sniffled.

"Just don't use it to blow your nose, okay?" She nodded her head up and down. "Are you going to look at me?"

"No."

Brian put a finger under her chin and, despite her protests, tipped it up. "I'm not going anywhere." He searched her eyes and saw a hurt there that he didn't know what to do about. He hadn't known he could hurt her like that. She always seemed so strong and nonchalant about their relationship. Now he was realizing she was going through the same pain and confusion he was.

He brought his lips gently to hers. When her lips trembled at his touch, a piece of his heart broke. He rested his forehead on hers and rubbed his hands up and down her arms. "I wasn't supposed to care this much for you. Damn, babe," he said with a smile.

"You damn me, and yet you can't stay away." Her eyes were

clearing up, but her nose was still running. "I need to get a tissue." She ducked into her car and reached for the glove compartment.

Brian admired the view until he heard a horn blow. He'd managed to block someone else in with his car. "Sorry," he called out with a wave of apology. "I'll meet you at home?"

Serena nodded, and he gave her a quick kiss goodbye.

On the way home Brian stopped at a little shop and picked up some daffodils. They were sunny and sweet. He smiled when he pulled back on to the road and found himself behind her. But then Serena's car gave out a loud cough and lots of smoke. Brian shook his head. He had known the car was a piece of shit, but Lord almighty, it was also an embarrassment. Brian watched as the car changed gears and another puff of smoke came out. He should get Darren to write a citation if she didn't either let him fix it or get it off the road. That would get her to see things his way. A grin spread across Brian's face. It would also piss her off.

When he pulled into his driveway, he could see Hope's car parked in Serena's drive. Not what she needs right now, he thought, and ran a hand through his hair. He could see they had gotten into a heated discussion. Their arms were gesturing wildly with stern and rigid movements. Serena tried to walk away from Hope, but she was stopped by something that was said. As much as Brian wanted to see her, the flowers were going to have to wait. There was no way he was going to get into the middle of a family brawl.

* * * *

"If I choose not to talk to him, then that's my choice." So much for her day getting better. "I'm not a little girl anymore that needs her older sister looking out for her, or telling her what she's doing wrong."

"Well, apparently you do. Otherwise, I wouldn't have to make excuses for why you haven't called Dad since you've been back."

"I don't need you to make excuses for me. I don't need you to scrutinize every decision I make, either."

"What was I supposed to tell him? That you just don't want to talk or see him ever again?"

"You can tell him anything that will make you happy. But don't expect me to pretend to feel something that I don't for the man. I owe him nothing."

"You really don't care about other people's feelings, do you? The man is your father!"

"The man left us for the bottle! We did everything possible to help him and all he did was screw us in the end." Serena could feel her face getting red and her body tremble.

"Tell me. Is there anything in your life that you care about? I mean besides yourself." Hope crossed her arms and glared at Serena. "I didn't appreciate the fact that I had to tell our father you've been back for months. Serena, you should have called him. I don't like having to listen to his sad tale of how his youngest daughter hates him so much, and he can't understand why. I'm sick of making excuses for you because I always seem to be caught right in the middle."

"I care for many things besides myself." Serena was not going to be wrapped into this game again. If Hope always felt she had to fix everything that was her problem. "You know Hope, you should really learn some things are best left alone, because sometimes you do more harm than good."

"Name something that means more to you than your own selfish needs." Hope uncrossed her arms and took on a fighting stance.

"The woman inside that house." Serena gestured with her hands. "We both know that if I didn't care, I wouldn't be here." She felt tears sting her eyes. "Both you and I have turned our lives around so that we could do what was right for her. She has supported us in every way. She's done her best to be a great mother, and she is. But Dad?" Serena let out a small laugh. "The only thing that man has ever done is lie, steal, and drive a wedge between all of us. No, Hope. I do not care about that man."

"He's your father," Hope argued.

"He's a man who fathered children and then left them to be raised and loved by anyone else who would do it. He's taken advantage of me for the last time, and I would hope the same would go for you, too." Serena didn't feel the tears that were streaming down her face. They were overpowered by the contempt she had for a man she was related to, but who was a stranger nonetheless.

"You really need to get over this anger you have," Hope choked out.

Serena gave out a large sigh. "Maybe we both have to get over our anger." With that said, she turned and walked into the house, past her mother who was coming out to see what was going on, and to her bedroom where she closed the door softly and locked it. Serena wanted to be alone. She wanted to cry her eyes out until there was nothing left and sleep was the only thing she could do.

It was hours later when she heard the knock. It had woken her out of the fitful sleep she was having. In the dark, she was disoriented and groggy. As she got out of bed to go to the door, she heard it again. However, this time she realized it was coming from the window. Changing directions, she ran right into her desk.

"Careful, babe," she heard his voice after her long trail of swears. "You have some mouth on you."

Serena tugged the screen up and poked her head out. She was instantly overcome by the smell of flowers.

"I'm not supposed to let boys in my room." The flowers made her smile. She wasn't feeling so cold and alone anymore.

"That's okay. I was hoping I could talk you into sneaking out."

Her eyes had adjusted to the dark and she could see him smiling up at her.

"Give me a minute." She disappeared back inside and found some shoes. It had been a long time since she'd snuck out her window. She only hoped that she didn't break her neck doing it.

They walked over to his house, where she could smell the aromas of a home-cooked meal permeating the inside.

"I figured you hadn't eaten supper yet. Hope you don't mind chicken Cacciatore." As they walked in, she saw the table was already set, with candles lit, and she heard soft music coming from the stereo.

"What if I had refused to come over?" She turned toward him as he popped the cork on the wine.

"Then I would have had to barge into the house and carry you over here." He handed her a glass and lifted his to hers in a silent toast.

What did I do to deserve this man? He always seemed to know the right thing to say, the right thing to do.

"What's going through that pretty little head of yours?"

"That you're too good to be true. And I'm either going to wake up at any moment, or you're going to reveal that you have some deep dark secret, and to find it out I'm going to have to go on Jerry Springer."

Brian almost spit out the wine in his mouth. "I can guarantee you're not sleeping." He put his wine down and wrapped his arms around her. "Though, I hope you'll be sleeping with me, in my bed, tonight."

Serena tossed her hair back and put down her own wine. "So you must have some deep dark secret that I need to know about." She tilted her head up at him. "Gosh, you are pretty. Did you use to be a woman?"

"No sweetheart. I'm all man." Brian picked her up and tossed her over his shoulder.

"Have you lost your mind? What the hell are you doing?"

Brian walked over to the stove and turned down the heat. "Only a man can do what I'm going to do to you. And the only secret I've got is… well, I can't tell you. Then it wouldn't be a secret." He flung her on the bed and then jumped on top of her.

"I'm hungry, Brian," she managed to say between giggles. "I mean it."

"I'm hungry, too." He bit her ear.

"You're a shit!" She twisted and turned trying to get out from under him. But, as Serena soon discovered, she only succeeded in arousing him more. His hands became possessive, molding and exploring. Her blood boiled and her body began to betray her. "Really, honey," she said breathlessly. "I'm hungry... for food."

Brian propped himself up on his elbows and looked down at her. "You're really hungry?"

"Yes."

"You're not making an excuse?"

"No."

"You'll stay the night?"

"Yes. But only if you feed me first."

He was grinning when he hopped off the bed and pulled her to her feet. "Well, then. Let's eat!"

Serena walked lamely, following him into the kitchen. She felt her stomach do flips when the smell of food reached her senses, and had to sit down right away before she fell.

"When was the last time you ate?" Brian asked.

"I had breakfast, this morning." A line appeared between her brows. "You know, I don't think I had lunch."

Brian put a large heaping of food on her plate. "Eat up," he said gently and kissed her on the head.

It didn't take long. Serena looked better and was talking away about what her sister had come over for. "I should call my mother. She probably thinks I'm still in my room sulking."

"You weren't sulking. And she knows you're here." He peered up from his plate. "I called her when you went to the bathroom. I also asked if she minded if we have a slumber party here tonight."

"You did not!"

"Well... not in so many words." He rose from his seat and picked up their plates. "Come on. Help me clean up and we'll sit outside and listen to the crickets and frogs."

They spent the rest of the evening talking, laughing and making love. Serena had a few bad moments about all the complaining she had done, but Brian reassured her that if he was ever in the position of needing an ear, she had better be ready.

When she woke to the early morning light, Serena realized she was alone; Brian had already left for work. Today will be different, she told herself. During the night Serena had made up her mind to take things as they came. She'd call Hope first thing and tell her they needed to talk and come to an understanding, even if it killed one of them. She felt better as she jumped out of bed and dressed. She was putting on her shoes when Bart came over and put his head on her lap.

"You are so cute." Serena was scratching his ears as Bart made moaning noises. Serena smiled remembering how he had tried to get in between Brian and her on the bench last night. Then he tried to get in bed with them, and almost pushed Brian right out. She had felt bad about Brian scolding the dog, but Brian made her feel better about it. Much better.

"Time to face the world," she said to Bart. "Want to come?" He gave out a sound of agreement, and tromped to the door. "Let's see if Mom has some biscuits for ya."

They walked into the crisp morning air that showed it was going to be a clear day. The night before had brought the promise of cooler nights and shorter days as the season drew to an end. Summer always seemed to pass quickly in New England. Soon the trees would reveal their exquisite colors, enticing people from afar to travel and enjoy. With this would come the cool windy days when Serena would bundle up in her softest, comfiest sweaters and pick apples and pumpkins while the leaves billowed around her. But for Serena, there was nothing like the first snowfall. Others didn't consider it as special as one on Christmas Eve, but the flurries were remarkable to her, nonetheless. The season revved her up for holiday parties and gifts, something she always looked forward to. Serena took a deep breath of fresh air. It was good to be home.

Chapter 19

Serena glanced around at the children playing. The world seemed so innocent through their eyes. All they worried about was 'when is snack time,' 'when can we go home,' and 'why do I have to wait my turn?' Serena often wondered that one herself. She spotted one red-faced demon across the park. There's always a screamer, she acknowledged with a smile.

The thought about what it would be like to be a parent crossed Serena's mind. The world she was observing was completely different from her own. Serena felt something pull on her heart. She let out a long sigh as a little girl ran up to her mother with some treasure she had just found. It must be one of the most wonderful things to be called 'Mommy'. What a giant responsibility, what a glorious thing to do. To teach, mold and love something so precious. She could see the undeniable love in the way parents and children looked at one another, and in the way they touched.

Serena scrubbed her hands over her face. Since when had she been thinking about having children? She didn't want children. She didn't even want a husband. She tried to sit up straighter as she watched Lizzy dart away from her mother to play with the other children. She's so beautiful. Serena sighed.

"Damn you Brian," she said aloud. "I'm not falling in love with you!"

"Are you talking to yourself again?"

Serena skewed her head up at Hope and smiled. "I'm the only one who will listen, and sometimes even I don't do that."

Hope grinned and sat down beside her on the ground. "You seemed a little lost when I was walking over."

"Do you ever regret the life you've chosen?"

"Sometimes." Hope turned away from her sister to watch her daughter laugh and play with the other children. "But it's only for a fleeting moment. It's not easy. There are moments when I feel like I'm really going to lose it from all the responsibility. There's nothing glamorous about being a parent. Or a wife," she added with a laugh. "But there is something so fulfilling about being loved and loving someone unconditionally."

Serena peered over at the children playing on the swings and slides. "But what if it doesn't work out?" She shifted to stare into her sister's eyes. "I mean, what if you end up an only parent? Look what Mom went through."

"You do your best, I guess. And as far as I'm concerned, if it doesn't work out, I got the best part of Will. I'll always be thankful for that." Hope glanced in the direction of her daughter. "What's with all the questions, Rena?"

The use of her childhood nickname had Serena smiling. "I don't know. I think I'm going through an early mid-life crisis." Serena started plucking at the grass and running it through her fingers. "Everything is so different now. I don't mind the change. I don't even mind being back. It actually feels right being here." She let out a long sigh and lifted her face to the warm afternoon sun. There was a small breeze, which barely kissed her face. "I think I'm just reevaluating my life."

They sat for a time not saying anything. They watched the children play, and let the sun warm their skin. Every now and then, Lizzy would wave and blow kisses. When the silence finally broke, it was due to a little boy who decided he was going to water the grass. His mother came running up behind him, completely mortified.

"You know, Hope," Serena said, in a breathless laugh, "we need to do this more often."

"Yes, we do. What did you want to talk to me about?"

"Seeing each other more often. And I think we need to learn to talk."

"Talk? You mean to each other?"

Serena wasn't going to let any confrontations get in the way of what was turning into a good day. She could hear the caution in her sister's voice. "It's something we don't do a lot of, or do nicely." Serena turned to study her sister's face. "I think we should start practicing."

"Well," Hope said after a moment, "I'd say today we've started off pretty good." With that, she got to her feet. "How about Sunday, I come over with Will, you invite Brian, and we'll all play some cards?"

Serena glanced up shading her eyes from the sun with her hand. "Sounds like a plan."

"Good. I'll bring the cards and beer."

"I'll have the chips, dip and wine."

"You can be on Will's team."

Serena gave a weak smile. "Thanks. Give me the handicap."

"How do you know you're not the handicap?"

Serena got to her feet. "Great. Put the two most likely to lose together. You know, we might surprise you."

After embracing, they walked over to get Lizzy. Serena kissed her niece and watched them drive away. It was the first time in a long time she could remember smiling after a visit with her sister, and it really felt good.

* * * *

August melted into September, the morning smells bringing

memories of school days past. Everywhere he looked there were signs of autumn. It wasn't just in the trees, it was in the way people started decorating their homes. The way the signs went up for winter tires and school clothes. People were talking about cleaning their gutters after the leaves fell, and about all the unfinished projects they needed to complete. Pools were now being closed, as the beaches had been. Then there was the talk about the dreaded Christmas shopping, and the day after Thanksgiving sales.

"You need a new heater." Brian wiped his grease covered hands on a black rag.

"I do not." Serena stood with her hands on her hips glaring up at Brian. "You only need to bang it a couple times and it'll work."

"Well, that explains all the dents." He glared down at the car and swore he could hear it begging to be put out of its misery. At least he'd been able to fix the smoke coming out the back end.

"And I can't afford a newer car right now."

Brian let out an inpatient huff. "I told you—"

"I know what you told me. And I'm not going to borrow your car when mine works fine."

"Fine?" He stared down at her with disbelief. "If the car was fine to drive I wouldn't be fixing it every week!"

"That's your choice. And, if it's such a problem, I'll find a new mechanic." Serena crossed her arms across her chest and stood firm.

"For goodness' sake, Serena! Be reasonable! The car is tired." I can be just as stubborn, he told himself, and kicked one of the tires.

"Hey, whatever you break, you fix," she stated while poking him in the chest.

"There isn't much more that can be broken on it. I'm shocked the thing even starts." Brian turned and smirked at the car. "When it starts."

"You're not being very nice." Serena turned her voice silky smooth and fluttered her lashes. "If you didn't fix my car, then what would be your excuse for seeing me so much?"

"I would have thought of something." His voice was flat and his eyes bore into hers.

Serena took a step forward and ran her hands up his arms to rest around his neck. "If it doesn't get fixed," she purred, "then I'm going to be really cold come winter."

"Don't bother with that woman in distress act. Both of us know you can take care of yourself, and that you're your own worst enemy. Case in point," he said, thumbing toward the car.

"I don't particularly like you today, Brian." Serena folded her arms once again and turned her back to him.

"That's okay. There are some days when I don't particularly like you."

Serena wheeled around. "When?"

"When you're being stubborn and pig-headed about things that you know are inevitable." He wasn't sure if he was still talking about the car. Wasn't he as pig-headed and stubborn when it came to her?

"Yeah, well." She threw her chin up in the air. "That's one of the things you like about me. And don't try to deny it."

"Admit you need a new car."

"I only need a new heater."

"Would you like me to make a list of what that hunk of junk needs?"

"No."

"Then admit you need a new car."

She pressed her lips together and glanced over at her car.

"Come on," he said, gesturing with his hands. "You can do it!"

"You're such an ass." After that pronouncement, Serena dropped her head and mumbled under her breath.

Brian cupped his hand to his ear and grinned. "I'm sorry, babe. I couldn't hear you."

"I said..." She took a deep breath. "That I might need a new car."

"I guess that's close enough." Brian walked over to her and put an arm around her shoulder. "Now let's talk about you and me going away for a weekend."

"That sounds awfully nice..."

"But?"

"Well... Mom just finished with her treatments, and... I don't know if I'm ready to leave her yet."

"I can guarantee she's ready to be left by you." It warmed Brian's heart to hear the laughter escape from her.

"That may be true."

"It is. And your sister has said, more than once, she'd be willing to look in on her if we ever decide to go anywhere."

"You have it all planned out, don't you?"

Brian's smile gave him away. "What do you say? Some place quiet?"

"Can I think about it?" she asked with a guilt ridden voice.

Brian tried not to let the hurt show. He really wanted some time when it was only the two of them. He needed to know if this was going to work. If she wanted marriage, children, white picket fences. The idea of it was becoming more and more appealing to him every time he was with her. "Don't take too long," he said, giving her a wink. "I'd like it to still be warm."

* * * *

Brian was finishing up the dishes when he heard the knock at his door. Throwing down the drying cloth, he went to see who it was. It wasn't late, but he hadn't been expecting any company. Serena left hours before and she didn't need to knock any more.

Brian opened up the door and found Mark standing there. "Come on, Brian!" he exclaimed, while slapping him on the shoulder. "We're going to celebrate."

Brian moved aside to let him in. "What are we celebrating?" He felt his mood instantly perk up. Whenever Mark wanted to party it was always a good time.

Mark flung his arms out to either side and wore an expression of disbelief on his face. "I'm getting married. Can you believe it?"

"I'm sorry," Brian said, shaking his head. "What did you say?"

"I'm getting married." Mark paced around the kitchen, bursting with excited energy. "I don't know how it happened. I mean I've known Mandy for years, but I never thought she'd be serious about me."

"Are you—"

"I've never gotten serious with anyone," Mark interrupted, "hoping that she'd see I'm really not a jerk." Mark was smiling so hard that Brian's mouth was starting to hurt. "Now I know you've always told me that getting married is an awful thing to do. But it feels right."

Mark didn't notice Brian's eyes cloud over. "It's only awful if you marry the wrong person."

"I'm not worried about that. She puts up with my shit, and she likes it!" Brian could see the excitement in Mark's eyes. "I love the hell out of that woman."

"Well, congratulations then," Brian exclaimed, "and I'm buying!"

* * * *

It was after one when Brian tried to focus on his watch. "Damn thing," he said while shaking his wrist. "I never can tell what time it is. Can you?" Brian swayed toward Mark.

"Now how the hell am I supposed to?" Mark slurred out. "There aren't any numbers."

"Precisely my point." Brian looked down at his watch in disgust. "You spend all that money on a… a…" He cleared his throat and searched for his next words. "Watch! And it doesn't even come with… the works."

Both men surveyed the overcrowded bar. They could tell who the usual bar rats were, the ones who knew the bartenders by name. Then there were the ones drowning their sorrows in booze, sulking alone in their corner seats. A woman walked by in a tight shirt and a skirt that showed more leg than was decent. The two men grinned at one another while one of the other men they were with gave a low whistle.

Brian swung his arm around Mark. "Sure you want to do the marriage thing?" They both swayed forward and almost fell off their stools.

"Sure." Mark had a crooked smile on his face from pure inebriation. "You think you've changed your mind on the subject?"

"Yeah!" one of the other men said. "You've got a looker there, Brian." He drew out Brian's name as he lifted his beer in a salute. Brian's reply was only a grin, and a lift of his drink.

For the next hour, they threw themselves into the music, smoke, and the sights to be seen. Brian pondered on the fact there was nothing better than watching a bunch of people making idiots of themselves. He would reflect in the morning that they were probably the idiots.

"I've got to go." Brian tried to stand, but the room tilted a little too much. "It's like a funhouse in here." He laughed.

"I think you just haven't been this blasted in a long time." Mark went to get up and thought better of it when he almost tripped on his own feet. "I think maybe we should call the girls."

"Yeah… they're going to love this." Glancing around they noticed the place was closing up. Since their buddies had left them a while before, Brian took out his phone and concentrated on trying to find the numbers. "Why do they always have to make everything so small?"

Mark shook his head. "I don't know. They really should've… taken situations like… Damn, I need another beer." He ordered another beer for them as Brian tried to dial Serena's number.

"This is the last one for the night, guys. We're going to be closing up." The bartender slid the beers in front of them and smirked at Brian trying to dial.

"I got it!" Brian finally heard the phone ring on the other end after his tenth time trying to dial. "Hi, sweetie! It's Brian." There was a pause. "Brian Allen," he said cautiously. "Oh, sorry." He hung up the phone and laughed.

"What's the matter? She pissssed?" Mark asked in a whisper.

"Nope, d…dialed wrong number."

"Maybe…get the bartender to dial."

"Good idea! John! Can you dial something for us?"

"Sure." He dialed the number with an amused expression on his face. "There you go, buddy. Hope she's up."

"Hi, sweetie! It's sooo nice to hear your beautiful voice. I was afraid I might have the wrong number again."

Serena rolled over and checked her clock. It was just after two. "Brian?"

"Yeah. What's up?"

Serena let out a giggle. "What's up with you?"

"Did I wake you?"

"Of course you did, idiot," Mark proclaimed.

"Don't mind Mark. He's had… umm… a bit too much to drink." Brian switched ears and turned his back to Mark. "So... what are you wearing?"

Serena laughed. "Honey, I don't have a stitch of clothing on." It was a lie, but what the hell.

"Can you come get us at TJ's?" He let out a long breath. "Hurry."

"I'll do what I can." Serena hung up and switched on her light. She'd have to write a note for her mother. She had a feeling she wouldn't be back home tonight. Pulling on a shirt and pants, she laughed again. Serena could only imagine what shape they were in to have to call her for a ride. She knew they were celebrating because Mandy had called. Serena had been so excited she'd started crying on the phone. Not a usual reaction for her, but she had been happy for them.

She got in her car and prayed that it started. Lately, she had been seriously thinking about buying a new one. Had even gone so far as buying a wheeler-dealer magazine. However, she wasn't going to give Brian any satisfaction by telling him that. Within five minutes her hopes for any form of heat were dashed. The car just didn't have it in her. When Mark opened the back door and threw himself inside she knew they wouldn't even notice.

"I think that... that I'm going to regret this... tomorrow." Mark's words were slurred and both men gave off a heavy stench of alcohol.

"If I wake up with a hangover… I'm gunnin' for you." Brian leaned back over the front seat and gave his buddy a punch in the arm. "You know I didn't always like you... but," he said cheerfully, "you grew on me."

Mark gave Brian a crooked smile. "Glad to hear it."

Witnessing this male bonding had Serena in stitches. Both men began to sing to the radio, and Serena suspected they were giving it their best. By the time she got to Mark's home, he was passed out in the back. Of course, that didn't stop Brian from jibber jabbering at the both of them.

"Hey, buddy." Brian pushed at his friend. "Time to go to bed."

Mark grudgingly opened the door and rolled out of the car. "I'm okay."

Serena was laughing so hard, she thought she would pee her pants. She watched as Mark got unsteadily to his feet. Then he leaned toward the driver's side window and subsequently rapped his head on it.

"Are you okay?" she asked while rolling down her window.

"I wanted to thank you for bringing me home." He seemed pathetic standing there rubbing his forehead.

"Not a problem." She touched his cheek. "Can you make it in okay?"

"I'm not the one you're going to have to worry about." He smiled a big-toothed grin and faltered to his door.

"Yeah!" Brian exclaimed. "You don't have to worry about him." He ran his hand up Serena's thigh. "I'm the one in the car with you. And I'm feelin' frisky." Serena averted Brian who tried to lean over and nibble on her but was restrained by his seat belt. He swore under his breath as he tugged at it.

Serena patted his knee. "Trust me, honey. It's for the safety of everyone."

She kept her window partially down. The aroma of alcohol had Serena smiling over at Brian. He was quietly snoozing beside her when she pulled into his drive. She waited a moment just taking in the man that had made such a difference in her life. How could he know what he'd done? He made not only a change in her life but in her. She touched the tips of his blond hair and sighed. She'd screw this up sooner or later. It was her M.O. and something she couldn't help.

Shaking away the bad thoughts, Serena walked around the hood of her car. She opened the car door slowly because Brian was leaning on it.

"Come on, big boy." She grabbed him by the arm and pulled before he could teeter. "You need to help me out a little, Bri."

"Are you going to take advantage of me?"

"I don't think, at this point, that would be an option." She wrapped his arm around her shoulder and started their journey. They had a few tough moments getting up the stairs when they swayed up against the house. "Honey, you're going to hurt one of us if you don't try to help me."

"You know." Brian staggered through the door. "I really, I mean, really, care about you. I've never." He threw his arms out, barely missing Serena. "I mean, never." He wrapped his arms around her as she led them into his bedroom. "Let a woman, a woman! Spend the night."

"Oh? Have you let a man?" She knew she was making fun of him. Nevertheless, she figured, why not?

"No!" He seemed offended, and Serena had to laugh. "You're making light of what I feel for you?"

"I'm not making fun of your feelings, Brian." She managed to straighten him up at the end of his bed. "It's just hard to take anything you say seriously in your drunken state."

"My drunken state?" Serena saw that gleam in his eyes before. It was there when he had thrown her into his pool.

"Now sweetheart." She put her hands up and took a step back. "You need to sleep this off and—" The next thing Serena knew the wind was knocked out of her from being tossed onto the bed. Before she could get her breath back, his long hard body was on top of hers and rock-hard in a place she hadn't thought could work at this intoxicated level. Brian's hot mouth was at her neck, and then her ear. His hands ran up and down her passively. She felt a fireball form inside of her. It scorched from the tips of her fingers to the tips of her toes. All her nerves stood on end even as her pulse jumped, then scrambled. His skin was hot and damp under her touch. Serena grasped for some type of sanity but when he grabbed the front of her shirt with both hands and ripped, she knew he was going to have anything he wanted. The gasp she let out only succeeded in arousing them both more. Their hands became desperate to touch, their mouths to feast on heated flesh. She'd never been this desperate to mate with a man before. She'd give herself fully to him, any way he wanted. Someone whimpered, and not sure which one of them it was, Serena's needs heightened.

She felt the front of her bra snap, then his lips on her breasts, sucking and nipping with teeth. The ball of fire that had grown in the pit of her stomach exploded. She grabbed at his shirt and tugged it off, not caring about the seams she ripped. She was fighting for her life, and Brian was the breath she couldn't quite catch.

They attacked the remaining barriers of clothing, tugging and swearing at them along the way. When they were finally flesh to flesh, heat to heat, he plunged into her and all madness let loose. They rolled across the bed, both desperate to be the one in control.

Serena let out a cry of release as Brian worked faster to reach his goal.

"Go up again," he commanded her. "I want you to only ever want me. I only want you."

Their eyes connected and Serena felt her heart and body let go. She clasped around him, in an almost painful release.

Brian's body shuddered as he collapsed on top of her. He snuggled into her hair and breathed in her scent.

"Stay the night," he whispered, "I want you here." He rolled off of her and then pulled Serena close before she could respond. She lifted her head to say that she would, but found he was already sound asleep. When she shifted to grab the blankets, Brian held on tighter. He wasn't going anywhere, she remembered him saying, and neither was she. It was then Serena realized no matter what she said, or what she did, she was helplessly lost to him. She nuzzled closer and came to the realization that she didn't even want to do anything about it.

CHAPTER 20

Brian woke the next morning with bugles playing in his head. Rolling over, he groaned and wished that part of his body could be removable. What had he been thinking when he decided to get that drunk? Brian peeked over at the clothes that were scattered on the floor. Just those slight movements made his head sing with pain. It hurt to open his eyes, and it hurt to close them. He wished for a quick and sudden death.

"Sweetheart," he heard someone say, "I have some aspirins and water for you."

Brian decided it was the voice of an angel because she brought exactly what he needed and couldn't get up to get himself. Opening an eye, Brian tried to focus, but his vision was blurry and everywhere he looked there were rings of light.

"It's okay. Here, I'll help you." Serena held up his head and helped put the aspirins in his mouth. "Now drink up, if you can. You don't want to get dehydrated. I'm going home and clean up. Then I'll come back and make you some soup." She kissed him on the forehead and was gone.

Brian awoke a few hours later. His head didn't feel like it was going to roll off anymore, but his stomach felt terrible. He picked Serena's ripped shirt off the floor, teetering. She must have worn one of his home, he concluded. A small smile formed, then faded when it sent pain rippling through his head. Brian brought his hands up to cradle it. He felt a little dizzy, and a little sick. Sitting back on the bed, he decided sleep was probably the best thing for him. When he spotted the crackers on the side of his bed, Brian thanked the Lord he had a good woman. He rode out the spinning in his head until it brought him into the dark tunnel of sleep. His last thoughts were of the woman with red hair and a heart of gold.

The sun was low in the sky when Brian pulled back the curtains. When his stomach growled he took it as a good sign. Walking into the kitchen, he thought about giving Serena a ring. He hoped she would be there when he woke, and found himself disappointed that she wasn't. She has things to do, he told himself. She doesn't have to answer to you, and you don't have to answer to her. Nevertheless, he still found himself searching around the kitchen for a note she might have left. He swore softly under his breath. What was he doing? Brian damned her once then opened up the refrigerator to try and find anything to soothe his knotted stomach. He welcomed the cool air that escaped from it like an old friend. Grabbing a sports drink he headed to the window. With creased eyebrows, Brian noticed Serena's car was still in his drive, but her mother's was gone from theirs. An uneasy thought crossed his mind, and he hoped he was wrong.

Where the hell is she? It was after ten and she was nowhere to be found. He'd tried her cellphone, and there was no answer. He'd tried their home phone, even walked over and knocked on the door. No answer. He hadn't wanted to look or act like a jealous or nervous boyfriend, but that was exactly what he was doing. On the other hand, what choice did he have? She wasn't at work. She wasn't with any friends that he knew about. He kept telling himself if something serious had happened she would've called. But what if something serious had happened to her, and no one called him? Brian felt anger rise up from inside his gut. Someone should've at least called him. He was her boyfriend after all. Her boyfriend? Brian stopped pacing long enough to think about what their relationship was. A sensible non-commitment, that's what they had silently agreed upon. It was what they both wanted. Right? Wrong. Screw sensible non-commitment, it was too late for that now.

Brian looked up from his pacing when the headlights shone through his windows. Bullshit! He was her boyfriend and he'd just spent a good amount of the day worrying about her when he should've been nursing his headache. Not making it worse. He stomped toward the door and threw it open as Serena came up to it.

"Where the hell have you been?" His voice was dark and angry. His stance was erect and defensive. "You could have called! I've been worried sick!"

"I don't have enough energy to fight with you, Brian." Serena turned away from Brian, and started for home.

"Where do you think you're going?" Brian grabbed her arm and spun her around. It was then he noticed the tears that were brimming in her eyes. She was still wearing his shirt, and her hair had been pulled back in a bad excuse for a ponytail. He quieted his voice, and started running his hands up and down her arms. "Talk to me. I'm so sorry, babe. Please, talk to me."

Hot tears streamed down Serena's face. Brian pulled her to him and wrapped his arms around her. He was petting her head, and making soothing noises as he would to a crying child. Serena let out ragged sobs, and her hands fisted into the back of his shirt.

When her sobs slowed down, Brian led her into the house. He pulled out a kitchen chair for her to sit in, and then went to the sink to get her a glass of water. He berated himself the whole time.

"I'm such a shmuck." He placed the glass in front of her and hung his head. Even Bart, who had his head resting on Serena's lap, was giving him dirty looks.

Serena wiped away at the tears. “Yeah, you are,” she choked out. “Sorry I didn’t get to call. There were other things on my mind.” She got up and headed to the door. “I can’t do this with you tonight. Obviously I shouldn’t have come here.”

Brian stopped her half-hearted attempted to escape by wrapping his arms around her from behind. He buried his face in her hair, taking in the familiar scent. When Serena tried to struggle out of his hold Brian held her tighter until she relaxed against him.

“Why can’t you just let me go? It would be so much easier on the both of us.” Serena sniffled loudly, and her voice began to crack. “Can’t you tell that I don’t like you, you’re a pain in my ass?”

“That may be true.” He turned her around so she’d look into his eyes. “But I’m nothing compared to you.” Brian kissed her softly on the lips. “So is this one of those times you don’t like me very much?” He smiled down at her, and Serena gave out something between a laugh and a sob. He pulled her back into his arms, and hoped he could soothe her breaking heart.

“It’s my mom.” Serena buried her face in his chest. “I need a tissue or else I’m going to use your shirt.”

“It’s dirty anyway.” He kissed the top of her head.

“I need a tissue.”

He let out an exhausted breath that had Serena trying for a smile. “If you must.” He walked into the bathroom and came out with an entire box. He hoped it was enough, because, after that box, he was fresh out.

They settled on the living room couch and Brian waited patiently for her to finish with her nose. Why hadn’t he noticed before how fragile she was? She appeared as if she was going to fall into a million pieces at any moment. He yelled at himself again for not paying close enough attention. Anyone could have seen that she had had an awful day, but not him, he thought grudgingly. It was part of the reason his first wife found comfort in the arms of another man. Brian had never paid close enough attention. He ran his hand up and down Serena's back. She glanced up and gave him another weak smile.

"Don't beat yourself up, Brian. I know I should have called." She looked down at her hands. "I didn't want to wake you, plus I forgot my phone. And, for the lack of a better excuse... I'm not used to someone caring. At least, not in this way."

"Neither am I." He took her hands and hoped she was done crying. A man just didn't know what to do with a leaky woman. "Tell me."

"She's going to leave me." Serena sniffled. "We all just started to make something that resembles a family. How could this happen? The three of us were never given the chance to see what we could do together." She fiercely pushed up from the couch. "It's like fate is working against us all the time!"

Brian took a deep breath. "What is it?"

"The cancer moved into her lymph nodes," Serena said very matter-of-factly. "She'll have to either enter a place that can take care of her. Or…" Now she took a deep breath and sat back down. "Or we try to finance some home care."

"There are lots of places that can help you." Brian took her hands in his. "If you need anything..."

"I know. But what I need right now isn't what's important."

"Yes, it is." Brian said it so strongly that he even surprised himself. "You can't lose yourself in all of this. It'll eat you alive." Isn't that what it almost did to him? Didn't he go running into a marriage with the wrong woman, only to realize that she couldn't replace his mother? Then berated himself for years over the mistakes he'd made that hurt the people he loved.

"I just want a chance to feel like I belong to a family. That sounds silly and selfish." She bent her head and concentrated on her feet where there were shoes with no socks. “I was heading to my room when I heard my mother calling. I’ll never forgive myself for not being there.”

“Don’t say that. You did nothing wrong and it’s not silly or selfish. I think there’s a point in everyone’s life when they feel they want to be a part of something.” He cupped her chin so she’d look at him. “You still need to live your life, Serena. You’re going to go on living.”

“It’s not fair.” Quiet tears slid down her face.

“I know.” He wrapped his arms around her once more and began to rock. Turning his eyes up toward the heavens, he said a silent prayer for things to go quickly.

* * * *

Things had gone quickly. Within the span of two weeks, Katherine’s condition worsened drastically. The cancer spread from her lymph nodes into her liver, leaving little hope. The slight yellowing of her skin was only a prelude to what would come. She was in and out of the hospital seeing this doctor or that doctor. There was a horde of medications she took on a daily basis, and her sleep became ever more fretful. Serena had to start making a daily regimen on what medications to take at what time. Then there were the ones that couldn’t be taken together or they’d make her sicker. It was all to make things easier on her, the doctor had said. However, it sure didn’t seem that way.

Katherine stared down at the piece of paper in front of her. She had taken to writing things down about what she wanted to be done with everything once she was gone. When she had tried to talk to Serena or Hope about such things, they both had insisted it wasn’t something they needed to talk about. Katherine knew that they just weren’t ready.

She stiffly shifted on her bed; even that had become an effort. She felt weaker with every passing day, as she watched herself wither away in the mirror. Letting out a long sigh, Katherine glanced at the picture next to her bed. Reaching over she caressed her fingers on the happy faces. It was one of the few photos that had the three of them together. Katherine remembered what a great day it had been. It was the year before Serena had "escaped the coop," as she liked to call it. They had been at a big family gathering. There were lots of people there that she hadn't seen in years, and whose names she couldn't remember for the life of her. Katherine could still almost hear the grill sizzling and the children laughing. The day had been sunny and warm. She had brought a potato salad. Funny the little things you remember about certain times in your life. Hope had just started dating Will. God must love that man, because he's a saint. Katherine always laughed a little when thinking about her son-in-law. He was funny, kind, and the best thing to happen to Hope. He helped her believe in love and trust again. It was something that had been taken away from her girls, with the help of their father. Katherine scowled to herself. What a waste of a man. At first, he was a knight in shining armor. He had been romantic and fun. He brought gifts home all the time for the girls and her. How quickly had things changed. He had striped all of her self-worth, and then cast her aside as if she was nothing. Oh, what those girls have been through. She looked at their cheerful images and smiled. They did all right by themselves, with her pushing and shoving all the way. Katherine had no doubt they would be okay without her. She really hoped they wouldn't kill each other.

Katherine laughed softly; they were more alike than they would ever admit. That's why they butted heads so often. She thought about how they'd started working together with all that was going on. There weren't any drag-out fights any more, although Brian did have to get in the middle of them once. It was, he'd confessed to Katherine, not a pleasant experience. Poor Brian. He was like an adopted son to her. This must be so tough on him. Sadness washed over her in a wave. He always said she was like a second mother to him. When Brian had moved next door, he'd seemed so lonely and lost. When she had come over with a batch of cookies for him, she was rewarded with the look of a child given his most cherished gift. Katherine had known from the moment she met him that he and Serena would be great together. Not that she had wanted to play matchmaker. Still, she'd thought it would be fun to put them together, and see what would happen. However, fate had other things in mind. It had taken years for them to meet. If something good came out of her illness, it was that. They were funny to watch, always picking on each other, always careful not to touch each other too much. They were trying to keep it casual by fighting commitment any way they could. Everyone knew, except them, that they were in love with each other. Katherine shook her head. The two of them were so pig-headed. She thought about the charity ball the following week. If she could only make it past that, if she could only convince Serena it was something she should go to. Katherine knew Brian's ex-wife would be there. Not that she was a threat, but she would love to hear about the expression on her face when she got a load of Serena and Brian together. They were a good looking couple.

Katherine caught a glance of herself in the bedroom mirror. She was getting more and more yellow everyday. She was starting to resemble a canary. At least she still had some humor. She had tried it on the girls, but only Serena understood. She always did have a dark side.

Katherine shifted again, and gave out a muffled oath. Staring up at the ceiling, she hoped the inevitable wouldn't be too much longer. Putting down the pen and paper on her nightstand, she decided some sleep would do her good. Before Katherine could finish her last thought, sleep had already taken her.

* * * *

Serena peeked in on her mother. She knew Katherine had been

writing her will. She had seen to the papers yesterday, legal and otherwise. It broke her heart to think the woman she loved was preparing to die. Katherine had tried to talk to her about it, and Serena had refused. She wasn't ready to go over all the logistics of her death. She wasn't ready to let go and start dividing everything up between her sister and her. Serena didn't think she would ever be ready.

Serena placed a glass of water on her mother's nightstand. The room smelled stale and the curtains were drawn. She thought briefly about opening a window, but didn't want to chance getting her mother sick. Her immune system was in less than poor condition, and she was looking worse with each precious day that passed. Serena fell to her knees next to her mother's bed. The cancer was taking with it every ounce of her being. Serena's heart felt as if it was being ripped out of her chest. It ached so bad she moaned. Serena knew there was nothing more she could do, but she couldn't help feeling there had to be. She'd never been one for praying, but under the circumstances, she felt there was little else she could do. She wasn't praying for herself, she was praying for her mother. She wanted the pain and suffering to stop and for her mother to finally be at peace. Serena felt something brush her side. Turning her head, Serena saw Hope kneeling next to her. With tears streaking down their faces, they both went back to prayer.

CHAPTER 21

What was she doing spending the weekend at Brian's family home? She should be back at home, with her mother and sister. How the heck had they talked her into going to the charity ball? She wasn't in the mood to dance and laugh. She just wanted to lock herself in a dark room to cry her eyes out. What good would that do, though? It wouldn't change anything, it wouldn't stop the inevitable; yet it would make her feel better. She sat with a plop on the large plush bed. It had spindle arms that reached up toward the high ceilings, stopping short to hold the lace canopy above. The room was done in quiet muted colors, soft browns and feathery creams. She wouldn't call the room feminine, even with the bed. She wouldn't call it masculine, either. It was the right mix of both. She fell back onto the bed and closed her eyes. Brian had told her this was his favorite room in the whole house. It was away from everyone else, and it had a great view of the water. However, even the ocean with its repetitive laps against the sandy shore couldn't soothe her troubled mind.

Her thoughts moved at a dizzying pace. Reverting back to the same place they began: her mother. Sometimes in the morning, things were too much to bear and Serena would be sick in the bathroom for what seemed like an hour. She was making herself ill over all the responsibility she had. She knew this, and yet, couldn't stop the worrying.

* * * *

Brian hadn't wanted to disturb her, but he was worried. Serena hadn't been feeling well lately from all the stress. She hadn't said too much on the ride down to his dad's. She had also made sure everyone knew she didn't feel right about leaving. Damn woman was so stubborn. He had hoped she'd ease up a little with the distance, but it had only succeeded in making her drift farther away from him. He needed to hold her, make her feel safe. Why wouldn't she let him? She'd been slowly putting a distance between them since her mother had taken a turn for the worse. He couldn't help but feel it was personal when she told him she hadn't wanted to come. Thank God Hope and Katherine had insisted that she did.

He walked down the hall trying to think of some excuse as to why she should let him in the room. Brian hadn't been able to touch her in a week. It was driving him crazy. He stopped in front of her door and raised his hand to knock.

"Bullshit," he said to himself. This was his house. Therefore, he would be damned if he was going to be intimidated by the woman he loved. Loved? Since when had he been thinking he was in love with her? Who said there was any thinking about it? It just was. He swore under his breath and turned away from the door to pace back and forth in front of it. She'd snuck her way into his heart. He didn't know how, or when, but she was there and there was nothing he could do about it. Brian rubbed at the pain in his chest. She needed him, he reminded himself. She needed him more now than she ever did.

"What's the matter?" Brian looked up to see his sister watching him from down the hall. He started stomping toward her. "You know Brian, if you had wanted it to be easy, you could have stayed married to Susan."

Brian stopped in the process of walking around her to go back downstairs. "What the hell is that supposed to mean?"

"It means that, with Susan, you knew she was after your money. There was no surprise with that." Jacqueline gestured with her hand toward Serena's door. "With her, you're going to have to decide if chancing heartache is something you're ready for." She turned away from him and started toward the other end of the hall. "That is, of course, if you've figured out you're in love with her, and aren't too much of a wuss to do something about it."

Jacqueline left him there with his mouth hanging open. How did she manage to know something he had only figured out moments before? Brian cursed women one more time and stomped back to Serena's door. He didn't even hesitate. He opened the door, closed it behind him, and then locked it. He walked through the small sitting room to the bedroom with a fierce and determined step. She was lying on the bed with her eyes closed and the whisper of a smile on her lips. Silently Brian slipped off his sneakers and dove on top of her. Serena's eyes flew open with surprise and her hands went against his chest in defense.

"What are youuu… smiling about?" Brian said with a playful lopsided grin on his face.

"I was just thinking about how I had to pick you up last week." Her breath hitched when he nibbled on her ear. "Brian."

"Yes," he whispered into her ear.

"This is your father's house..."

"It was his cabana, too." Brian moved to her neck. It felt so good to feel her close. She smelled like peaches and cream, and her skin felt as soft as velvet. His hands began to roam where they chose to.

"Brian." Serena was trying to sit up but he had her pinned. "Brian!"

"Yes?" He propped himself up on his elbows and smiled down at her.

"I really don't think..."

"That we should do this with the shades open?" He grinned.

"No. That—"

"Let me guess." He covered her mouth with one of his hands. "You haven't shaved your legs." She shook her head no, and licked his hand. "Yuck!"

"Let me finish."

He could see the anger building up inside of her. That's good, he thought. She needed to let it out. Brian offered her a patient expression, and was rewarded with a shove.

"Get off me!"

"Okay." Brian wrapped his arms around Serena and rolled until she was on top. "There. Now I'm off and you're on."

"That's not what I meant." Serena struggled to get out of his arms and only proceeded in getting herself caught closer. "I don't know what has gotten into you, Brian. But I'm not in the mood to be harassed."

She feels right, was the only thing going through Brian's mind. Her breasts were pressed firmly against his chest, and her breath was heaving from controlled rage. He slid one hand down her back to squeeze her bottom. He couldn't believe how a woman in temper could arouse him so.

"Brian," she said through her teeth, "I'm not in the mood to play with you."

"I know." He tightened his hold and rolled. "So let's see what you're in the mood for." He grabbed her hands and cuffed them above her head with one of his own. "You know, one of us might not make it." He nipped at her bottom lip. "But it's going to be a whole lot of fun."

* * * *

Serena was sitting at the dining room table when a shiver ran through her body.

"Are you cold?" Daniel had an expression of concern on his face.

"No, I had a chill." From the turbulent sex your son and I had not too long ago, she put in silently. Serena glanced across the table where Brian was seated. He simply grinned at her and took another sip of wine. Jerk, was all she could think. Arrogant, selfish jerk. She narrowed her eyes at him and took a sip of her own wine. How dare he make her feel this way? She wasn't interested in having a relationship with him anymore. She had to figure out a way of getting out of this before it went any further. She sent him another sneer. He blew her a kiss.

"So tell me, Serena." Daniel sent a glare Brian's way. "Is my boy causing you some distress?"

Serena turned to Daniel and smiled. "Nothing I can't handle."

"Good. I'd hate to see you have to go tomorrow without a date."

"Daniel," Rosa said very sharply, "stop teasing the children."

"Why? It's good for them. Builds character," he replied while shaking a fist in the air.

"We have enough character, Dad." Gabriel shot Serena a charming smile. "Besides, if Serena decides she's sick of Brian's boyish antics, I'm more than willing to step into his place," he finished with a wink.

"Never could resist leftovers."

"Donald." Jacqueline swatted her husband in the arm. "That's an awful thing to say."

"It's okay, Jac." Brian turned toward Serena. "There won't be any leftovers here to take." Serena shot him another killer sneer. "Whether she likes it or not." He raised his glass once more, and was rewarded with a kick in the shin by Serena. "Ouch."

"I'll decide what I like and don't like."

"Tell 'em Serena!" Jacqueline cheered her on.

Serena leaned forward on the table. "Maybe your bother has more to offer in the gentleman department."

"You don't like gentle men." Brian smoothed out the last word and Serena felt her temper rising once again.

"He's baiting you Serena. Don't fall for it." Jacqueline sent Brian a warning look.

"Now children." Daniel slapped his hand on the table. "I want to talk about my grandchild." He turned to Jac. "Sweetheart, how are you feeling?"

"Very good, Daddy. We had the ultrasound this week." Donald and Jacqueline beamed at one another.

"Yes! Yes! What did the doctor say?"

"Daniel. Stop badgering the poor girl. She's been answering all of your questions very patiently for months."

"Rosa, I just want to make sure that my little girl is getting the best care possible."

"You should not have to worry about—"

Daniel slammed a fist on the table. "I can worry if I want to, woman."

"Don't you cut me off in the middle of a sentence."

"It must be a family trait." Serena put in glaring at Brian. She shouldn't have looked at him. She could hear them all talking and arguing about Jacqueline, but couldn't hear the words. Brian had begun to undress her with his eyes. She felt another chill run through her body when his gaze became hard and determined. Serena tore her eyes away and concentrated on the conversation at hand. Damn him. How am I supposed to do what I have to do when he can turn me inside out with a look? She should head home. She should excuse herself and tell everyone she really didn't feel comfortable being away from her mother for even those few days. Serena frowned and scolded herself. She should not be using her mother as an excuse. That was wrong. She should be able to face Brian with the truth. She was in love with him. Damn it! When had she fallen in love with him? Serena's pulse jumped and her palms began to sweat. She felt the mixture of confusion and relief run through her body. Love had happened slowly, she realized. It snuck up like a thief in the night, and in the morning Serena discovered she was missing something. That something was her heart.

Serena got up swiftly from the table and everyone stopped talking.

"Are you okay, my dear?"

"Yes, thank you, Rosa." Serena glanced at all of them, and then settled her eyes on Brian. He deserved so much more than she could offer. Brian appeared smug and content that he'd set her off balance. She cursed the fact he could get to her. She cursed herself for letting him.

"You know, I'm not feeling quite myself. If all of you will forgive me, I'm going to bed early." Serena turned and left the room before anyone could say anything. As she climbed the steps to the second floor she had to ask herself where all her insecurities were coming from. When she opened the door to her rooms, she had a flash of what it had been like that afternoon with him. She slowly lowered herself into a chair. Serena had thought she was in love once, a long time ago. She even thought she might be falling in love with Brian a couple times. However, when the reality of it hit her square in the face at a dinner table full of people, it became a completely different story. Now she had to worry about how he felt about her.

* * * *

"Well, go get her, boy." Daniel gestured toward the door. "You go and drag that girl back here, and for God's sake, tell her—"

"Daniel. It's none of our business."

"Rosa. It's quite clear to everyone in this room how the two of them feel about each other. Now boy, get your head on straight. That girl." He pointed toward the door, again. "Is the best damn thing to happen to you. Now don't be an idiot, go get her."

"Sorry, Brian. I have to agree," Jac said to Brian, who was

smiling.

"I'm only giving her five minutes to let the fact that she loves me sink in." Brian took another sip of his wine while Daniel let out a whoop and Gabriel slapped him on the back.

"Rope her in Bri." Donald cheered.

Brian got up from his seat. "I'll see all of you in the morning."

"Don't be pushy," Jac told him when he kissed her cheek.

"For God's sake!" said Rosa. "Be a gentleman." Brian kissed her nose.

"Show her who's boss!" Everyone turned and stared at Gabe. "I was feeling left out."

"Did you want me to kiss you, too?"

Gabe puckered out his lips at his brother and without any warning Donald leaned across the table and took Gabe's face in his hands. "Don't even think about it!" Gabe struggled against Donald's grip.

"We don't want you to feel left out."

"Great!" Daniel waved Brian off. "Maybe the poor girl's scared of this family. Damn kids," Brian heard him say, as he headed for the stairs.

Brian found Serena sitting in the chair. She seemed a little lost and confused, but she still met his eyes when he kneeled in front of her.

"Go away."

Brian smiled. There hadn't been any punch to her words. "Now that wouldn't be any fun, now would it?"

"I'm not interested." Serena folded her arms across her chest and turned away from him.

"You're always so cute when you pout."

"I don't pout."

"Yes, you do. It's one of the things I love." Brian caressed her cheek with his hand. "We can do this the hard way, or the easy way. But either way, neither of us are leaving until we have this resolved."

"There's nothing to resolve. We both know that this is a—" She faltered for a second. "Casual affair."

"No it's not." Brian gave her a look when she opened her mouth to argue. "Easy way or hard way?"

"I don't know." Serena helplessly stared up at the ceiling. "This is new to me."

Brian took her hands in his and brought them to his lips. "Serena—" He struggled out, then dropped her hands and began to pace the room.

"Is there something you wanted to say?" Serena stood to face him. "Or are you just going to make a wear mark in the rug?" Serena took a big breath. It might be cowardly, but she was going to take her way out. She'd known all along it would end at some point; she'd hoped it wouldn't hurt so bad. "I need to pack. I'm not comfortable with staying h—"

"I'm in love with you."

Serena felt it like a shot. A hot burn burrowed through her heart. Slowly she lowered herself back into the chair. Never in a million years had she expected him to come out and say it. Her chest started to burn. She knew she should say something, but her mouth wouldn't work.

"Breathe," he commanded, and Serena felt the air whoosh out of her lungs.

"Thanks." She sat there and blankly stared at him some more.

"Is that it? I tell you I love you and all you can say is thanks for helping me breathe?" Brian started pacing wildly. "Do you know how hard that was for me to say? Do you understand what that means to me?" Sometime during his ranting, Serena had knocked out of her trance. She was up and standing behind him when he turned to pace back the other way. Brian came to an abrupt halt, all words caught in his mouth.

"Do you ever shut up? Or do you just like to hear yourself bitch?"

"I like to hear myself."

Brian had made no move to touch her, yet she could feel his eyes pleading with her to give him some sign that he could. "I love you, too." The world started whirling, not because of her declaration, but because Brian had picked her up and was spinning around the room with her. "Honey, you're going to make me sick."

Brian plopped her back on her feet and kissed her fiercely. "Say it again."

"I love you!" Serena threw her arms around his shoulders and wrapped her legs around his waist. She felt so free. Who knew? She always thought people exaggerated when they said love was one of the most wonderful things you could feel. Yet, here she was, experiencing it for herself.

"I love you, Serena," Brian said against her mouth. He tightened his hold and carried her into the bed. It was there they showed each other with slow caresses and soft whispers what love could bring to them. It felt like a dream filled with tranquil hollows and turbulent peaks. There were bright flashes of color and gentle soothing pleas of desire. Every time they thought the other couldn't possibly give more, there was more. Together they experienced for the first time what it was like, not to fall asleep in your lover's arms, but to fall asleep in your love's arms. They discovered there was a difference.

CHAPTER 22

He woke the next morning to the sun shining in the bedroom. Brian had a magnificent feeling that something was different, but he couldn't put his finger on it. When Serena shifted in her sleep to snuggle closer, his heart did a flip. Reaching out to brush her hair away from her face, Brian had a moment of hesitation. Everything suddenly became so clear to him. How could he have not seen it earlier? This was the woman he wanted to spend the rest of his life with. He took in slow deep breaths as the recognition of feeling complete overcame him. Snuggling closer so they were face to face, he ran his finger along her jawbone, then the back of his hand along her cheek. Serena's eyes fluttered open. A smile crossed her face to settle in her eyes. It only took the slightest movement of his head to have Brian's lips meet hers.

"Good morning, beautiful," he whispered. "Did you sleep well?"

Serena shifted into him and the covers a little more. "Yes, I did." Her eyes were still heavy from slumber and her body serene. "You make a great bed warmer," she said in a sleep-soaked voice.

"Thank you." He closed his arms around her and pulled until her head was on his chest and her body pressed completely to his. Serena gave a long satisfied sigh.

"Why don't we stay right here all day?" he said. "It's way too cozy to move."

"Mmm. You're right. I was just thinking the same thing."

"Yeah?"

"Yeah. Of course," she said, sliding a hand up his chest, then raking her nails down it, "we do have some place to be tonight." Serena shifted to run a trail of hot wet kisses down his chest. Brian's body reacted instantly. When she tried to move out of his arms, he pinned her back down. "And I have to go get my hair and nails done."

"Serena," Brian proclaimed breathlessly, "I can't get enough of you." He nibbled at her neck.

"I'm sorry, sweetheart." Brian's head popped up and they both smiled at one another. "I have to meet your sister in..." She cranked her head and gasped. "Twenty minutes!" She felt Brian's hand cup her breast. "Save it for tonight." She hopped out of bed and headed for the bathroom.

"Hey!"

Serena paused for a moment. "Yeah?"

"I love you."

Serena's eyes sparkled and she whispered, "I love you, too."

* * * *

"Damn women!" Daniel was complaining. "They'll always make you late."

"Serena wouldn't even let me in the room."

"Jacqueline did the same thing."

"See!" Gabriel said, while gesturing with his drink. "That's why I don't take dates."

All three men turned to glare at him. "The only reason you don't have a date is because everyone in the surrounding area knows what a dog you are."

"Donald, my sister found out too late what a dog you are. Lucky for you she's forgiving."

Brian gave a chuckle and earned a swat to the head from his father. "Hey! Why don't you ever do that to Gabe?"

"You were closer. Now," he said, pointing to the door, "go get the women."

"Like they're going to listen to me," Brian grumbled. He fixed his hair and glared at Gabe once more. "Send him. He's the one bragging that he doesn't have to put up with a woman tonight."

"Right." Daniel nodded. "Go get 'em."

"If I've learned one thing about women, it's that they don't like being rushed. You want them so bad," Gabe told his father, "you go get them."

With that, the door to the study opened and Rosa walked in. She had on a long, sleek black dress that complemented her full-figured body. The hair that was usually worn in a bun was left loose to curl to her shoulders, and she had on the ruby earrings Daniel had given her the night before. She no longer resembled a housekeeper and Daniel was determined to make sure she got it through her thick head that she no longer was.

"Sweetheart," Daniel said, holding out his hands to take hers. "I never imagined you could be more beautiful. But, once again, you have proved me wrong." He kissed her quietly on the lips. "Now, where the hell are the other ones?"

"Daniel," Rosa said with her thick accent, "no rushing the women. They need to be beautiful"

"They already are," Daniel huffed. Rosa shook her head while accepting the wine that was offered to her.

Sensing the uneasiness Rosa was experiencing, Gabriel kissed her on the cheek. "Just stick with me and you'll do fine," he whispered. "You look wonderful."

She smiled up at him. "Gabriel, why do you not have a woman?"

"Because they're trouble. Besides, I have you to keep me company tonight."

"Hanging out with an old woman—"

"You are not old," Brian chimed in.

"If you're old, then what am I?"

"Dad, you're old and cynical." Gabe managed to duck out of the way when his father tried to swat him. "See Brian, you only have to be quick. Ouch!"

"I'm still quicker than you," Daniel announced.

"All right, children," Rosa announced, "I believe I hear the other women."

"About time."

"Yes, yes, yes. Now Daniel, behave yourself."

"I always do," he grumbled, following the rest of them out of the room.

Brian came to a halt when he saw his sister and Serena coming from the foyer. Jacqueline had on an emerald green silk gown with an empire waist. It helped, not so much to hide her pregnancy, as to keep her comfortable. She'd been very happy with her choice of dress when she had woken up that morning to a belly no longer flat enough to conceal. Her dark hair had been swept up in a series of complicated twists and there were diamonds winking at her ears.

"Sweetheart," Donald took her hands and kissed them. "You're stunning." She blushed and turned to kiss both her brothers and her father.

Brian couldn't tear his eyes from Serena. He gave Jacqueline an absent kiss, and stepped toward the woman who was his future. Letting out a long breath and shaking his head, Brian realized he was speechless. The deep purple made her eyes come alive. Her hair was pulled back from her face so it could cascade down her back to show off her soft features. Unlike Jacqueline's dress that had cap sleeves, Serena's dress was off the shoulders with long fitted arms. The gown was snug enough to show off her figure, and loose enough not to be risqué. Brian's eyes followed the trim line of the dress down to where the toes of her shoes peeked out. When he brought his eyes back to hers, she shifted her feet.

Brian saw Serena wringing her hands. Her eyes darted over to glance at his father and the rest of the family. Idiot, say something.

"You look..." Brian lost all words again and chose to just show her. He encased her in his arms and dipped her over in a passionate kiss. When he pulled her back up to her feet, she visibly had to compose herself.

"Stop manhandling that poor girl, boy." Daniel pushed his son out of the way to give Serena a kiss on the check. "My son is an idiot, and you're beautiful." He smiled down at her and ran his hands up and down her arms. "You'll do fine," he whispered. It was exactly what Serena needed to hear and it made her smile.

Gabriel propped out his arm. "May I escort you to the car?"

"I don't think so. Get your own woman." Brian and Gabe exchanged a brotherly grin while Donald passed out champagne and sparkling cider for Jacqueline.

"We have an announcement to make first." Donald held up his glass and waited for everyone to get quiet. "Honey, why don't you do the honors?" He turned and kissed his wife. Together, the two of them looked elated.

"Donald and I have decided we're going to name our daughter Sofia. After Mom." She waited as the news sunk in. A tear ran down her father's face, telling her she'd done the right thing. Rosa stepped forward with tears brimming in her own eyes.

"My dear child, she would be so happy. You have done your mama's memory good." She kissed Jacqueline's cheek and stepped back.

"Now look what you did," Gabriel exclaimed. "You went and made all of us love you more." He gave his sister a bear hug and was swatted by his brother.

"She has a delicate condition, Gabe." Giving her a hug of his own, Brian whispered, "I love you."

"I love you, too," Jacqueline whispered back.

Serena smiled at her. "I told you it would be okay."

"You knew about this?" Daniel asked accusingly. "I should know first." He cupped Jacqueline's face with both his big hands. "You do me proud."

"Don't make me cry, Daddy. I'll spend another hour fixing my makeup."

"Then let's go, quickly."

* * * *

Serena had to keep from running her hands along the sleek leather seat of the limo. She had only ridden in one once when her sister had gotten married, and it had been nothing like this. The light gray interior was smooth as silk. There were lights around the ceiling inside and along the bar. It fit all seven of them comfortably with room for at least four more. Music was playing softly out of the speakers and Serena felt an uneasy edge to all the excitement.

The bunch of them enjoyed glasses of champagne and cider as the streetlights blinked by. Serena could see people pointing and whispering to one another, as she had done so many times before when a limo drove by. She turned her attention back to Brian's family. They all seemed so comfortable, as if fancy dresses, diamonds, and galas were an everyday thing. She felt Brian take her hand in his and squeeze.

"Relax," he told her, low and comforting.

"Easy for you to say, you're used to it." She shifted in her seat and concentrated on the argument at hand. It seemed they were always teasing each other. Never a dull moment in this family, Gabe had said to her once.

Serena leaned into Brian. "Do they ever stop?"

"No." He started playing with her fingers, something that had become a habit. "It's gotten only worse since Rosa has finally given up on keeping her and Dad's affair a secret."

Serena looked over at the two of them. She witnessed the sparkle in Daniel's eye as he tried to prove his point once again.

"She'll keep him young," Serena said while trying to get her hand back. Brian brought it to his lips.

Brian leaned to her ear. "You're the most beautiful creature I have ever seen. I love you."

Serena couldn't conceal the sigh. He made her feel as if the two of them were the only ones on the planet. "I love you too... now give me my hand back." She grinned and gave him a peck on the lips as the limousine pulled to the curb.

The building was magnificent. It resembled something straight out of Greece with its large pillars and marble entrance. When the car pulled to a stop, it took all of Serena's efforts not to stick her nose to the glass like a child and stare. The driver signaled to Daniel then got out and opened the door with a smile.

"Behave yourself, Daniel," he said under his breath.

"Be careful, Leo. I just might fire you again."

"I believe that will make three times this week."

"I guess I'm slipping."

When Leo helped Serena out, she thought she was going to faint from the excitement pumping through her veins. There were so many people. They were dressed to the hilt in silks and satins. There were diamonds sparkling on the men as well as the women while they held glasses of champagne in their elegant hands. Serena felt small and homely next to them all. She asked herself again why she was there. She had no business being at something like this. She wasn't raised to attend these things.

"Don't be nervous. They're all people like you and me. Just some aren't as nice." Brian flashed a grin and kissed her lightly on the lips.

"I'll try to imagine all of them naked."

"That could be interesting." Brian gestured toward the big man at the entrance to the lobby. "What does your imagination see with that one?" he asked.

Serena made a face. "I'd rather not say."

"I'm so glad you came. I don't think I could have handled this alone."

"So if you have to suffer..."

"Then you're suffering with me," Brian finished.

"Well... at least we're all doing it together."

"As a family," Gabe chimed in while taking one of Rosa's hands to put through his arm.

"I don't think it's that bad." Jacqueline said while eyeing her big brother.

"Don't look at me that way, Jac. I like being single," Gabe told her. "So don't go trying to set me up with one of your friends."

"I really don't like to see you alone."

"I never leave here alone."

"He's right Jac." Brian took both ladies' coats and handed them over to get their slips. "Gabe never leaves empty handed."

"And he smiles about it the next day." Donald shifted in his shoes when his wife turned and jokingly glared at him. "I'll go get you something to drink." He wiggled his eyebrows at Gabe and Brian then disappeared to find some juice.

"She's just looking out for you," Serena insisted. "If you were my brother, I'd do the same thing."

"Thank you, Serena. Now let's go powder our noses and talk trash about our men." Jacqueline wove her arm through Serena's and guided them both to the powder room.

It amazed Serena how many people Jacqueline knew. They would nod to her and say how they'd catch up later. The men glanced at her admiringly, while women watched her with envy. Serena was sure she was playing a part in someone else's life, because none of this could be real. It felt too much like a dream.

Serena had admired the inside of the lobby with its giant chandelier and water fountain. However, she soon discovered the restrooms were something to revere. The long plain mirrors on the walls welcomed her to admire and see all of herself. The marble counters were smooth and cool, with porcelain sinks resting in them. The colors in the room were soft and complementary to every woman's skin tone. There would be no harsh glare to overcome when beautifying oneself in here. Even the toilets seemed to have a polished appeal to them.

Serena caught sight of the striking blonde at the end of the counter. She was leaning into the mirror and applying fresh lipstick. She wore a butter cream silk dress that flowed to the floor with a small train at the back. The dress showed off the woman's tiny waist and her small but full breasts that peeked out the top. Serena felt an instant dislike for the woman. She couldn't explain why, but it was there. When their eyes met in the mirror, a flash of disgust was exchanged between the both of them. Serena knew instantly that it was Susan. Her hand balled into a fist before she realized it.

"What a nice feeling that would be. I'd love to see you deck her," Jacqueline whispered into her ear. Serena turned and checked her own makeup in the mirror.

"Only if she decides to try and make trouble."

"Why, hello, Jacqueline. I hear you are expecting. Isn't that just wonderful." The woman turned and gave Serena a glance over. "And who is your little friend?"

"Serena," Serena said, without turning from the mirror to extend her hand.

"Serena," Jacqueline announced, "this is Susan." Serena turned to take a closer inspection. Susan was tall and pencil-thin, even with her subtle curves. Serena could tell she had bottle blonde hair, which brought her some amusement.

"So this must be your first time at one of these. I've never seen you before." Susan gave Serena a calculated smile.

"This is my first, with Brian. Jacqueline's brother," she put in, just in case Susan wasn't clear on it.

"Oh. I didn't know he was doing favors for your friends, Jacqueline."

"Actually, I met Serena through Brian." Jacqueline turned and smiled at Serena.

"Brian's so fond of his family that I couldn't wait to meet them." Serena flashed Susan a killer smile. "Of course, it doesn't mean much when the family isn't fond of you. Don't you agree?"

"That's something you will never have to worry about, Serena. Everyone loves you, including Daddy." Jacqueline turned to Susan. "You know how hard of a man he is."

"He's not fooling anyone." Serena waved Jacqueline off. "Daniel's a big teddy bear." Serena turned and took one more glance in the mirror. "Speaking of which, you know how the men get when we dilly-dally. It was a pleasure meeting you..." Serena pretended to think for a minute. "Susan."

Both women turned and left Susan before anything else could come out of her open mouth.

"Serena, my dear, I think we are going to be long-time friends."

"Gosh, I hope so."

"What are you two up to?"

"Gabe, I wish you could have seen Susan just now in the bathroom. Serena handled herself like a pro."

Gabe gave the two of them a mischievous smile. "You didn't

think she could?" He swung his arm around Serena's shoulders. "I can't wait to hear how you plan on driving her nuts all night."

"Driving who nuts? And Gabe," Brian said while pushing his brother's arm off Serena's shoulder, "get your own." He wound his arms around Serena's waist and kissed her loving and longingly on the mouth. Out of the corner of Jacqueline and Gabriel's eye, they saw a very flustered and envious Susan. Both tried to sustain their laughter but chuckles escaped.

"I want to know what's going on, now." Brian eyed Serena, then Jacqueline, then Gabe.

"Hey, I only came in on the tail end," Gabe said, while throwing up his hands.

"Hello, Brian." At the sound of the voice beside him, Brian knew what his women had been up to.

"Hello, Susan." Brian turned to her while keeping his arm tightly around Serena's waist. "This is Serena," he stated cheerfully.

"Yes. We met in the ladies room." She turned to Brian's brother. "Gabriel. Single?"

"Just the way I like it." He rocked back and forth on his heels and looked maliciously at his brother's ex-wife. The mutual distain for one another was obvious by the hostility in the air.

Susan turned back to Brian and smiled. "Could I talk to you for a minute?" When she flashed her bright baby blues at him, Brian couldn't help but think about how stupid he must have been to get involved with someone like her.

"I don't think so. You know how busy we get at this."

"Brian, dear." Serena placed a hand on his chest. When he looked down at her, he felt as if he was going to burst at the seams from trying to restrain his laughter. "If she really needs to speak with you, by all means..." Serena turned and gave Susan an expression of pity. "She seems like she has something she needs to get off her chest."

Susan noticeably composed herself. With one hand she flicked back her hair and leveled her chin as if to say, 'that little bitch isn't going to get the best of me'. "Yes, I do."

"Sorry, Susan," he said, shaking his head. "We men have been waiting a while for these beautiful women to be ready. And you know how my dad gets."

"Speaking of which," Donald chimed in with Jacqueline's drink in his hand, "your father told me to round up the troops."

Looking at Susan, Brian shrugged his shoulders. "Maybe later." He steered Serena toward the large doors that had just been opened to the main room. He could feel Serena's side convulsing from holding in the laughter. "You enjoyed that."

"More than you will ever know." Serena turned her face up and met his lips with hers. "Hope you're not mad. But Jac and I couldn't resist."

"You gave her a hard time in the bathroom?"

"She started it," Serena pointed out.

"I'm sure she did."

"Do me a favor?" Serena asked.

Brian turned toward her and played with one of the curls that framed her face. "Anything."

"Wait as long as you can to talk to her. It'll drive her nuts!"

"Why don't we start with this?" He pulled her close and gave her a kiss that turned more than a few heads. "That wasn't for her, it was for us. If it drives Susan crazy, then she'll just have to deal with it." He cupped the back of her head and brought his cheek to hers. "I'll wait as long as I can," he promised.

* * * *

The room was filled with flowers and sparkling crystal. Everywhere Serena looked, there were portraits of women who had either won their battle with breast cancer or ones who were taken because of it. The reality of the night struck her like a fist to the gut. Her mother would not be a statistic here, she realized. However, someday soon, she would be one elsewhere. Serena glanced over at the hors d'oeuvre table. On top of it was an ice sculpture of an angel. Her wings were spread wide while she peered down at the people with a compassionate face. Her arms were stretched out, as if ready to embrace anyone in need. She made a powerful statement to anyone who glanced her way.

"She's beautiful, isn't she?" Serena turned to the sound of Jacqueline's voice.

"Yes, she is."

"Every year I try to find something that will make you stop and look, the way you just did." It was clear to Jacqueline her friend was in pain and this was exhausting for Serena to be a part of. Yet, she was still here to support Brian, even though everyone knew she wanted to be someplace else.

"It does get better. The first year we did this was the hardest." Jacqueline glanced down at her glass of juice. "Now it's an honor to do this for my mother. She's helping so many people." Jacqueline gave Serena a weak smile. "I gave up faith at one point. I think we all did." She looked back up at the sculpture and said, "We must believe everything happens for a reason."

"That's not easy, sometimes," Serena mumbled.

"No it's not, Serena. That's why we have family and friends to remind us."

Some time later in the night, Jacqueline's words echoed in Serena's head. Serena tilted her head up at the sparkling sky. The stars winked at her like small festive lights cheering on the party. She'd needed some air and space to breathe. It was getting a little too stifling in that large room. There were too many people, too many questions. What's your name? Where are you from? Have you known the Allens long? Just a few minutes, that was all she needed. Just a few minutes to get her head to stop reeling and her stomach to settle. Damn it, I should have brought those antacids.

Somewhere between the food, dancing and beautiful people, Serena had come to the realization that she was going to lose her mother. Therefore, the only person she wanted to be with, the only person who could possibly understand, was the man she loved and she needed to go find him.

* * * *

Susan saw her the moment she stepped onto the terrace. She was going to let this little candy dish know that Brian was not someone she could take. Susan had made up her mind and she was going to get him back. Financially life was getting too hard. Brian had been the best thing to ever happen to her and if she had to sell her soul, she'd get him to realize how much he still wanted her. As she stepped toward Serena, Susan could see the faraway expression on her face.

"A bit chilly tonight."

"Yes. But it's so beautiful." Serena gazed up at the stars.

"Why are you here with Brian?"

Serena looked Susan straight in the eye. "Because I love him and he needs me to be here, with him and his family."

Susan was taken off guard by the genuine honesty of Serena's words. "Yes... But how could you possibly understand what he is going through?" Susan knew it was small of her. She knew what she was trying to do. Break this woman, berate this woman, and she couldn't stop herself.

Serena turned to Susan with a whisper of despair in her eyes. It was something Susan didn't miss. "My mother is dying of cancer." Serena turned and left Susan baffled and standing alone in the twilight.

Susan hurried in after her. It had taken a moment, but she realized she needed to apologize. She and Brian hadn't been together for years now. Yet lately she'd had this fantasy about them getting back together. It hadn't been a completely loveless marriage. They'd had some good times, hadn't they? She tried to think of one when they weren't fighting. Susan stopped short when she entered the crowded Grand Room. Her mother told her she was a selfish person the last time they talked. Was that true? Was she really a spoiled little rich girl with nothing to show for the years she'd been alive? She'd been evaluating her life lately, and found very few redeeming qualities. Even her friends seemed self indulgent. Maybe she should take the retreat her mother had mentioned. No phone, no TV, nothing but meditation and listening to her inner soul. Susan had laughed at her mother then. Now she was searching for the solace a place like that could give.

Glancing across the room Susan spotted Brian and Serena. His hand was caressing her cheek while he studied her eyes with loving concern. It occurred to Susan he'd never looked at her like that. It was more than love that she saw exchanged between them. It was an intimate understanding only soul mates could experience. It was in the lack of words even while they soothed. Why hadn't she been able to find something like that with him? Because she was always too busy with manicures and shopping.

Brian met Susan's eyes from across the room. He didn't appear happy. She watched him march across the room toward her, a mad man on a mission.

"Let's talk," Brian said, and grabbed her arm.

"Brian," Susan said in a low voice, "you're hurting my arm."

"You'll be lucky if that's the only thing I hurt."

They walked out onto the terrace where Serena and herself had been only a few minutes before. He walked her down the steps and out onto the grass, all the while keeping her arm imprisoned in his grasp.

"Serena won't tell me what the hell you said to her. But you will, or you'll never again be welcome here or at the many gatherings you like to attend that include my family." He sneered down at her with fire blazing in his eyes. "Everyone will know what a bitch you are, and we all know how important your social life is to you. So tell me."

Susan had seen him this angry before. However, it hadn't been for her. It had been for his mother. The woman she would never meet, but had been shocked to realize she was jealous of. "I said something I shouldn't have. She doesn't deserve—"

"To be treated this way," he completed.

"Don't start finishing my sentences, Brian. And let go of my arm!" Susan yanked it away and began to rub the tender spot. "I was about to apologize to her when I spotted her talking to you."

"What did you say to her?" Brian's voice was low and angry.

"It doesn't matter now." She looked up at him with a whisper of a smile. "She makes you happy, doesn't she?"

"Yes," Brian said cautiously.

"I could never have done that?"

"No."

"Why?"

Bewilderment covered his face. "What…? Why does it matter?"

Susan threw her chin up and tried to appear dignified. "I have the right to know why."

Brian pulled a hand through his hair. "I wasn't ready to get married." He took a step back and examined the woman in front of him. "I wasn't very fair to you. I wasn't fair to either of us."

"It was very mutual, Brian." Susan took a step toward him. "I'm glad she makes you happy." She looked up to where the music was floating down to them. "She needs you right now. She's going to need you a lot more soon." Susan cleared her throat. "Tell her I'm very sorry to have upset her. I hope her mother... well... I hope she's comfortable." Susan hung her head and began to walk away.

"Thank you, Susan," Brian called out to her.

Susan stopped, glanced back, and smiled. "It's time to move on, Brian." She left the party feeling free. She was starting a new life, a new her. When she stepped into her waiting limousine, Susan called her mother.

* * * *

"My dear, I do believe it's time that you danced with me." Daniel hadn't missed the expression on Serena's face when she came in from the terrace. He also hadn't missed his son drag his ex-wife back out on to it.

"I warn you, Daniel." Serena eyes sparkled up at him. "I can make your feet ache. Literally."

Daniel gave out a hoot of laughter. "My love, no one was worse than the children's mother." He took her hand and placed it through his arm to lead her to the dance floor. "That woman broke more toes on my feet than I care to count."

"That's so wonderful."

"She was a free spirit, that girl. Always was." He led her into an uncomplicated box step. "Just like my daughter, just like you." His eyes were so intense that Serena missed a step and walked on one of his feet. "Oh yes!" he boasted. "You could make my feet ache."

Serena thought she was going to cry. She had only met this man a few months earlier and yet she already thought of him as a surrogate father. "I'm so sorry, Daniel, I didn't mean to do that." She stepped on him again. "Or that."

He grinned down at her. "Relax," was all he said, and brought her close to him.

That was how Brian spotted them. His big burly father with his arms wrapped possessively around the woman Brian loved. She was so small compared to a lot of the women in the room. Yet he could see the strength in her eyes. Brian grabbed a glass of champagne from a passing waiter. He stood where he was, studying the woman that was dancing with his father. He could see Serena's eyes were closed as she danced, her head resting on his father's broad chest. He was talking quietly to her, and Brian saw her laugh. Then she gazed up and Brian saw the undeniable affection they had toward one another. It was the look in his father's eyes that had Brian reflecting on the thought of never being married again. Daniel had looked at Serena the way he looked at Jacqueline; with love, respect, and humor. Then she stepped on his foot. Brian had to cover his mouth for fear of sending the contents in it flying. His father laughed so loud he could hear him above the rest of the crowd. Serena was red as a beet. Time to save her. Brian dropped his drink off with a waiter on his way. Quickly and efficiently, he worked through the crowd of people who wanted to talk to him.

He tapped his father on the shoulder. "May I cut in?"

"Do you have steel toes?" Daniel leaned down and gave Serena a kiss on the cheek. "Just kidding." Daniel gestured to his son with a hand. "By all means."

"Thank you." Brian took Serena's hand in his and her waist with the other. They moved across the dance floor not saying anything until the music changed.

"So, do you come here often?"

"No." Serena giggled. "This is my first time."

"Good." He led her out into the gardens. "Then you won't know my reputation for picking women up at these things."

"Oh? Is that what you're doing? Picking me up?"

Brian turned and gazed straight in her eyes. "Only if you marry me."

"Well…Ummm… Do you always propose to women that you pick up?"

The moonlight danced on her hair while giving her skin a silver glow. It reminded Brian of another night. The night he first met her and she was standing alone by the water seeming lost. How could he have known it was he who was lost, and with her, found?

"No, I don't. You just feel special." His voice was quiet and humbled. When he knelt down on one knee, Serena's eyes grew large as she stared down at him.

"You didn't answer my question." Brian kissed the hand that laid in his. "Will you marry me, Serena O'Neal?"

"I don't know what to say, Brian," she stumbled. "To be perfectly honest, I didn't know you... I didn't think... us, we... marriage?"

Brian stood slowly and took her face in his hands. She's scared, he realized, really scared. "I'm not a patient man, Serena."

"No shit."

"I'm serious."

"So am I." She let out the breath she'd been holding.

Brian gazed down at the woman he'd just asked to spend the rest of his life with him. "I'll give you room and time to think about it. But that doesn't mean I'm not going to nudge you along."

"Don't get pushy with me, Brian." Serena poked a finger into his chest.

Brian narrowed his eyes. "You haven't seen how pushy I can be."

She rested her head on his heart. "Can this sit in for a little while?"

"I see no problem with that." Brian felt the smallest of breaks in his heart. She could do that, she could break his heart. "Just don't go running away on me." Brian cupped her chin and brought her face up to his. "I'm head over heels in love with you, Serena O'Neal. That's a big thing for me to accept and admit."

"I love you too, Brian Allen. I simply don't think right now would be the time for me to make a decision concerning the rest of my life."

"Then I'll wait." He wrapped his arms around her, and asked himself, why did she feel already gone?

CHAPTER 23

It was a brisk morning. The air had a bitter scent and when Serena breathed in deep, tiny ice crystals formed in her lungs. The wind slapped her face with an unpleasantness that made her cheeks burn. There wasn't a cloud to be found in the sky on that lonely wintry day. The rays from the sun left a cold glare on everything she looked at. Under her feet, she could feel the grass creaking from the arctic blast.

Katherine Jean O'Neal had left behind two daughters, a son-in-law, and a granddaughter. She had passed quietly in her sleep, with all of her wishes known. Toward the end, there was only peace. She had slipped into a deep sleep and days later, in the night, she decided it was time to sleep forever. There had been no pleas to stay, no last requests or regrets. She had simply left and the machines had stopped beeping. The room had been filled with the people who loved her, people whom she loved in return. There had been tears and moans from their broken hearts. However, the knowledge that she was in a better place, that she was no longer left here to suffer, made the loss somewhat more bearable.

Serena stared on in an almost hypnotic state. She knew she was holding her sister's hand, but the numbness that had overcome her body wouldn't allow her to feel it. When they lowered the casket, she heard a gasp, and couldn't distinguish if it had been hers or Hope's. In the end it really didn't matter, they were there to comfort each other.

Flowers were taken from the many wreaths that were sent. They would be pressed and kept as a reminder of a loved one lost. Afterward, people would gather in a restaurant and talk about the good times they had had, and the arguments that now seemed so petty. The many people there would come up one more time before excusing themselves, and say again how sorry they were. Everything was a blur. Names, faces, even past events didn't register through Serena's grief. She moved like a well-oiled machine. There were no tears shed, no signs of faltering. Her back remained straight, and an appreciative smile set on her face. Yet inside, Serena was as fragile as a porcelain vase. It took all she had to keep from crawling into a corner and letting all the unnecessary guilt and natural grief take over.

Serena turned her attention to Hope, who was sitting quietly with Lizzy on her lap. She was bouncing the little girl on her knee, making soothing sounds to help heal the gaping wound in their hearts. Serena turned away. Who was soothing whom? she wondered. Turning to leave the room, she spotted Brian. He had given her space. That was what she had wanted. She wanted no one hanging on her, asking if she was all right; no one following her, waiting for her to fall to pieces. Serena straightened her shoulders. She didn't need anyone for such things. She always handled them quite well on her own. So why was it that she wanted to be wrapped in Brian's warm safe arms?

She needed fresh air to breathe, something to tell her that she was still alive. She needed to get away from the 'I'm sorry' that everyone seem to be saying. She nodded to the man as he opened the door to let her out. She couldn't remember what color his hair was, let alone his suit. That is, if he was wearing one. Her system was shut down from every emotion it held. Serena was a shell waiting to crack under the constant pressure, and knew it was only a matter of time before she did.

She hurried around the side of the building and found a curb to sit on. Inside the stagnant room she could feel the grief starting to overwhelm her. Yet now, out in the cool open air, she felt undeniable relief.

"Come here often?" Brian sat down next to her and let out a long breath. "I don't think it's ever been this cold in late October." He glanced over at her. "What do you think?"

"You're sweet." She went to lean her head on his shoulder, but he lifted his arm and she was brought tight to his chest. "No, I don't think it's ever been this cold."

"You should be wearing a jacket."

"I know." She felt safe, warm, and loved.

Brian kissed the top of her head. "People getting to you?"

"Yeah."

"You think you'll be up for a nap after this?"

Serena tilted her head up to him. "I have a million and a half—"

"Things that can wait till tomorrow," he interrupted. "You're asleep on your feet. I'll make some soup, and then we'll just sleep."

"I hate when you interrupt me, and when you're right." She burrowed her head back into his chest one last time. "I have to get back in there."

"Okay." They got up together and went their separate ways once inside. It had felt good when she leaned on him outside. Although it was only for a minute, she knew what a large step it was for her. She also knew that without his strong presence there, she would have surely fallen to pieces.

The drive home was agonizing. Serena hardly said two words while she stared out the window. When they drove over the small hill and their homes came into sight, Serena closed her eyes while silent tears rolled slowly down her cheeks. Brian pulled into his drive and cut the engine.

"It gets easier," he said softly with his head back against the seat. "You'll never forget. But it will get easier." Brian lifted his hand and started stroking her hair. “Honey... Hey.” He leaned over and swaddled her in his arms. Serena’s body shook from the shock of burying her mother. Her breath rushed in and out and her tears fell like a torrid rainstorm. They rocked back and forth in an attempt to soothe their pain.

They carried one another inside, and then dismissed the idea of soup for bed. Sleep would come quickly, and be a welcomed escape. Brian had taken the phone off the hook and the doors were all locked. They were not going to be disturbed. Under the covers, they nestled close for emotional support. Nevertheless, the warmth of the body couldn’t melt an ever-cooling heart. Serena stared up at the ceiling as she listened to Brian’s deep slumber. Never again would she lose someone she loved. Never again, she vowed to herself. It wasn’t right how people can be taken away with no regard to the others who have to pick up the pieces afterward. She thought about her sister and how she had sat with her daughter on her knee while the service was being read. Tears were streaking down her face as she held her Lizzy close and tight. They said not a word to one another, yet they received all the reassurance they needed. Willie’s arm had come up behind them and he cradled the two in his refuge. It was a moment that would live forever in Serena’s mind. A moment captured for her to relive any time she needed to. Someday that flash of remembrance would give her comfort and reflection in times of need. It would also be remembered as the moment when she felt something break inside of her.

* * * *

Brian woke a few hours later to an empty bed. He searched through the house, and found only dust and clutter. He went outside to walk next door, but thought better of it when he didn’t see a car. Going back inside, Brian went into the bathroom. I should clean up first, take a shower and brush my teeth. Then make a small meal with a salad; nothing heavy tonight that could upset our stomachs. Brian’s thoughts went still when he saw Serena's toothbrush was missing. At first, he dismissed it and began to brush his own. Then slowly he turned toward the bedroom door. Something wasn't right. He could feel it in every inch of him. Brian spat out the rest of the paste and darted to the bedroom closet. The side where she had been hanging some of her clothes was empty. Serena had been slowly filtering things into the house since they had started dating. Neither of them had said anything about it, it was just something that had happened.

Brian stumbled back from the closet in disbelief. He already knew the drawer with her panties in it would be empty, too. She was gone and she didn't even write a note. Somehow, he had known sooner or later she would leave. He sat on their bed and thought about what he was supposed to do next. When nothing came to mind, Brian fell back on it and felt his heart break for a second time that day. It wasn't possible, he kept telling himself. She wouldn't leave like this, yet she had. He rolled over and took in the aroma she'd left behind. How could she be gone? he kept asking himself.

At the sound of cars in his drive, Brian darted to the door. When he saw Mark and Mandy, Darren and Meg getting out, he felt the disappointment and rejection run through his body once again. She was gone, and he'd have to resign himself to the fact that Serena was not going to be someone he could get over easily.

When everyone filed into the house, Brian was pouring himself a shot of whisky. He saluted them as they waited patiently for him to explain what was going on. They knew he only drank like this if something was seriously wrong.

"How are you doing?" Meg asked cautiously. She walked over and gave him a kiss on the cheek. He never even looked up from his glass. Brian downed the contents and turned to pour some more. They all glanced at one another, judging what the best thing to say and do was.

Mandy cleared her throat. "Is Serena here?"

"No." Brian downed the shot and set up another one as Mark stepped forward.

"Take it easy, Brian. We men get pretty stupid when we drink like that," Mark advised cautiously. "We don't want Darren here to arrest us for bad behavior."

"I haven't started with bad behavior, yet." He turned his back to them and poured himself some more. "I think all of you should leave. I'm not going to be very good company pretty damn soon. I appreciate you coming by."

"That's bullshit!" Darren stepped forward and grabbed the glass from Brian. "I hate seeing you like this and I'm not going to stand here while you get yourself cocked."

Brian tried to be as pleasant as he could. "I really want to be alone."

"Brian. I have known you for too many years to not know something else is eating at you. Spill it!"

"She's gone!" Brian opened a cabinet and took out another glass. "She left no note. She said no goodbye. She just left." He decided the hell with a glass and drank straight from the bottle. "Guess she didn't know how to tell me she didn't want to get married." Brian shrugged his shoulders. They felt heavy, even though the rest of his body was starting to feel light. Good, that means the stuff is finally starting to work.

Meg took a step forward. "You asked her to marry you? When?"

"The night of the dance, it was even romantic. Even though I didn't have a ring." Brian shrugged this off as if it was no big deal. "Not that it would have made a difference," he slurred, "she obviously doesn't care enough about me to even say goodbye."

"Wait a minute." Mandy was confused. "So… she didn't say goodbye? She didn't leave a note that she was leaving? And you haven't talked to her since when?"

"A few hours."

"So how do you know she left you? How do you know she's not coming back?"

Brian took a swig from the bottle and grinned at his friends. "She took all of her clothes while I was asleep. While she was supposed to be sleeping." He threw his hands up in the air splashing liquor all over the floor. "Then left without as much as a goodbye."

"Did you check at her mother's house?"

"No! Now why the hell would I check there? It would seem too obvious, don't you think?"

"Brian." Both Mark and Darren took a step toward him.

"What? The two of you ganging up on me now?" Brian threw a glass to smash against the wall.

"No." Darren motioned for Mandy and Meg to leave. "I think you should probably chill out."

"Brian. No one doubts that today was tough on both of you. But you need to deal with this in a little less asshole-like way. Maybe she simply needs some time to clear her head."

Darren purposely lowered his voice. "You know how women are. They can never make up their minds. I'm sure she'll be back before you even sober up."

Chapter 24

Serena wasn't back, and it started to look like she wasn't coming back. She had taken off, destination unknown. Hope made it very clear to Brian: if either of them heard from her, they should call the other. She had no idea what her sister was doing, or where she was. The anger Hope had initially felt when she realized her sister had gone was overrun with concern about what Serena was doing. In the five weeks since she'd disappeared, Hope had heard from her only through the mail. Serena had simply stated she was all right and she would be home as soon as she could. Hope had even gone so far as to call her ex-roommate, Rob. He had assured Hope that he hadn't heard from her, and if he did, he would call. It felt like a dead end. Everything with their mother's estate had been carefully planned and taken care of before she passed. Serena knew she didn't have to be there for the selling of the house or the reading of the will. However, Hope needed her there. They'd come so far with their relationship in such a short time. It was a betrayal all around and there was no other way Hope could think of it, no other way to feel about it.

* * * *

Brian peered out his window at the two For Sale signs. He was doing the right thing by leaving. The place held too many memories. He turned and sneered at all the boxes in what used to be his dining room. The movers would be coming in a week, and he would be more than ready. Next door, they were having more luck with the selling of the house. It had been on the market for a week, and already people were biting. Brian didn't care how long it would take to sell his house, as long as he never had to come back to it.

"Are you sure this is what you want to do?" Darren looked over at his friend with reservation in his eyes. "It seems like such a drastic move."

"And what should I do? Wait here for a woman who obviously isn't coming back?" Brian felt bitter. He could taste it in his mouth, feel it in his gut. No amount of time that passed would ever change his feelings for her. "My dad has more than enough room, and besides, I have to decide what I'm going to do from here."

"Maybe you should just think about it a little more."

"I was going back and forth about moving down there anyway. Jac's going to be having a baby, and she's going to need help."

"Well, I guess if you have to come up with an excuse, that's as good as any." Darren frowned at his friend. "Does her sister know where she is?"

"No." Brian busied himself with packing the stuff in the upper cabinets. "Only thing she says is that she's all right and she's sorry." Brian tossed a small glass up and down in his hand. His gaze swept to the window where he could see the pool he had thrown her into. Everywhere he looked, she was there. He couldn't get away from the memories and feelings. At first, he blamed himself for pushing her at the wrong time in her life. Then he searched for reasons she'd want to leave him. Then finally he came to the conclusion she wasn't the person he thought she was. He flung the glass against the wall where it rained in a thousand pieces to the floor.

"You know, Brian. You keep up with this type of behavior and you're going to run out of dishes." Darren went to the closet and took out the broom. "If you want to sell this place, you'd better stop smashing it up." He glanced over at the hole in the kitchen wall. It was the perfect size of Brian's fist. After he had realized Serena was gone, and had enough liquor in him, Brian had decided to take it out on the wall. It was too bad he hadn't known there was a beam there. Nevertheless, a couple broken knuckles was nothing compared to his heart.

"I'll fix that tomorrow." Brian nodded to the hole. "I just had to wait till my hand was better." He flexed his fingers and bent to pick up the remaining shards of glass.

"I told you I'd help."

"I don't need anyone's help." Brian threw the shards of glass into the wastebasket. He was sick of everyone trying to help him.

"Yeah, I know you don't. But when someone picks up and runs, there's usually a good reason."

Brian's blood boiled. "I'm not running!" He turned to his friend ready for battle.

"I wasn't talking about you."

Brian swore under his breath and walked back to lean on the kitchen sink. "I'm sorry, Darren." He pulled his hands through his hair. "I haven't been sleeping well. I might go some place hot for a while. Just get away." He looked up at Darren, pleading with his eyes for answers that no one seemed to have. "Do you think she had a good reason for leaving?"

"Yeah."

"Do you think I should try and find her?"

"No."

"So, I should do nothing?"

"Yes."

"Could you give me more than one word answers?"

"I don't have any answers."

"Well, someone should." Brian turned and started packing again.

He slammed his dishes into the box, not caring if they broke. Maybe getting away for a while would be good for him. He could drink as much as he wanted. Lie around in the sun and surf. There would be no one making him feel like a lost puppy. And wasn't that the shit of it? Feeling lost? Every day that went by it didn't seem to get any better. The funk Brian was in felt like a bag of sand attached to his back. The worst part about it was that he almost welcomed it. Tomorrow's another day, he'd tell himself, another day closer to finding out why she left. It was something he needed to know. He had a right to know. Brian cursed her again, and the fact life went on. Even for someone as miserable as he was.

* * * *

Serena was miserable, too. What had she been thinking? She hadn't been, she concluded. She'd been so overwhelmed with her own grief, she hadn't realized what she was doing until it was done. She had lived out of friends' homes for a while. Then Serena finally settled at Rob's. He had insisted she call her sister right away. When she had, her sister only reinforced the fact she'd been wrong.

But at that moment, Serena wasn't thinking about her sister. At that moment, she didn't know if she was going to go on living. Serena stared down into the white porcelain bowl where she'd just finished bringing up her lunch. Her head was spinning and her stomach was rolling. It's nerves, she kept telling herself. Just nerves. She leaned against the adjacent wall and held her head in her hands. Something wasn't right. She knew it, but wasn't about to admit it. When she tried to stand, the room tilted and she came down hard on the floor.

"Serena... Serena." She heard the voice and felt the cool cloth on her head. "That's it. Take it easy." When she tried to open her eyes, they were heavy and her body felt weak.

"Brian." She opened her eyes to a distorted face then slipped back into the dark.

* * * *

"Ms. O'Neal. Come on now, we know you can hear us." The nurse checked her signs again and continued to talk to her. "Time to wake up."

Serena's eyes fluttered open. The light from the window was a rude intrusion to the deep dark she had come out of. "Where... am I?" She tried to sit up but was easily restrained by the nurse's hands.

"You're in the hospital, Ms. O'Neal. You were quite dehydrated when you came in." The nurse took a penlight and shone it into her eyes. "Good. You only needed some fluids and rest." The women looked Serena squarely in the eyes. "You should know better in your condition."

Serena shook her head in confusion. "What condition?"

The nurse glanced at Serena with a sparkle in her eyes. "Why Ms. O'Neal, you're expecting." From the baffled expression on Serena's face, the nurse could see it wasn't something that had been planned. "You're going to have to find yourself a doctor. Do you know when your last period was?"

Serena was still dumbstruck, looking at the nurse while her mind went in a million different directions. "I don't know. Oh... the end of June. I just thought... since I was under so much stress, that..." She faded off as the reason for her recent weight gain clicked.

"By my calculations you're a little over four months. Have you been getting sick at all?"

"Well… I thought it was simply nerves. It started, oh... a... a few months ago. Just recently it's gotten worse."

"There are a lucky few that experience no sickness. I had it with all of mine." The nurse was cheerful and peppy. Serena had a hard time disliking the woman, even though she wouldn't stop poking and prodding at her. "You've probably been sick due to the lack of fluids." The nurse went back to Serena's chart and started jotting down something.

Serena straightened in the bed and for the first time saw Rob waiting patiently in a chair. “Rob? I...”

“Need to go home,” he said quietly. “As much as I love you, you need to be home.”

“Ms. O’Neal can leave tomorrow if everything checks out all right. I scheduled an ultrasound for this afternoon. Try to get some sleep. And congratulations.” She placed a comforting hand on Serena’s shoulder. “I’ll be back later.”

“Thank you.” Serena looked over to Rob and frowned. “I’m sorry to get you wrapped up in this.”

“Hey, that’s what friends are for.” He waited a beat. “I called your sister. I didn’t know what was wrong with you. I thought she should know what’s going on.” He got up and sat on the side of her bed.

“It’s okay, Rob.” Serena took his hand to hold in her own. “I’m just flabbergasted, that’s all.”

“Me too.” His face became serious, and Serena knew what was going to come next. “I think you should call him.”

“He moved, last week.”

“You can find him.”

“He won’t want to talk to me.”

“Then ask him to listen.”

Staring out the windows, she could see the first flurries fall from the expected storm. “I will. In my own time.”

“You need to call your sister. I had to talk her out of coming down here.”

“Thank you.”

“Here.” He handed her the room phone. “Call her.”

“Fine, Dad.” Serena rolled her eyes and took the phone from him.

“I’m going to go and get something to drink.” He left the room as Serena stared at the phone. Should she tell her? It wasn’t as if this was something Serena was going to be able to hide.

She dialed the number and Hope picked it up on the second ring.

"Hello."

"Hi." Serena tried to sound cheerful but she couldn't muster up the strength.

"Don't you, 'Hi' me! What the hell is going on?"

"I was a little dehydrated, that's all."

"That's all?"

"Yeah."

"What else? I know you're not telling me everything."

"And how would you know that?" Serena cringed on her end of the phone. She had always been terrible at covering things up.

"You're pretending to be happy. What is it?"

"I'm pregnant." The silence on the other end had Serena shifting in her bed.

"Really? Well, I guess... well I don't know. Are you sure?"

"The nurse seems to be."

"Then it's probably pretty final."

"Yeah."

"I hope it's a boy."

Serena took a gulp of air. "Lord knows I wouldn't be very good with a girl."

"You got a fifty-fifty chance."

"Yeah." Serena didn't know what else to say to her sister. Everything was still sinking in for her. A baby? She was going to be a mother? How was she supposed to feel about that? How was Brian going to feel?

"How far?"

"A little over four months. They're doing an ultrasound a little later. Rob's here with me."

"Coming home, Rena?"

"Yeah, it's time."

"Good. Call me after the ultrasound."

* * * *

Hope hung up the phone and sank into a chair. Staring out the kitchen window, she could see her little girl playing in the snow. She was bundled up like a little pink Michelin baby. She knew her cheeks would match her outfit when she came in, all rosy and sweet. Her little hands would be chilled along with her feet, like tiny icicles. All the same, the little girl would be happy. Yes, definitely happy. Hope couldn't imagine life without the hellion. Lizzy had completed her life.

Hope's mind wandered back to Serena. Her sister was having a baby. The thought purely mystified her. Serena would be a good mother. She'd snuggle and coo. She'd kiss and dote. What a sight it was going to be, and what a strange twist in fate God brought upon their family. Smiling, Hope walked to the door and called her own angel in. What a wonderful event. Hope was completely elated.

CHAPTER 25

Brian stared out at the cold waters of the ocean. Hope had called to tell him Serena was coming home. What home? he asked himself. She didn't have one. Her mother's house had been sold. She certainly wasn't going to be staying with him. Why the hell had Hope called? Brian picked up a shell and whipped it in the water. It made a plunk noise when it hit and then sank. He was over her, he told himself. Hadn't he just gone out on a date the week before to prove it to everyone? Or was it to prove it to himself? Swearing heavily, Brian picked up another shell and threw it with all his might. Tomorrow was Christmas. He remembered what he had fantasized about, once upon a time. He had them sharing Christmas dinner with his family, laughing and talking about wedding plans. He was going to surprise her with a trip to some exotic place where they could enjoy the sand and sun. Of course, he ended up doing that alone and almost ended up in bed with some sweet tart. It wasn't that she wasn't beautiful, she was. She had made great conversation, and would have had no strings attached. Nevertheless, as soon as he touched her, it was over. Her skin didn't feel the same under his hands. When he kissed her, the lips weren't full and pouted. He stepped back immediately, feeling like a fool. "Sorry," was all he could say. When she came toward him to change his mind, he pretty much ran from her. Brian pelted another shell into the turbulent water. The ocean was like his mood, dark and erratic. He remembered another day when the water hadn't been so cold, and neither had he. They both had opened themselves fully to each other, or he thought they had.

Brian stopped asking himself, a while ago, the reasons for her departure. Jacqueline had reminded him that everyone takes to grief differently. And wasn't he a shinning example of that? Hadn't he run?

"No!" He shouted aloud.

"You're going to catch a death."

Brian heard the Spanish accent and smiled. She had been like a little mother hen since he had moved home.

"Well, Rosa. Then it'll be no one's fault but my own." He turned to her with his fists on his hips.

"You only look that way when she is bothering you."

"Her sister called." Brian absently picked up another shell and started running it through his fingers. "She's moving back home."

"So she's coming home?" Rosa pondered it for a few seconds. "You go to her?"

"No." He threw the shell back to where it had come from.

"Then you are a bigger fool than I thought."

"She left me, remember?"

"She left no one but herself. You have right to be angry. Yes? You also have a right to know why."

"It doesn't matter anymore." Brian turned back to the ocean, his thoughts as tempestuous as the water. "I don't care."

"I'm not a fool." Her tone demanded he look at her. "If you do not care, why you sad?"

He grinned at her. She always did see right through him. Brian was sad. He suddenly became distinctly aware that he still wanted what could have been, what could still be.

"You deal with your anger, Brian." She touched his check with her gloved hand. "Remember, she's had to deal with hers."

Brian watched her walk away. Damn women. Just when you think you've got everything straightened out, they come and screw it up. Stuffing his icy hands in his pockets Brian headed to the house.

* * * *

Christmas came with giant snowdrifts and ice-covered lights. They blinked on and off with a slowed rhythm due to the bone-chilling temperature. The plastic Santas and Frostys became brittle and cracked. When house doorknobs were touched, they were cold, even inside. Traveling became optional on days like these. New England in the winter could be as fierce as a woman scorned.

Serena looked out her sister's living room window and sighed. There was no getting out, so everyone was stuck in. She'd made it to Hope's before the worst of the storm had hit. Now she wished she'd been stranded in some motel somewhere, anywhere, alone.

Serena discovered the noise one child could make at Christmas time was deafening. She, herself, had bought Lizzy some really noisy toys. She hadn't thought about how she'd be stuck listening to the small, but loud, karaoke machine. The little girl could screech out a song.

Serena turned and saw the pained expression on Hope and Willie's faces. She mouthed 'sorry' and turned back to the window.

Hope put a hand on her shoulder. "I really think you should lie down. You look beat."

"It was a long ride." Serena attempted to smile. "I'll sleep in a little bit. Right now," she stated enthusiastically, "I want some pie."

"Sounds good to me." Willie made a beeline for the kitchen.

Hope playfully put her hands on her hips. "You had to say pie, didn't you?"

"I've got a healthy appetite these days."

Hope placed a hand on Serena's small round tummy. "Have you talked to him?"

"I don't want to talk about it."

"I'll take that as a no." Hope frowned at her sister. "I'll drop it for now."

"Good. I'm starving." Serena headed to the kitchen in time to have Willie slice her a piece. Hope joined them a short time later, after putting Lizzy to sleep. Hope carefully avoided the chair that their mother would have occupied. They spoke little about her absence. More was spoken of the years that had passed, and the memories of adventures gone by.

As the night went into wee hours, things quieted down. The dishes were done, leftovers put away. Presents that were wrapped with love and care and now opened, put back under the tree. There would be only a select few brought to rooms to snuggle with or use.

Serena sat on the sofa with her new throw quilt that Hope had made. Its colors were bright and bold, the texture soft and warm. She knew it would be something to cherish in the years to come. Serena thought about what it would be like to sit in a rocking chair with it, and have her baby in her arms. She'd read to the little one, feed bottles, and then burp him. Then after rocking the baby to sleep, she'd slip next to Brian on their couch, and talk quietly about their day. Serena let out a long sigh. She needed to talk to him. She'd known about the baby for weeks now, and she was being a coward when it came to telling him.

The house was quiet but for Hope and Willie talking in the kitchen. Serena looked outside to see ice had formed on everything, magically making it all appear to be crystal. She frowned as a thought ran through her mind. What was Brian doing? Was he happy? Sad? Was he wondering the same thing about her? Saturday, she decided. She would go and see him on Saturday.

* * * *

Brian looked up from his plate. "I'm sorry Dad. I didn't hear what you said."

"I said! Get the stick out of your ass, and go see her!"

"Daniel! I'm shocked!" Rosa leaned over and patted Brian's hand. "If the boy needs to be idiot, let him."

Gabe tried to cover a snort with his wine and almost choked. "With a family like this, do you really wonder why I don't bring anyone home?"

"Your day will come, Gabe." Jacqueline turned to her other brother with pity. "Brian, I have to agree with Dad."

"Great!" Brian threw his hands in the air. "It's Christmas, and as usual everyone's trying their hardest to cheer me up." He rose from the table. "Well, I don't need anyone's advice, I'm doing just fine. If you don't believe me, that's too bad."

"Sit down, Brian."

Brian shot his father a glare. It wasn't often Brian's temper showed completely, and when it did, everyone needed to watch out.

"Boy. Don't look at me with that tone. I'll eat you alive." Brian lowered himself into his chair. "We only say this because we love you, and you love her. It's been months, and with each passing one you get more miserable. Work it out." Daniel stabbed the air with his fork. "Then you marry her. She's right for you. Even if she is a little unstable." He said the last with a lowered voice, and Rosa kicked him under the table. "Damn, woman. What the hell did you do that for?"

"You're intolerable." She turned her attention to the whole table. "I'm sure Brian is sick of this subject, so let's change it."

"Good idea," Brian grumbled.

"Yes, let's change it. Jacqueline." Daniel turned his attention to his only daughter in time to see her roll her eyes. "Don't you look at me that way!"

"You badger her."

"Gabe. Stay out of it." Daniel gave him a warning stare, and then turned to smile at Jacqueline. "Now dear, how are you feeling?"

Jacqueline turned to Brian, who was grinning at her because all the pressure was off him.

"Wonderful." She stuck her tongue out at her brother. Daniel missed it because he was pouring himself more wine.

"Very good. More wine, dear?" His eyes sparked at Rosa, who offered her glass.

"Thank you."

* * * *

What was she doing? Was she smiling and laughing, or was she as miserable as he? Brian turned from his bedroom window. Going to his nightstand he opened the drawer. You're torturing yourself. He pulled a framed picture from its safe spot. It was the Fourth of July party, he remembered. They had been sitting at the table with Jacqueline, making fun of Darren's cooking. Mandy had popped up with the camera and told them to say cheese. Brian remembered wrapping his arm around Serena's shoulders, and her leaning into him. When the snap was done, he brought her even closer for a smacker of a kiss. Brian looked to the ceiling and wondered for the thousandth time, why? He was so sick of wondering; he felt his soul choking on the very existence of that single word. Deep down, Brian knew why. Hadn't he gone through the same thing himself? He didn't need any explanations from her. Except the one on why she hadn't trusted him enough to lean on him. Brian threw the picture back into the drawer and fleetingly thought about burning it. That would make him feel better. For about a second.

Climbing into bed, Brian decided tomorrow he was going to start getting himself together. It was about time he did it and moved on. So what if she's back from wherever she went? If she had wanted to talk to him, she would have called. He turned off the small table lamp next to his bed. Who was he trying to kid? He was still in love with her.

CHAPTER 26

She shouldn't have come. He wouldn't want her there. The trip to the house had been grueling. Construction. That's all Connecticut was. Construction. Serena couldn't understand how anyone could live with such chaos on a daily basis. Stop-go. Stop-go. She thanked the good Lord her mother had had an automatic.

Serena hesitated before ascending the stairs to the wide front porch. Would he even speak to her? Would he even see her? She would understand if he didn't.

Taking a deep breath Serena raised her hand to knock. Then hesitated, and decided to ring the bell. They wouldn't hear the knock if they were out back. However, they wouldn't be out back, she told herself. It was thirty-four degrees.

* * * *

Brian watched her from the window. A smile tugged at his lips watching her indecisiveness. Then he felt a dark shadow blanket his thoughts. Marching to the door, he flung it open, taking Serena by surprise. He grabbed her arm in time so she wouldn't fall back from fright. The touch was too much contact for both. They stared at one another for what seemed like eternity.

"I didn't know whether you were going to stand here talking to yourself, or ever knock." Brian searched her face. "I figured I'd decide for you."

"Brian! Who is out there? Don't you let them freeze to death." Rosa came to a halt when she saw who it was. "Let that poor girl in!"

Brian stepped out of the way and motioned Serena in. "After you." Something was different with the way she looked. He angled his head to get a better view of the back of her. When her jacket slid from her shoulders, he saw the extra weight. She must have really taken her mother's death hard.

"Would you like something to drink?" Rosa asked Serena.

"No thank you, Rosa."

"I have some ginger tea."

Serena understood what she was saying. Ginger had become her best friend to battle the nausea. "That would be nice, thank you."

Brian watched as Rosa disappeared and Serena wrung her hands. What the hell did she want? He placed his hands on his hips and waited, glaring at her. Brian wanted to make her nervous, make her uncomfortable. He wanted her to suffer in some way as he had. Serena's eyes met Brian's and he felt the ice around his heart begin to thin. "What do you want, Serena?"

"We need to talk."

"Maybe I don't want to."

"Brian, get that girl out of the doorway!" Daniel appeared like a father bear protecting his cub. "Well, girl. Haven't seen you around here in a while."

"Nice to see you too, Daniel." Serena attempted to smile but couldn't quite pull it off. "I hope I'm not intruding."

"Not at all, not at all. Come in, sit." One of his large hands rested on the small of Serena's back. As he steered her into the living room, Daniel glanced back at his son, who clearly wasn't happy. "You look tired. Is Rosa getting you something to drink?"

"Yes, she is. Thank you." Serena sat and folded her hands on her lap.

"Sit," Daniel commanded as he pushed Brian into a chair. "I'll be right back. And don't look at me in that tone of voice, boy!"

Brian turned an unsympathetic sneer on Serena. "So you decided to come out of hiding?"

He was going to make this harder than she had imagined he would. It wasn't that she thought he'd run into her arms. It was just she didn't think he'd look so cruelly at her. Examining him, she realized Brian's usually short hair was long and ragged. He kept brushing his bangs out of eyes that were lined with dark circles, eyes that cruelly stared at her with a gray as cold as steel. He'd lost weight, she noticed. His usually full face was creased and worn.

"I'm sorry, Brian." Serena gazed down at her folded hands. "I don't know what I was thinking—"

"You weren't," he interrupted.

Serena's head snapped up at his sharp words. She felt a tear slide down her cheek and quickly wiped it away.

"You'll get no sympathy here." Brian shifted in his seat.

"I'm not looking for pity," Serena snapped. "We need to talk."

"No," Brian said slowly. "You need to leave."

"There's something I need to tell you." Serena said desperately.

"No." Brian was up and out of his chair.

Serena watched as he came over and grabbed her arm, pulling her to her feet. They were so close they could feel the energy vibrating off one another.

* * * *

Daniel and Rosa backed silently into the kitchen after seeing Brian and Serena staring into each other's eyes.

"That boy better not make that poor girl suffer any more than she has." Daniel glanced at the closed door with concern in his eyes.

"He'll mess it up."

"You're a real optimist," Daniel grumbled.

"He has too much anger, and he's an idiot." She busied herself with putting away dishes. "Men are pig-headed."

Daniel gave out a huff. "And you're going to tell me you're not."

"No, I am not. I'm smart."

Daniel grabbed her shoulders and whirled her around. "If you're not pig-headed," he said using her words, "then you'll marry me."

"You..."

"Asked you to marry me, again." Daniel searched her eyes for a hint of an answer. "Rosa, my world fell apart when Sofia died. I never thought I'd love again. Then, there you were. Fighting with me every chance you had."

Rosa's chin shot up in the air. "Had to get you out of my house. You kept messing it up."

"You made me feel challenged and alive." He brought a hand to her cheek. Daniel could see tears brimming in her eyes. "Don't you dare say you don't deserve me! You're a part of this family. Have been for a long time." He moved in closer, trapping Rosa between himself and the counter. "Marry me, Rosa. Life's too short to not share it with someone you love."

Rosa felt the tears stream down her face. "You are idiot, Daniel. With all the time we spend together, I only love you more."

"Say yes," Daniel demanded.

"Like I have choice."

They grinned at one another. Daniel let out a hoot, and before Rosa knew what was happening, she was whisked up and kissed enthusiastically.

"Let's go make love!"

Rosa laughed. "First let's make sure Brian's okay."

* * * *

Brian's breath came short and fast. She was so beautiful standing there, close, too close. She stared up at him with wounded puppy dog eyes. His lips crushed hers. One more touch, that's all he wanted, just one more taste. Serena's body yielded to his need. But when her hands touched his face, Brian jolted back with contempt in his eyes.

Tears spilled full force down her face now. Serena laid a hand on her stomach "Brian…" Her eyes pleaded with him.

Brian simply grabbed Serena by the arm and dragged her to the door. "I don't ever want to see you again." He pushed her out and slammed the door. His body fell against it as tears came to his own eyes.

"What the hell are you doing?" Daniel wanted to know. "I am not happy with the way you just manhandled that girl. She may deserve a bit of the cold shoulder, but she also deserves her say."

"Stay out of it, Dad." Brian pointed a finger at his father. "I'm a grown man."

"Yes, you are." Daniel's reply was quiet. "What did she say?"

"Nothing." Brian pushed himself off the door. He heard her car start and begin to leave the drive. Silently, he hoped she'd have a safe ride home.

"Did you give her the chance?"

"What does it matter? She's out of my life!"

"Is that what you want?"

"Yes!" Brian turned to storm up the stairs.

"What about the baby?" Rosa's voice was low and definite. Both men turned in astonishment.

"What did you say?" Brian descended the few steps he had managed to climb.

"Are you both blind?" Rosa's eyes went from Brian's to Daniel's and back again. "The girl is with child."

"She said we needed to talk."

"No shit!" Daniel exclaimed. "I thought she just put on some weight. I'm going to be a grandpa!"

Rosa released an exasperated breath. "Idiots." She went to where Brian had slid in a chair. "Brian." Rosa knelt in front of him. "Sweetheart. You going to be a daddy with the woman you love." His eyes focused on hers. "Now stop sitting there like a dummy and go after her." She stood up quickly and pointed to the door. When Brian didn't move she simply grabbed him by the ear and twisted. "Go!"

Brian snapped out of his trance and gave Rosa a smacking kiss on the cheek. "Marry him," Brian demanded as he ran to the door.

Rosa turned to Daniel with her hands on her hips. She narrowed her eyes as she walked toward him.

"I have a smart boy, love." He flashed her a charming smile, Rosa only smirked. "Now," Daniel said while taking steps to her, "let's make love!"

* * * *

Brian raced down the highway at ninety. He just threw the best thing to happen to him out his father's front door. He swore at all the Connecticut traffic and construction. Why bother. As soon as they're done fixing one spot, they'll start ripping it all back up again.

Brian leaned on his horn. Apparently, the person in front of him didn't know the Connecticut highways' unspoken rule. If the sign says sixty-five, it means go eighty or more. Brian stepped down on the gas pedal and passed on the right. Why is it when you're in a hurry, everyone's always trying to get in your way?

"Idiot!" He proclaimed aloud. It took a second, but it occurred to Brian, he wasn't talking to the driver in front of him. How could I have been so stupid? How could he have not seen that she was pregnant? They were both to blame. Neither one was at more fault than the other. Brian glanced in his rearview mirror and swore heatedly. The red and blue lights were only going to be another delay in getting to the woman he loved.

* * * *

Tears streaked down Serena's face with the force of a river overflowing. She wiped at them with the sleeve of her cloak jacket. A sob escaped her mouth with the howl of a wounded animal. He turned me away, was all she could think. He never wanted to see her again. He would never be there for her and the baby. What was she going to do now that he was gone? She pulled over on the side of the highway to get a hold of herself. Laying back her head on the rest, Serena took mental notes on her condition. "Blurry eyes, from crying so hard," she announced to herself. "Nose won't stop running." She wiped at it again with her sleeve. "Look for tissues, nose is starting to hurt." Serena let out another sob when she leaned over to the other seat to grab her box. "And, of course, sobbing so hard… I can't breathe." She blew her nose with an impatient persistence. She was going to feel even worse when she was done with this crying session. Serena wiped her eyes and glanced in the rearview mirror for coming cars. When Serena came into eye contact with herself, she frowned. "I'll make it through this," she told herself. "We'll make it through this." Serena laid a hand on her belly while glancing down. "Let's take the long way home."

* * * *

One hundred and fifty dollars! It was worth it, Brian thought. Looking ahead of him, he couldn't believe he hadn't caught up with her. She hadn't left that long before him. Brian silently hoped Serena was driving carefully, and not like a crazed fool. He cursed them both again as he took the next turn. What if she hadn't headed home? Brian glanced at the field to the left of him. Her sister lived around the next bend. He would have caught up with Serena by now, he repeated in his head.

Brian's throat felt tight as he drove by the small house. No car. Slamming his fist on the steering wheel, he cursed loudly and prepared to head back the way he came. He had a feeling he knew where she'd be.

"Damn woman!" he swore. "Has me driving all over kingdom-come to find her!" Well, I will find her, Brian thought with confidence, even if it takes all night. Then he'd choke her.

Brian drummed his fingers restlessly on the steering wheel waiting for the red light to change. He searched frantically around him at the passersby. Everyone seemed to be enjoying the cold but beautiful day. Brian's gaze settled on a woman and man bringing their baby into a house. His fingers stopped suddenly in the middle of a frantic and hard tempo when the thought of becoming a father overwhelmed him. The baby was high upon its father's shoulder, peering over at the world still beyond its reach. What would it be like to have something that precious and trusting? Scary, Brian decided. A baby loves you unconditionally. They count on you for everything. A thousand 'what ifs' ran through Brian's mind even as a joyful tear slid down his face. Then the child he was watching let out a squeal of delight before the family disappeared into the house. Brian suddenly realized that's what he wanted. A family. And he wanted it with Serena. Smiling, Brian turned back to the road and continued his journey toward his new life.

* * * *

Serena pulled into the small but crowded restaurant. Mark had told her Mandy was there dropping some stuff off to a friend. As Serena opened the door, Mandy was walking out.

"Serena?" She pulled her into the lobby and took a serious examination of her friend. "Oh, dear," she said in a voice coated with concern.

"I know what I look like." Serena's head was bent, her hands stuffed into her pockets. "I really need something to eat."

"Come on." Mandy wrapped her arm around Serena and steered her to the back of the restaurant. "I'll buy whatever it is you're craving."

Serena grinned up with a mischievous grin. "Anything?"

"Anything," she promised.

The waitress came and took their orders as Serena blew her nose and gave Mandy a weak smile. "Do I look as bad as I feel?"

Mandy gave out a long breath. "Maybe. What happened?"

"He threw me out. Didn't even let me say anything."

"Bastard!" she hissed.

"Well, I did deserve it." Serena played with the straw to her drink. "I was the one who got up and ran."

"You had a tough time dealing with your mother's death. Brian, of all people, should understand that."

"Maybe." Serena was running her hands through her hair. She had dark circles around her red-rimmed eyes.

"So what are you going to do now?" Mandy asked her friend.

"I don't know." Serena looked down once again. "What can I do?"

* * * *

"Son-of-a-bitch! She has me chasing her all over the place!" Brian tugged a hand through his own hair. Frustration was a mild word for what he was feeling at that point.

"Sorry, Bri. Mandy was bringing some stuff to a friend. Serena said she was going to try and catch her there."

Brian looked hopelessly around Mark and Mandy's kitchen. They had moved in together only weeks before. Things were just being hung on the walls. Empty spaces still remained, waiting for memories and loving moments to be captured and hung. This was what Brian wanted. A life of making memories with someone he loved.

He pointed at Mark. "Call her. Don't let her tell Serena that I'm on my way. It's going to take me a good five minutes." He was out the door before Mark could respond.

* * * *

Mandy's phone rang, and interrupted what she was saying.

"Shoot. Let me just get this, it's Mark." She smiled. "Hello."

"Don't let Serena know. Brian's on his way."

"Oh, that's great, honey."

"It's going to take him about five minutes."

Mandy glanced at Serena and beamed. "I think we're going to be a while, anyway."

"Good. Love you."

"Love you, too." Mandy hung up the phone and placed it back in her purse. "Why don't you call him in a few days?"

"No," Serena stated simply and finally. "I'm not going to throw myself at him. Besides, he won't want to hear from me. He made it very clear when he threw me out of the house."

"Literally," Mandy said, with disgust.

"Literally," Serena grumbled. "I'm going to get going. I'm so tired."

Mandy placed her hands on her friends. "I know you're feeling pretty miserable right now. But you will get through this. Things will get better."

Serena gave her a weak smile. "I'm so glad we became friends."

"Me too."

* * * *

Brian raced down the car-packed road, and felt disgusted over his behavior. He played the scene back again in his mind. He did manhandle her. Grabbing her by the arm and tossing her out the door like a bag of trash. But how the hell was he supposed to know she was pregnant? Just had to look, he replied to himself with repulsion.

Brian threw the car into the restaurant's parking lot. Parking next to her car, he stormed out of his.

* * * *

"I really need to get some rest." Serena took a large swig of her juice.

Mandy glanced up and saw Brian standing behind Serena. "I'm going to… I'm just going to go." Mandy pushed back her chair abruptly to flee, while Serena gaped at her. "Brian." Mandy nodded at him, and then patted his shoulder.

"Thanks. Serena, we need to talk." Brian was out of breath and a little out of sorts.

"I know." She stared down into her juice.

Brian pulled out a chair and turned it around to straddle it. The back of the chair created just enough of a barrier between them to make him feel somewhat comfortable. He examined her slowly, taking in everything he'd missed last time he saw her. Then Serena shifted in her seat, the natural light shadowing the conflicting planes in her face. It was rounder, due to the weight gain. Her eyes were puffy, and her complexion pale.

"I was going to call you in a few days," she told him quietly.

"Why?"

Serena took a deep breath. "I needed to get away, for a little while."

"We could have done that together." When her eyes fixed on his, a revelation came to him. "You needed to get away from me?"

"Somewhat." She stirred her drink with the straw. "By the time I got myself together, it seemed too late to come back."

Brian gripped the rungs on the back of the chair. He needed to relax. "It was, the moment you walked out the door."

Serena winced. "Why are you here?"

"Because I don't believe you would do something like this without good reason." Brian's voice was raising, and Serena matched hers to it.

"If I recall correctly, you did the same thing at one time!"

"That was different!" He jabbed a finger at her. "I didn't leave someone high and dry!"

Clearly uncomfortable, Serena shifted in her seat.

"Excuse me." Both Brian and Serena looked up at the waitress. "I'm afraid you're going to have to take this outside. If you need anything," the waitress directed to Serena, "let us know." She gave one last warning glance at Brian, and then walked away.

Brian stood, dug some bills out of his pocket, and threw them onto the table. "I'll meet you outside," he said, and walked away.

"Well," Serena said to herself, "you're stuck now." She got up from the table. "A fine mess you've gotten yourself into."

Outside, the cold was a bitter reality. "Talk to me." Startled by his sudden appearance behind her, Serena let go of the front of her jacket and cupped the bottom of her belly.

"Do you enjoy scaring the shit out of me?"

"Yeah!" he yelled back. "It gives me sick pleasure. Now..." His words trailed off as his gaze fell on her stomach. When his eyes lifted to hers, he could see the divine turmoil swirling in them. His eyes went rapidly back to her stomach and then to her face again.

"Surprise?" Serena gave a weak smile.

"No kidding. Just when were you going to tell me, anyway?"

"I tried! You kicked me out!"

"You deserved it!"

"I know that." Silence fell when they realized they were getting nowhere. Serena took a step back from Brian, then felt his hand clasp down hard on her arm.

"Brian, I'm cold."

"Then we'll go back inside."

"We got kicked out!"

"Right." Brian searched around them until his eyes settled on his car. "Come on," he said dragging her to it.

"Brian, I'm very emotional right now. If you don't stop dragging me around, I can't guarantee what I will or will not do to you." He let go of her arm and she breathed a sigh of relief.

"I really don't want you disappearing on me again. I've driven around for hours trying to find you."

"I probably wouldn't have disappeared the first time if I'd known where all the emotions were coming from." He actually turned and smiled at her while opening the car door.

"Get in. I'll find a place where we can talk." Brian drove down the snow-trimmed road for about a mile, and then turned into a motel parking lot.

"Nice," Serena drawled out.

"Hey, it's not like either of us has a place nearby."

"Do you bring all your expectant mothers here?"

"I don't know what the hell to say to you!" He glared out the windshield and slammed a fist on the wheel.

Serena crossed her arms on her chest. "If you're going to yell at me, the least you could do is wait till we're inside the room."

"Fine." Brian slammed out of the car and marched up to the door with the 'office' sign. When he came back out with a key, he stopped to watch Serena climb out of the car. She looks adorable. Brian watched as she walked across the parking lot. She had a little waddle in her step and Brian couldn't help but grin.

"Stop smiling." Serena had a warning in her voice. "If you say how cute I look, I'll blacken your eye."

Brian held up his hands. "I was only thinking it." I still love her. Months had passed and yet it seemed his feelings were only stronger. It felt so right to be there with her, even with everything they had to work out.

She followed him to the room where he opened the door and motioned her inside. Enthusiastic laughter instantly burst from Serena.

"Oh God!" she exclaimed. "It's so much seedier than I imagined!"

Brian surveyed the room and grinned. "I like the fine plastic art."

"And look at the wonderful polyester spread!" Serena covered her mouth with her hand. "I want one," she choked out.

"It's you." Brian took off his jacket to hang on one of the folding chairs that went with the small but efficient table. He turned in time to see a side view of Serena as she slipped her own jacket off. She did look cute and radiant, all at the same time. He walked to her in silence, their eyes never leaving one another's. Running his hands up and down her arms, he fell to his knees. Pressing his cheek to her stomach, Brian choked back a sob.

"I'm so sorry, Brian." Serena took a deep cleansing breath and looked to the ceiling. "I didn't know what to do when I found out. I didn't want you to feel like I'm trapping you." Tears flowed down her face like a harsh spring rain. "I didn't want to show up at your doorstep and say, 'guess what, you're going to have a son.'"

"A son?" Brian's arms squeezed a little tighter.

"I was thinking about calling him Daniel."

"It's a good name," Brian said solemnly.

"Well, then I..." Serena struggled with her own tears and words.

"It's okay, Serena."

"No, it's not." She broke from his hold to pace the room. "I should have come to you right when I found out. I should never have left." She turned to face Brian when he placed a hand on her shoulder. "I don't blame you for turning me away. I would have done the same thing."

Gently, Brian led Serena to sit on the bed. He wiped his eyes, and blew his nose with the tissues that the room provided. "Don't try the tissues," he warned. Serena let out a quiet laugh and then a sigh when Brian picked up her hand to play with her fingers.

"I love you, Brian. I know right now it's not fair for me to say, but I do."

Brian looked up from their joined hands. "I love you, too." He leaned over and gently kissed her lips. “Let’s just pretend for a while that there’s nothing between us. I need you.” Brian lowered her back onto the bed so he could run his hands over her body. It was glorious to be next to her again. The feeling swept over him and into her. Their lips met over and over, each time more hungry. It was wrong. They both understood it wouldn’t solve anything. In the back of their minds, they knew they should be talking. However, need is a strong emotion, and that’s what they were functioning on.

As clothes were peeled away slowly, they rediscovered each other. The room filled with soft moans, and feelings of elation. Nothing had ever felt so right as that moment. When she filled herself with him, Serena’s whole body was overwhelmed. Tears streaked down her face for all the past mistakes and the forgiveness.

After, they lay in each other’s arms basking in the rightness they felt. Serena opened her eyes and stared up at their reflection. Laughter over the room escaped her once again. “Please tell me you paid for more than an hour.”

“It’s mandated three. Besides.” He nuzzled closer, and rubbed her belly. “I like the mirrors on the ceiling.”

“You would.” Serena gave him a quick impulsive kiss on the lips. When he jumped off the bed to find his pants, Serena sat up, confused about his burst of energy.

“Brian—”

“No!” he pointed and interrupted her. “You will not, and I mean not, stop me.”

Serena was baffled. He was going through his pockets like a mad man. Finally, he found what he was searching for in his jacket. Brian leaped back onto the bed next to her. When she opened her mouth to say something, he covered it with his hand.

“No. I understand why you left. I understand why it took so long to tell me about—” He gazed down and smiled at her belly. “—

Daniel." Once again, Brian had to cover her mouth with his hand before she could say anything. "Sometimes, sweetheart, you talk too much. This is one of those times. Be quiet. " Brian waited to be sure she would be, and then pressed on. "We both have done some things that were very selfish." He saw Serena stick her tongue in her cheek. Something she did when she was getting impatient. "Relax." She made a face at him. "Smart ass. Anyway." He took her left hand in his and kissed it. "You can't say you want to think about it. You're also not allowed to say no. I'm crazy in love with you Serena. I don't just want to be a part of his life. I want us to be a family, marry me." After a second or two, he said, "You can speak now."

Serena looked up from the ruby ring blinking on her finger to jump into Brian's arms. "We'll see how you feel about that during midnight feedings."

About Rebecca Rose

Rebecca Rose lives to find romance in ordinary life doing everyday things by believing you just need to be conscious enough to look for it.

Divine Turmoil was her first adventure in writing novel length stories. After finishing this work of love, inspired by the death of her Grandmother, she felt the need to find out what happened to the other characters in the book. And a series was born.

This started a new and exciting life for Rebecca and her family who live in Western Massachusetts. She's also had numerous short tales published with her hometown magazine.

Rebecca's Website:

http://www.authorrebeccarose.com/

Reader eMail:

authorrebeccarose@yahoo.com

Breinigsville, PA USA
16 September 2010

245535BV00001B/1/P

9 781616 501860